Alberto Moravia was born in Rome in 1907, the son of an architect. He wrote his first novel in 1925 and became foreign correspondere for *La Stampa* and G   ing his years in England   hen in Bloomsbury, whe   Yeats and H. G. Wells.   books were banned and   ...articles under a pseudonym. During the German occupation of Italy he went into hiding in the mountains and was liberated by the Americans in May 1944. He now lives in Rome and Capri and is incontestably the foremost contemporary Italian novelist.

'The most autonomous of contemporary novelists. His work has a purity, a singleness of purpose, that ensures an immense "rest and refreshment" to the common reader' *New Statesman*

'One of the greatest literary craftsmen of our time' *The Observer*

By the same author

Fiction

The Woman of Rome
The Conformist
Two Adolescents (*Agostino* and *Disobedience*)
The Fancy Dress Party
The Time of Indifference
Conjugal Love
Roman Tales
Bitter Honeymoon
Two Women
The Wayward Wife
The Empty Canvas
More Roman Tales
The Fetish
The Lie
Command and I Will Obey You
Paradise
The Two of Us
Lady Godiva
The Voice of the Sea
Time of Desecration

General

Man as an End
The Red Book and the Great Wall
Which Tribe Do You Belong To?

Play

Beatrice Cenci

ALBERTO MORAVIA

A Ghost at Noon

translated from the Italian by
Angus Davidson

GRANADA
London Toronto Sydney New York

Published by Granada Publishing Limited in 1983

ISBN 0 586 05704 8

First published in Great Britain by
Martin Secker & Warburg Ltd 1955
Published in Italian under the title of
Il Depresso
Copyright © Alberto Moravia 1955

Granada Publishing Limited
Frogmore, St Albans, Herts AL2 2NF
and
36 Golden Square, London W1R 4AH
515 Madison Avenue, New York, NY 10022, USA
117 York Street, Sydney, NSW 2000, Australia
60 International Blvd, Rexdale, Ontario, R9W 6J2, Canada
61 Beach Road, Auckland, New Zealand

Printed and bound in Great Britain by
Cox and Wyman Ltd, Reading
Set in Times

Granada ®
Granada Publishing ®

I

During the first two years of our married life my relations with my wife were, I can now assert, perfect. By which I mean to say that, in those two years, a complete, profound, harmony of the senses was accompanied by a kind of numbness – or should I say silence? – of the mind which, in such circumstances, causes an entire suspension of judgement and looks only to love for any estimate of the beloved person. Emilia, in fact, seemed to me wholly without defects, and so also, I believe, I appeared to her. Or perhaps I saw her defects and she saw mine, but, through some mysterious transformation produced by the feeling of love, such defects appeared to us both not merely forgivable, but even lovable, as though instead of defects they had been positive qualities, if of a rather special kind. Anyhow, we did not judge: we loved each other. This story sets out to relate how, while I continued to love her and not to judge her, Emilia, on the other hand, discovered, or thought she discovered, certain defects in me, and judged me and in consequence ceased to love me.

The less one notices happiness, the greater it is. It may seem strange, but in those two years I sometimes thought I was actually bored. Certainly, at the time, I did not realize that I was happy. It seemed to me that I was doing what everyone did – loving my wife and being loved by her; and this love of ours seemed to me an ordinary, normal fact, or rather, to be in no way precious – just like the air one breathes, and there's plenty of it and it becomes precious only when it begins to run short. If

5

anyone had told me, at that time, that I was happy, I should even have been surprised; in all probability I should have answered that I was not happy because, although I loved my wife and she loved me, I felt a lack of security for the immediate future. This was true: we barely managed to rub along on what I earned, with great difficulty, as film critic on a daily paper of secondary importance, combined with other similar journalistic activities; we lived in a furnished room in a lodging-house; we often had no money for extras, sometimes not even for necessities. How could I be happy? Thus I never had so much to complain of as I did during the time when in truth – as I came to realize later – I was completely and profoundly happy.

At the end of those two first years of married life our situation at last improved: I got to know Battista, a film producer, and for him I wrote my first film-script – a job which, at the time, I considered to be merely a stop-gap, particularly in relation to my more exalted literary ambitions, but which was fated, on the other hand, to become my profession. At the same time, however, my relations with Emilia began to change for the worse. My story, in fact, begins with my own first beginnings as a professional script-writer and with the first deterioration of my relations with my wife – two occurrences that were almost simultaneous and, as will be seen, directly linked together.

Looking back, I am aware of having preserved a confused memory of an incident which appeared at the time to be irrelevant but to which, afterwards, I was forced to attribute a decisive importance. I see myself standing on the pavement of a street in the centre of the town. Emilia, Battista and I had dined at a restaurant and Battista had suggested finishing the evening at his house and we had accepted. All three of us had been standing beside Battista's car, a red car, very expensive, but with a narrow body and only two seats. Battista, who was already sitting at the wheel, leaned over and opened the door, saying: 'I'm sorry, but there's only room for one. You'll have to find your own way, Molteni . . . Unless you'd rather wait for me here: in that case I'll come back and fetch you.' Emilia was beside me, in her black silk evening dress, the only one she had, a low-necked, sleeveless dress; and over her arm she was holding her fur cape: it was October and still warm. I looked at her, and for some reason noticed that her beauty, usually so serene and placid, had in it, that evening, as it were a new kind of restlessness, almost a disturbed look. I said gaily: 'Emilia, you go on with Battista . . . I'll follow in a taxi.' Emilia looked at me and then answered slowly, in a reluctant tone of voice: 'Wouldn't it be better for Battista to go on, and for us two to go together in the taxi?' Then Battista put his head out of the window of the car and exclaimed in a joking way: 'You're a nice sort of person. You want me to go all alone.' 'It's not that,' began Emilia, 'but . . .'; and then I suddenly noticed that her beautiful face, usually so calm and harmonious, was now darkened and, one might even say, distorted by an almost pained perplexity. But in the meantime I had already said: 'You're right, Battista. Come on, Emilia; you go with him and I'll take a taxi.' This time Emilia yielded, or rather, obeyed, and got into the car. But – a further sensation that comes back to me only now, as I write about it – once she was seated beside Battista, with the door of the car still open, she looked at me with a hesitating glance, a glance of mingled pleading and repugnance. I took no notice of my own sensation, however, and, with the decided gesture of one who closes the door of a safe, I slammed the heavy door. The car moved away, and I, feeling very cheerful and whistling to myself, started off towards the near-by taxi rank.

7

The producer's house was not far from the restaurant, and normally I should have reached it in a taxi, if not quite at the same time as Battista, at any rate very shortly afterwards. But what should happen, when we were half-way there, but a mishap, at a crossroads: the taxi ran into a private car, and both sustained some damage; the taxi had a wing scratched and bent, the side of the other car was dented. At once the two drivers got out and faced each other, arguing and swearing, people collected, a policeman intervened and with some difficulty separated them, and finally names and addresses were taken. All this time I sat waiting inside the taxi, without impatience, in fact with a sensation almost of happiness, because I had had plenty of good food and drink and at the end of dinner Battista had proposed that I should take a share in the script of one of his films. But the collision and the subsequent explanations had lasted perhaps ten, perhaps fifteen minutes, and so I was late in arriving at Battista's. As I came into the sitting-room I saw Emilia sitting in an armchair, her legs crossed, and Battista standing in one corner in front of a bar on wheels. Battista greeted me gaily: Emilia, on the other hand, asked me, in a plaintive, almost melting, tone, where I had been all that time. I answered lightly that I had had an accident, realizing at the same time that I was adopting a tone of evasiveness, as if I had something to conceal: in reality it was simply the tone of one who attributes no importance to what he is saying. But Emilia persisted, still in that strange tone of voice: 'An accident . . . what d'you mean, an accident?' – and then I, surprised and perhaps even a little alarmed, gave an account of what had happened. This time, however, it seemed to me that I went into too many details, as though I were afraid of not being believed; and I was, in fact, aware of having made a slight mistake, first by being reticent and now by being over-precise. Emilia, however, did not insist further; and Battista, full of laughter and affability, put down three glasses on the table and offered me a drink. I sat down; and so, chattering and making jokes – especially Battista and I – we passed a couple of hours. Battista was so exuberant and gay that I hardly noticed Emilia was not so, at all. In any case she was always rather silent and retiring, because she was shy, and so her reserve did not astonish me. I was only slightly surprised that she did not take part in the conversation at least with glances and smiles, as she usually did: but she did not smile or look at us; all she did was to smoke and drink in silence, as though she were alone. At the end of the evening, Battista talked to me seriously about the film in which I was to collaborate, telling me the story, giving me information about the director and about my fellow script-writer, and finally inviting me to come to his office next day in order to sign the contract. Emilia took the opportunity of a moment's silence, after this invitation, to rise to her feet and say that she was tired and wanted to go home. We said good night to Battista, we left the room and went downstairs to the ground floor and out into the street, and we walked along the street to the taxi rank, without speaking a word. We got in and the taxi moved off. I was wild with delight at Battista's unhoped-for proposal, and I could not help saying to Emilia: 'This film-script comes just at the right moment . . . I don't know how we should have got along without it . . . I should have had to borrow money.' Emilia's only reply was to ask: 'How much do they pay for a script?' I told her the amount and added: 'So our problems are solved, anyhow for next winter'; and as I spoke I put out my hand and took Emilia's. She allowed her hand to be pressed and did not say any more until we arrived home.

2

After that evening, everything went, as far as my work was concerned, in the best possible way. I went next morning to see Battista, signed the contract for the script, and received my first advance of money. It was, I remember, a film of little importance, of the comic-sentimental type for which, serious-minded as I was, I did not imagine myself to be cut out, but which in fact showed me, as I worked on it, that I had an unsuspected vocation. That same day I had a first meeting with the director and also with my fellow script-writer.

While it is possible for me to indicate exactly the starting-point of my career as a script-writer, which was that evening at Battista's, it is very difficult for me to say with the same precision when my relations with my wife began to deteriorate. I could, of course, point to that same evening, as the beginning of this deterioration; but that would be what is called being wise after the event; and all the more so because Emilia gave no sign, for some time afterwards, of any change in her demeanour towards me. The change certainly took place during the month which followed that evening, but I really could not say at what moment, in Emilia's mind, the decisive turn of the scale occurred, nor what caused this to happen. At that time we were seeing Battista almost every day, and I could relate, with an abundance of detail, many other episodes similar to that of the first evening in his house; episodes, that is, which were then in no way to be distinguished – to my eyes, anyhow – from the general colour of my life, but which later acquired, more or less all of them, some special prominence or meaning. There is just one fact I wish to note: every time Battista invited us, which now happened very often, Emilia always showed, at first, a certain reluctance to go with me, not a strong nor a very decided reluctance, it is true, but curiously persistent in its expression and in its justifications. She always adduced some pretext or other that had nothing to do with Battista, in order not to come with us; always, in the same way, I proved to her without any difficulty that the pretext did not hold good, and insisted on trying to find out whether she disliked Battista, or what her reason was; always, in the end, her answer to my question, given with a slight touch of perplexity, was that she did not in the least dislike Battista, that she had no fault to find with him, and that she did not want to go out with us simply because these evenings tired her and, really and truly, bored her. I was not content with these vague explanations and returned to my point, hinting that something must have happened between her and Battista, even though Battista himself was not conscious of it, or had not intended it. But, the more I tried to prove to her that she did not like Battista, the more she seemed to persevere in her denial: her perplexity, in the end, disappeared altogether, and its place was taken by a wilful obstinacy and determination. Then, completely reassured with regard to her feelings towards Battista and Battista's demeanour towards her, I went on to point out to her the reasons that told so strongly in favour of her giving us her company on these occasions: how hitherto I had never gone out without her, and Battista knew it; how her presence gave pleasure to Battista, as was shown by his urging, every time he invited us: 'Of course, bring your wife'; how her absence, unexpected and difficult to justify as it was, might appear ill-natured, or, even worse, insulting to Battista, upon whom our living now depended: how, when all was said and done, since she was unable to show any valid reasons for her absence, whereas I was in a position to give many excellent reasons for her presence, it was preferable that she should put up with the fatigue and boredom required of her. Emilia usually listened to these arguments of mine with a dreamy and as it were contemplative attention: it might have been thought that it was not so much the reasons themselves, as my face and my gestures while expounding them, that interested her; then, in the end, she would invariably give in and start silently dressing to go out. At the last moment, when she was ready to go, I would ask her, once more and for the last time, if she really disliked coming with me – not so much because by now I was doubtful of her answer, as in order to leave her no doubts about her freedom of decision. She would answer, in a categorical manner, that she did not dislike going, and then, out we would go.

All this, however, I reconstructed later, as I have already mentioned, patiently retracing in memory a number of occurrences which – at least at the time – had seemed insignificant, and which had passed almost unobserved by me at the moment when they took place. At the time I had been aware merely of a change for the worse in Emilia's demeanour towards me, but without explaining or defining it to myself in any way; in the same way one becomes conscious, through a change and a heaviness in the air, of the approach of a thunderstorm though the sky is still serene. I began to think she loved me less than in the past, because I noticed that she was no longer so anxious to be near me as in the first times after our marriage. In those days I would say: 'Look, I've got to go out, I'll be out for a couple of hours, but I'll come back as soon as I can'; and she would not protest, but she showed, by her expression of mingled sadness and resignation, that she did not like my being away. So much so, indeed, that often I either gave up going out, excusing myself somehow or other from my engagement; or if possible, took her with me. Her attachment to me, then, was so strong that one day, when she had gone with me to the station from which I was to leave for a very brief journey to North Italy, I saw her, as we were saying good-bye, turn away her face to hide the tears that filled her eyes. That time I pretended not to notice her grief; but during the whole journey I was haunted by remorse for that shamefaced but uncontrollable weeping; and from then onwards I ceased completely to travel without her. But now, instead of assuming the usual, beloved expression with its slight suggestion of mortification and sadness, all she would do, if I announced that I was going out, was to answer calmly, often without even looking up from the book she was reading: 'All right, I understand; then we'll see each other at dinner . . . don't be late.' Sometimes she seemed actually to want my absence to last longer than I myself intended. I would say to her, for instance: 'I've got to go out . . . I'll be back at five'; and she would answer: 'Stay out as long as you like . . . I've got things to do.' One day I remarked in a light tone of voice that she seemed to prefer that I shouldn't be there; but she made no direct answer, merely saying that, since I was busy, one way and another, almost all day, it was just as well that we shouldn't meet except at meal-times, and so she would be able to get through her own jobs in peace. This was only partly true: my work as a scriptwriter obliged me to be out of the house only in the afternoons; and hitherto I had always arranged matters so that I could spend the rest of the day with her. From

13

that day onwards, however, I took to going out in the morning as well.

In the days when Emilia gave me to understand that my absences were displeasing to her, I used to leave the house with a light heart, well content, in reality, at her displeasure, as being yet another proof of the great love she felt for me. But as soon as I became aware that not merely did she show no disappointment, but even seemed to prefer to be left alone, I began to experience an obscure feeling of distress, as if, all of a sudden, I had felt the ground give way beneath my feet. I went out now not only in the afternoons to go and work at the film-script, but in the mornings too, as I said, and often without any other purpose than to test Emilia's indifference, so utterly new and, to me, so bitter; and yet she did not show the slightest displeasure, in fact she accepted my absences with placidity if not actually – so it seemed to me – with ill-disguised relief. At first I tried to console myself for this coldness by arguing that, after two years of marriage, habit, even though it may be an affectionate habit, creeps into love with fatal effect, and the assurance of being loved takes away all character of passion from a married couple's relationship. Yet I felt that this was not true: I felt it rather than thought it, for thought is always more fallible, even in its apparent preciseness, than obscure, confused feeling. I felt, in fact, that Emilia had ceased to be displeased at my absences, not because she considered them inevitable and without consequence to our relationship, but because she loved me less, or indeed not at all. I also felt that something, without doubt, must have happened to change her feeling, which had once been so tender and so possessive.

14

3

At the time I first met Battista, I found myself in an extremely difficult, not to say desperate, situation, and I did not know how to escape from it. My difficulty consisted in my having, just at that time, acquired the lease of a flat, although I had not the money to complete my payment for it and did not know how I should be able to procure it. We had lived, Emilia and I, during our first two years, in a large furnished room in a lodging-house. Any other woman but Emilia would perhaps not have put up with this provisional arrangement; but, in the case of Emilia, I think that, by accepting it, she gave me the greatest proof of love that a devoted wife can give to a husband. Emilia was, indeed, what is called a born housewife; but in her love of home there was more than the natural inclination common to all women; I mean that there was something that resembled a deep, jealous passion, almost a hunger, which went beyond her own self and seemed to derive its origin from some ancestral situation. She came of a poor family; she herself, when I first came to know her, was working as a typist; and I think that her love of home was an unconscious means of expression for the frustrated aspirations of generations of disinherited people who were chronically incapable of setting up an abode of their own, however modest. I do not know whether she was under the illusion that, with our marriage, her dreams of domesticity would come true; but I remember that one of the few times I ever saw her weep was when I was forced to confess, shortly after we

15

became engaged, that I was not yet in a position to provide her with a home of her own, even a rented one, and that we must be content, at first, with a furnished lodging. It seemed to me that those tears, quickly suppressed as they were, were an outward expression not only of bitter disappointment at seeing her cherished dream thrust away into the future, but also of the actual power of that dream, which for her was, as it were, more a reason for living than just a dream.

And so we lived, those first two years, in a furnished room; but how meticulously tidy and bright and clean Emilia always kept it! It was obvious that, as far as possible – and in a furnished room it is possible only to a limited degree – she wanted to deceive herself into believing that she had a home of her own; and that, lacking her own household furniture, she wanted at least to infuse her own concentrated domestic spirit into the lodging-house-keeper's shabby utensils. There were always flowers in a vase on my desk; my papers were always arranged with loving, inviting orderliness, as though to encourage me to work and guarantee me the greatest possible privacy and quietness; the tea service always stood ready on a small table, with napkins and a box of biscuits; never was a garment or other intimate object to be found where it should not be, on the floor or the chairs, as so often happens in similar cramped, temporary abodes. After the first, hurried cleaning by the servant-girl, Emilia would subject the whole room to a second, more scrupulous, personal cleaning, so that everything which could shine and reflect *did* shine and reflect, even the smallest brass knob on the window-frame or the least visible strip of wood on the floor; at night, she insisted on preparing the bed herself, without the help of the maid, laying out her own muslin nightgown on one side and my pyjamas on the other and carefully turning down the sheets and arranging the twin pillows; in the morning she would get up before me, and, going to the lodging-house-keeper's kitchen, would prepare the breakfast and bring it to me herself, on a tray. She did all these things in silence, discreetly, without drawing attention to herself, but with an intensity, a concentration, an eager, absorbed solicitude that betrayed a passion too deep to be openly proclaimed. Nevertheless, in spite of these pathetic efforts on her part, the furnished room remained just a furnished room; and the illusion that she sought to create for herself and me was never complete. And then, from time to time, in moments of excessive weariness or discouragement, she would complain – gently, it is true, and almost placidly, in accordance with her character, but not without evident bitterness – asking me how long this provisional, this inferior, way of living would have to continue. I was aware that it was a real sorrow that lay behind this very moderate expression of displeasure; and I worried myself with the thought that, sooner or later, I would somehow have to satisfy her.

In the end I decided, as I said, to buy the lease of a flat; not because I had the means to do so, for such means were still lacking to me, but because I understood how she was suffering and how her suffering would perhaps, some day, overcome her powers of endurance. I had put aside a small sum of money during those two years; to this sum I added some more money which I had procured on loan; and so I was able to pay the first instalment. In doing this I did not, however, experience the joyful feelings of a man preparing a home for his bride; on the contrary, I was anxious and sometimes seriously distressed, because I did not know in the least how I would manage when, a few months later, the time came to pay the second instalment.

At that time, in fact, I was so desperate that I had almost a feeling of rancour against Emilia, who, by the tenacity of her passion, had in a way forced me to take this imprudent and dangerous step.

However, the profound joy of Emilia when I announced that the matter was settled, and, later, the unaccustomed feelings – strange to me, both in their quality and their intensity – which she displayed on the day we went, for the first time, into the still unfurnished flat, made me for some time forget my troubles. I have said that, with Emilia, love of home had all the characteristics of a passion; and I must add that, on this occasion, that same passion appeared to me to be bound up with, and mingled with, sensuality, as though the fact of having at last acquired a flat for her had made me, in her eyes, not merely more lovable, but also, in a wholly physical sense, closer and more intimate. We had gone to inspect the place, and Emilia, to begin with, walked round all the cold, empty rooms with me while I explained the purpose of each of them and the way in which I thought to arrange the furniture. But, at the end of our visit, as I was walking over to a window with the intention of opening it and showing her the view to be enjoyed from it, she came close up to me and, pressing her whole body against me, whispered to me to give her a kiss. This was quite a new thing for her, usually so discreet, so almost shy, in any expression of love. Excited by this novelty and by the tone of her voice, I kissed her, as she wanted; and all the time the kiss lasted – certainly one of the most violent and most abandoned we ever exchanged – I felt her clinging more and more closely with her body against mine, as though inviting me to greater intimacy; and then, wildly, she tore off her skirt, unbuttoned her chemise, and thrust her belly against mine. The kiss over, in a very low voice

18

that was like an inarticulate breath and yet was melodious, melting, she murmured in my ear – or at least it seemed to me – that I should take her; and meanwhile, with all the weight of her body, she was pulling me down towards the floor. We made love on the ground, on the dusty tiles, under the sill of the window I had meant to open. Yet in the ardour of that embrace, so unrestrained and so unusual, I was conscious not only of the love she felt for me at that time, but, more particularly, of the outpouring of her repressed passion for a home, which in her expressed itself quite naturally through the channel of unforeseen sensuality. In that embrace, in fact, consummated on that dirty floor, in the chilly gloom of the empty flat, she was giving herself, so I felt, to the giver of the home, not the husband. And those bare, echoing rooms still smelling of paint and fresh plaster, had stirred something in the innermost recesses of her heart that no caress of mine, hitherto, had ever had the power to awaken.

Between our visit to the empty flat and the day of our entry into it a couple of months went by, during which the necessary contracts were drawn up, all in Emilia's name, because I knew that this gave her pleasure; while we also collected together the small amount of furniture that, with my very limited means, I could afford to buy. Meanwhile, when the first feeling of satisfaction was over, I felt, as I have already mentioned, extremely anxious about the future, and at moments positively desperate. I was earning enough by now, it is true, for us to live in a modest manner and even put aside a few pennies; but these savings were certainly not sufficient to pay the next instalment on the flat. My desperation was all the more acute inasmuch as I could not even have the relief of talking about it to Emilia: I did not wish to spoil her pleasure. But I recall that time as a period of great anxiety and, in a way, of diminished love for Emilia. Indeed I could not help realizing that she was not in the least worried to know how I had managed to come by so much money, although she knew our real position perfectly well. This thought was vaguely surprising to me, and there were moments when it inspired me almost with irritation against her – she who now, all busy and cheerful, thought of nothing but going round the shops looking for things to furnish the flat, and who every day, in her most placid tone of voice, announced some new acquisition. I wondered how it came about that she, who loved me so much, failed to guess at the cruel anxieties that oppressed me; but I realized that, probably, she thought that if I had bought the lease of the flat I had no doubt also taken steps to procure the necessary money. Nevertheless, her serenity and satisfaction seemed to me, in contrast to my own wretched worries, to be a sign of selfishness, or, at the least, of insensibility.

I was also troubled, at that period, that even the image I had hitherto made of myself in my own mind had changed. Up till then I had looked upon myself as an intellectual, a man of culture, a writer for the theatre – the 'art' theatre, I mean – for which I had always had a great passion and to which I felt I was drawn by a natural vocation. This *moral* image, as I may call it, also had an influence on the *physical* image: I saw myself as a young man whose thinness, short sight, nervousness, pallor and carelessness in dress all bore witness, in anticipation, to the literary glory for which I was destined. But at that time, under the pressure of my cruel anxieties, this very promising and flattering picture had given place to an entirely different one, that of a poor devil who had been caught in a shabby, pathetic trap, who had not been able to resist his love for his wife and had overreached himself

20

and would be forced to struggle, for goodness knows how much longer, in the mortifying toils of poverty. I saw myself changed in my physical aspect as well: I was no longer the young and still unknown theatrical genius; I was the starving journalist, the contributor to cheap reviews and second-rate newspapers: or perhaps – even worse – the scraggy employee of some private company or Government office. This man hid his anxieties from his wife, so as not to worry her; he ran about the town all day long, looking for work and often not finding any; he would wake up in the night with a start, thinking of the debts that had to be paid; in fact he no longer thought of, or saw, anything but money. It was a touching picture, perhaps, but lacking in lustre and dignity, the picture of a wretched, conventional literary figure, and I hated it because I thought that, slowly and insensibly, with the years, I should end by resembling it, in spite of myself. But there it was: I had not married a woman who could understand and share my ideas, tastes and ambitions; instead, I had married, for her beauty, an uncultivated, simple typist, full, it seemed to me, of all the prejudices and ambitions of the class from which she came. With the first I could have faced the discomforts of a poverty-stricken, disorganized life, in a studio or a furnished room, in expectation of the theatrical successes that were bound to come; but for the second I had had to provide the home of her dreams. And at the cost, I thought in desperation, of having to renounce, perhaps for ever, my precious literary ambitions.

There was another factor which contributed at that time to increase my feeling of anguish and impotence in face of material difficulties. I felt that the metal of my spirit, like a bar of iron that is softened and bent by a persistent flame, was being gradually softened and bent by the troubles that oppressed it. In spite of myself, I was conscious of a feeling of envy for those who did not suffer from such troubles, for the wealthy and the privileged; and this envy, I observed, was accompanied – still against my will – by a feeling of bitterness towards them, which, in turn, did not limit its aim to particular persons or situations, but, as if by an uncontrollable bias, tended to assume the general, abstract character of a whole conception of life. In fact, during those difficult days, I came very gradually to feel that my irritation and my intolerance of poverty were turning into a revolt against injustice, and not only against the injustice which struck at me personally, but the injustice from which so many others like me suffered. I was quite aware of this almost imperceptible transforma-tion of my subjective resentments into objective reflec-tions and states of mind, owing to the bent of my thoughts which led always and irresistibly in the same direction: owing also to my conversation, which, without my inten-ding it, always harped upon the same subject. I also noticed in myself, at that same period, a growing sym-pathy for those political parties which proclaimed their struggle against the evils and infamies of the society to which, in the end, I had attributed the troubles that beset me – a society which, as I thought, in reference to myself, allowed its best sons to languish and protected its worst ones. Usually, and in simpler, less cultivated people, this process occurs without their knowing it, in the dark depths of consciousness where, by a kind of mysterious alchemy, egoism is transmuted into altruism, hatred into love, fear into courage; but to me, accustomed as I was to observing and studying myself, the whole thing was clear and visible, as though I were watching it happen to someone else; and yet I was aware the whole time that I was being swayed by material, subjective factors, that I was transforming purely personal motives into universal reasons. I had never wished to become a member of any political party, as almost everyone did during that uneasy period after the war, just because it seemed to me that I could not take part in politics, as so many did, for personal motives, but only from intellectual conviction, which, however, I had so far lacked; and I was therefore very angry when I felt my ideas, my conversation, my whole demeanour going very gradually adrift on the current of my own interests, slowly changing colour according to the difficulties of the moment. 'So I'm really just like everyone else,' I thought furiously. 'Does it only need an empty purse to make me dream, like so many other people, of the rebirth of humanity?' But it was an impotent fury; and in the end, one day when I felt more desperate or less firm than usual, I let myself be convinced by a friend who had been hovering round me for some time, and became a member of the Communist Party. Immediately afterwards I reflected that, once again, I had behaved, not like the young, unrecognized genius, but like the starving journalist or the scraggy employee into which I was so terrified that time would transform me. But the thing was done now, I was inside the Party and I could not draw back again. Emilia's reception of the news of the step I had taken was characteristic: 'But now only the Communists will give you work . . . the others will boycott you.' I had not the courage to tell her what I was thinking – which was that, in all probability, I should never have become a Communist if I had not bought the lease of that over-expensive flat, in order to give her pleasure. And that was the end of it.

At last we moved in, and the very next day, by a coincidence that seemed to me providential, I met Battista, and, as I have already related, was at once invited by

23

him to work on the script of one of his films. For some time I felt relieved and more cheerful than I had been for many weeks: I thought I would do four or five film-scripts to pay off the lease of the flat, and then devote myself again to journalism and my beloved theatre. Meanwhile, my love for Emilia had come back to me stronger than ever, and sometimes I went so far as to reproach myself, with the bitterest remorse, for having been capable of thinking ill of her and judging her to be selfish and insensitive. This brief bright interval, however, lasted only a very short time. Almost immediately the sky of my life clouded over again. But at first it was only an exceedingly small cloud, though of a decidedly gloomy colour.

4

My meeting with Battista took place on the first Monday in October. The day before, we had moved into the flat, which was now completely furnished. This flat, the cause, to me, of so many anxieties, was in truth neither large nor luxurious. It had only two good rooms – a big living room, of greater length than width, and a bedroom, also of good proportions. The bathroom, the kitchen and the maid's room were all three very small – reduced, as always in modern buildings, to the smallest possible size. Besides this there was a little windowless box which Emilia intended to make into a dressing-room. The flat was on the top floor of a newly-built block, as smooth and white as if it had been all made of plaster, in a narrow, slightly-sloping street. The whole of one side of the street was occupied by a row of buildings similar to ours, while along the other side ran the boundary wall of the garden of a private villa, with branches of great, leafy trees hanging over it. It was a beautiful view, as I pointed out to Emilia, and we could almost delude ourselves into thinking that this garden in which we could catch glimpses here and there, where the trees thinned out, of winding paths and fountains and open spaces, was not cut off from us by a street and a wall, and that we could go down and walk about in it as often as we liked.

We moved in during the afternoon. I was busy the whole day, and I do not remember where we dined, nor with whom; I only remember that, towards midnight, I was standing in the middle of the bedroom in front of the triple looking-glass, looking at myself and slowly undoing my tie. All at once, in the mirror I saw Emilia take a pillow from the double bed and go off towards the door of the living room. Surprised, I asked; 'What are you doing?'

I had spoken without moving. Still in the mirror, I saw her stop in the doorway and turn, as she said in a casual tone: 'You won't mind, will you, if I sleep on the divan bed in the other room.'

'Just for tonight, you mean?' I inquired, puzzled and still uncomprehending.

'No; for always,' she replied hurriedly. 'To tell you the truth, that was one of the reasons why I wanted a new home. . . . I really can't go on sleeping with the shutters open, as you like to do . . . I wake up every morning at cock-crow and then I can't go to sleep again, and I go about all day long with a sleepy feeling in my head. You don't mind, do you? . . . I do think it's better for us to sleep separate.'

I still failed to understand, and at first I felt no more than vaguely irritated at an innovation so completely unexpected. Walking across to her, I said: 'But this can't go on . . . We've only two rooms; in one there's the bed, and in the other, the armchairs and divans . . . Why . . . ? Besides, sleeping on a divan, even if it can be turned into a bed, is not very comfortable!'

'I never dared tell you before,' she answered, lowering her eyes without looking at me.

'During these two years,' I persisted, 'you've never once complained . . . I thought you'd got accustomed to it.'

She raised her head, pleased, it seemed to me, that I had taken up the point of the excuse she had made. 'I've never got accustomed to it . . . I've always slept badly . . . recently, in fact, perhaps my nerves are bad nowadays,

I've hardly been sleeping at all . . . If we could only go to bed early; but, one way or another, we're always late . . . and then . . .' She did not finish her sentence, and made as if to move away towards the living-room. I went with her, and said hastily: 'Wait a minute . . . if you like, we can perfectly well give up sleeping with the shutters open . . . It's all right – from now on we'll sleep with them shut.'

I realized, as I spoke, that this proposal was not merely a demonstration of affectionate compliance; in reality, as I knew, I wanted to put her to the test. I saw her shake her head, and she answered, with a faint smile: 'No, no . . . Why should you sacrifice yourself? You've always said you feel suffocated with the shutters closed . .. It's better for us to sleep apart.'

'I assure you, for me it will be a very slight sacrifice . . . I shall soon get used to it.'

She appeared to hesitate and then said, with unexpected firmness: 'No; I don't want any sacrifices – either great or small . . . I shall sleep in the other room.'

'And what if I say I don't like it, and that I want you to sleep with me?'

She hesitated again. Then, in the good-natured tone which was usual to her: 'Riccardo, that's just like you . . . You didn't want to make this sacrifice two years ago, when we got married; and now you want to make it, at all costs . . . What's the matter with you? Plenty of married people sleep apart and are fond of each other just the same . . . And you'll be freer in the mornings, too, when you have to go to work; you won't wake me up any more.'

'But you've just said that you always woke at cock-crow . . . I don't leave the house at cock-crow!'

'Oh, how pig-headed you are!' she exclaimed impatiently. And this time, without paying any more attention to me, she left the room.

Left alone, I sat down on the bed, which, despoiled of one of its pillows, already had about it a suggestion of separation and desertion, and so I remained for some moments in bewilderment, looking at the open door through which Emilia had disappeared. One question came into my mind: 'Did Emilia not want to sleep with me any longer because the daylight really annoyed her, or simply because she did not want to go on sleeping with me?' I was inclined to believe in the second of these alternatives, although I longed with all my heart to believe in the first. I felt, however, that if I had accepted Emilia's explanation, there would always have been a doubt in my mind. I did not admit to myself, but the final question, in reality, was: 'Has Emilia perhaps ceased to love me?'

In the meantime, while, absorbed in these thoughts, I sat looking about the room, Emilia was coming and going, carrying into the living-room, after the pillow, a pair of folded sheets that she took from the cupboard, a blanket, a dressing-gown. It was the beginning of October, and the weather was still mild, and she was going about the flat in a gauzy, tranparent chemise. I have not yet described Emilia, but I should like to do so now, if only in order to explain my feelings that night. She was perhaps not really a tall woman, but to me, owing to the feeling that I had for her, she seemed taller and, above all, more majestic than any other woman I had ever known. I could not say whether this look of majesty was innate in her or whether it was my own ravished glances that attributed it to her; I only remember that, on the first night of our wedding, when she had taken off her high-heeled shoes, I went up to her in the middle of the room and embraced her, and was vaguely surprised when I noticed that her forehead barely came up to the top of my chest and that I was taller than her by a head and shoulders. But later, when she was

28

lying beside me on the bed, there was a further surprise: her naked body now looked to me big, ample, powerful, although I knew that, in reality, she was not in the least massive. She had the most beautiful shoulders, the most beautiful arms, the most beautiful neck I had ever seen, full and rounded, shapely in form and languid in movement. Her complexion was dark, her nose pronounced and in form severe; her mouth full and fresh and laughing, with two rows of teeth of a luminous whiteness which seemed always to be wet and gleaming with saliva; her eyes very large, of a fine golden brown, sensual in expression, and sometimes, in moments of abandon, strangely relaxed and dazed-looking. She had not, as I have already said, a really beautiful figure; and yet she appeared to have – for some reason that I cannot explain; perhaps because of the supple slenderness of her waist which emphasized the form of her hips and breast; perhaps because of her erect, dignified carriage; perhaps because of the youthful boldness and vigour of her long, straight, well-shaped legs. She had, in fact, an air of grace and of placid, unconscious, spontaneous majesty such as comes from nature alone, and which, on that account, appears all the more mysterious and indefinable.

And so that evening, as she went backwards and forwards between the bedroom and the living-room, and as I followed her with my eyes, not knowing what to say, and feeling at the same time both displeased and embarrassed, my glance travelled from her serene face to her body, which was sometimes more, sometimes less visible through the thin stuff of her chemise, its colours and contours being veiled and broken up by the folds; and suddenly, the suspicion that she no longer loved me sprang into my mind again, in an abrupt, haunting sort of way, as a feeling of the impossibility of contact and communion between my body and hers. It was a sensation I had never felt before, and for a moment I was as it were stunned and at the same time incredulous. Love is certainly, and before all else, a matter of feeling; but it is also, in an ineffable, almost spiritual manner, a communion of bodies – that communion, indeed, which up till then I had enjoyed without being conscious of it, as something obvious and completely natural. And now, as if my eyes had been at last opened to a fact which was clear and yet, till that moment, invisible, I was conscious that this communion might no longer exist between us, in fact, no longer did exist. And I, like a person who suddenly realizes he is hanging over an abyss, felt a kind of painful nausea at the thought that our intimacy had turned, for no reason at all, into estrangement, absence, separation.

I came to a pause at this staggering notion; meanwhile, Emilia, who had gone into the bathroom, was washing, as I could tell from the sounds of water flowing from taps. I had an acute feeling of impotence and, at the same time, a violent desire to overcome it as quickly as possible. So far I had loved Emilia both easily and ignorantly; and my love had always manifested itself as if by enchantment, with a thoughtless, impetuous, inspired impulse which hitherto had seemed to me to spring from myself and from myself alone. Now, for the first time, I realized that this impulse depended upon, and nourished itself upon, a similar impulse in Emilia, and, seeing her so changed, I feared that I should no longer be capable of loving her with the same ease and spontaneity and naturalness. I feared, in fact, that that admirable communion, of which I had only now become aware, would be succeeded by, on my side, an act of cold imposition, and on hers . . . I did not know what her attitude would be, but I felt intuitively that if, on

30

my side, there was, as I have said, imposition, on hers there could only be a non-participating passivity, if not worse.

At that moment Emilia passed close to me as she came and went about the room. I leant forward with an almost involuntary lunge and seized her by the arm, saying: 'Come here . . . I want to talk to you.'

Her immediate reaction was to draw away from me, then, next moment, she yielded and came and sat down on the bed, though at some distance from me. 'Talk to me? What d'you want to talk to me about?'

For some reason or other, my throat now felt choked by sudden anxiety. Or perhaps it was shyness – a feeling which had hitherto been absent from our relationship and which, more than anything else, seemed to confirm the change that had taken place in it. 'Yes,' I said. 'I want to talk to you; I have an impression that something has changed between us.'

She threw me a rapid, sideways glance and answered with decision: 'I don't understand you . . . What d'you mean, changed? Nothing's changed.'

'I haven't changed, but you have!'

'I haven't changed in the least . . . I'm still just the same.'

'You used to love me more . . . You used to be sorry if I left you alone when I went out . . . You used not to mind sleeping with me then . . . on the contrary.'

'Ah, that's what it's all about,' she exclaimed, but I noticed that her tone was less assured. 'I knew you would think something like that . . . But why don't you stop tormenting yourself like this? I don't want to sleep with you, merely because I want to *sleep*, and with you I can never manage to – that's all.'

Now, strangely, I felt that arguments and ill-humour

were melting quickly away and dissolving into nothingness, like wax at the fire: she was sitting beside me, in that vaporous crumpled chemise through which it seemed that only the most intimate and secret colours and forms of her body were visible; and I desired her and felt it strange that she should not be aware of it and should not stop talking and embrace me, as had alway happened in the past at the mere meeting of our disturbed glances. On the other hand, this feeling of desire made me hope not only that I should be drawn with the old irresistible force towards her, but also that I should arouse in her a similar impulse towards me. I said, in a very low voice: 'If nothing's changed, prove it to me.'

'But I prove it to you every day, every hour!'

'No; now.'

As I said this, I leant forward and took hold of her almost violently by the hair and tried to bend her head back to kiss her. Obediently she allowed herself to be drawn towards me, but at the last moment she avoided my kiss by a slight movement of her head, so that my lips could only reach her neck. Letting her go, I said: 'Don't you want me to kiss you?'

'It's not that,' she murmured, rearranging her hair with characteristically wayward indolence. 'If it was just one kiss, I would willingly give it you . . . But then you go on . . . and it's late already . . .'

I felt hurt by these prudent, discouraging words. 'It's never too late for such things,' I said.

Meanwhile, I was trying to kiss her again, pulling her towards me by the arm. 'Ooh!' she cried out. 'You're hurting me!'

Now I had scarcely touched her, and I remembered how, at the time when we loved each other, I had sometimes clasped her violently in my arms, without drawing so much as a sigh from her. Irritated, I said: 'In the old days it didn't hurt you!'

'You've got hands like iron,' she replied: 'you don't realize . . . You must have left marks on me now!' All this was said in an indolent way, but, I noticed, without the slightest coquettishness.

'Come on,' I insisted sharply. 'Are you going to give me that kiss, or not?'

'Here you are, then'; and she leant forward and, in a motherly way, flicked me a light kiss on the brow. 'And now let me go to bed; it's late.'

I did not intend to put up with that; and I took hold of her again with both hands, just below the waist, where the bust fits into the broadness of the hips. 'Emilia,' I said, leaning towards her as she drew herself away, 'that's not the kiss I wanted from you.'

She thrust me away, saying once again, but now in a distinctly rough tone of voice: 'Oh, let me alone . . . You hurt me!'

'It's not true; it can't be true,' I muttered between my clenched teeth, throwing myself upon her.

This time she disengaged herself with two or three energetic, simple movements; then rose to her feet and, as if suddenly making up her mind, said, without any show of modesty: 'If you want to make love, all right then . . . But don't hurt me; I can't bear to feel myself squeezed like that!'

I was left breathless. Her tone was now utterly cold, I could not help noticing, and practical, without the faintest touch of feeling in it. For a moment I sat quite still on the bed, my hands clasped, my head bent. Then her voice reached me again: 'Well, then, if you really want to, let's get on with it . . . shall we?'

Without raising my head, I said in a low voice: 'Yes, I

33

want to.' It was not true, for by this time I no longer desired her, but I wished to endure this new, curious sense of estrangement to the bitter end. I heard her say 'All right,' and then I heard her walking about the room and moving round the bed behind me. All she had to do was to take off her chemise, I thought, and I recalled how in the past I had watched this simple act with enchanted eyes, like the brigand in the fairy tale who, when the magic word had been uttered, saw the door of the cave slowly open, revealing the splendour of the marvellous treasures within. But this time I was unwilling to look, knowing that I should be looking with different eyes, eyes that were no longer childish and pure, even if desirous, but that had been, by her indifference, made cruel and unworthy both of her and of myself. I remained as I was, leaning forward, my hands in my lap, my head bowed. After a little I heard the springs of the bed creak gently; she had got on to the bed and was lying on top of the bed-clothes. There was again a slight rustling as though she were changing position, and then she said, still in that horrible new voice: 'Well, come along then . . . What are you waiting for?'

I neither turned nor moved; but all of a sudden I wondered whether it had always been like that in our relationship. Yes, I said to myself at once, it had always been like that, more or less; she had always undressed and lain down on the bed: how else could it have been? And yet, at the same time, everything had been different. Never until now had there been this mechanical docility, cold and detached, such as was apparent from the tone of her voice and even from the creaking of the bed-springs and the rustling of the pressed-down bed-covers. Formerly everything, on the contrary, had happened in a cloud of inspired haste, of intoxicated unconsciousness, of ravished complicity. It happens sometimes, when one's

34

mind is absorbed by some profound thought, that one puts down an object of some kind – a book, a brush, a shoe – somewhere or other, and then, when the fit of absorption is over, one looks for it in vain for hours and, in the end, finds it in some strange, almost unbelievable place, so that a physical effort is required to reach it – on top of a cupboard, in a hidden corner, inside a drawer. That is what had happened to me, hitherto, in relation to love-making. Everything had always run its course in a mood of swift, feverish, enchanted absorption, and I had always come to myself again in Emilia's arms almost without being able to recollect how it had all happened and what I had done between the moment when we were sitting opposite each other, quiet and without desire, and that other moment in which we were joined together in the final embrace. This absorption was now entirely lacking in her and therefore in me also. Now I could have observed her movements with a cold, even if excited, eye, just as she, no doubt, could on her side have observed mine. All of a sudden, the feeling which was becoming clearer and clearer in my furious, disgusted mind took on the character of a precise image: I was no longer face to face with the wife I loved and who loved me, but with a rather impatient and inexpert prostitute who was preparing to submit passively to my embraces, hoping only that they would be brief and not too tiring. I had this image right before my eyes for a moment, like an apparition, and then I felt that it went, so to speak, round behind my back and became one with Emilia lying behind me on the bed. At the same moment I rose to my feet, still without turning round, and said: 'Never mind . . . I don't want to, now . . . I'll go and sleep in the other room; you stay here'; then, on tiptoe, I went to the door of the living-room.

The divan bed was ready, with the sheet turned down

and Emilia's nightdress laid out on top with the sleeves spread wide. I took this nightdress, the slippers she had placed on the floor, and the dressing-gown she had arranged on an armchair, went back into the bedroom and put them all down on one of the chairs there. But this time I could not help raising my eyes and looking at her. She was still in the attitude she had taken up when she lay down on the bed and called to me: 'Come along, then!' She was lying quite naked, with one arm behind her neck and her head turned towards me, her eyes wide open, but indifferent and as it were unseeing, and the other arm lying across her body so that her sex was covered by her hand. But now, it seemed to me, she was no longer the prostitute; she had become a semblance in a mirage, with a haze of impossibility, of nostalgia, about her, and infinitely remote, as though she were not only a few paces away from me, but in some far-off region, outside reality and outside my personal feelings.

5

I certainly had a presentiment, that evening, that a period full of difficulties was beginning for me, but, strange to say, I did not infer from Emilia's behaviour the results that might have been expected. There was no doubt that she had shown herself cold and indifferent; and it was perfectly true that I should rather have renounced love altogether than obtain it in that way. But I loved her, and love has a great capacity, not only for illusion, but also for forgetfulness. Next day – I don't know how – the incident of the previous evening, which later on was to appear so full of significance to me, had already lost, in my eyes, much of its importance, losing its burden of hostility and reducing itself to an insignificant divergence of opinion. The truth is that one easily forgets what one does not want to remember; and, furthermore, I think that Emilia herself contributed to my forgetfulness, for a few days later, though she still insisted on sleeping alone, she did not refuse my love. It is true that on this occasion she again behaved in the cold, passive manner which had previously roused me to revolt; but, as often happens, what had seemed intolerable to me on that first evening seemed, a few days later, to be not only tolerable, but even flattering. I was already, in fact, without being aware of it, in the slippery region where the coldness of the day before becomes, a day later – thanks to false arguments and the goodwill of a mind in need of illusion – warm-hearted love. I had thought that Emilia, that first evening, had behaved like a prostitute; but less than a week afterwards I consented to love her and be loved by her in exactly that way; and since, in the obscure depths of my mind, I had perhaps feared that she really did not want me any more, I was grateful to her for her cold, impatient passivity just as though it had been the normal attitude in our sexual relations.

But, if I continued to delude myself that Emilia still loved me as in the past, or rather, if I preferred not to put the question of our love to myself, there was one thing which betrayed that state of my heart towards the change that had come about between us. That was my work. I had, for the time being, given up my theatrical ambitions and devoted myself to the cinema, simply in order to satisfy Emilia's longing to possess a home of her own. As long as I had been sure that Emilia loved me, the work of script-writer did not seem to me too onerous; but after the incident of that evening it seemed to me, all of a sudden, that a subtle feeling of discouragement, of restlessness, of repugnance had crept into it. In reality – as I have already said – I had accepted this job just as I would have accepted any other, even more uncongenial and even farther removed from my own interests, merely out of love for Emilia. Now that this love was on the point of failing me, the work lost its meaning and justification and acquired, in my eyes, the absurd character of sheer slavery.

I want to say a few words about the job of script-writer, if only to give a better understanding of my feelings at that time. As everyone knows, the script-writer is the one who – generally in collaboration with another script-writer and with the director – writes the script or scenario: that is, the canvas from which the film will later be taken. In this script, and according to the development of the action, are minutely indicated, one by one, the gestures

38

and words of the actors and the various movements of the camera. The script is, therefore, drama, mime, cinematographic technique, *mise en scène*, and direction, all at the same time. Now, although the script-writer's part in the film is of the first importance and comes immediately below that of the director, it remains always, for reasons inherent in the fashion in which the art of the cinema has hitherto developed, hopelessly subordinate and obscure. If, in fact, the arts are to be judged from the point of view of direct expression – and one does not really see how else they can be judged – the script-writer is an artist who, although he gives his best to the film, never has the comfort of knowing that he has expressed himself. And so, with all his creative work, he can be nothing more than a provider of suggestions and inventions, of technical, psychological, and literary ideas; it is then the director's task to make use of this material according to his own genius and, in fact, to express himself. The script-writer, in short, is the man who remains always in the background; who expends the best of his blood for the success of others; and who, although two-thirds of the film's fortune depends upon him, will never see his own name on the posters where the names of the director, of the actors, and of the producer are printed. He may, it is true – and as often happens – achieve excellence in his inferior trade, and be very well paid; but he can never say: 'It was *I* who made this film . . . in this film *I* expressed myself . . . this film is *me*.' This can only be said by the director, who is, in effect, the only one to sign the film. The script-writer, on the other hand, has to content himself with working for the money he receives, which, whether he likes it or not, ends by becoming the real and only purpose of his job. Thus all that is left for the script-writer is to enjoy life, if he is capable of it, on the money

39

that is the sole result of his toil – passing from one script to another, from a comedy to a drama, from an adventure film to a sentimental film, without interruption, without pause, rather like a governess who goes from one child to another and never has time to grow fond of one before she leaves it and starts again with another; and in the end the fruit of her labours is enjoyed entirely by the mother who is the only one with the right to call the child her own.

But, apart from these disadvantages, which we may call fundamental and immutable, there are others also, in the job of the script-writer, which, though varying according to the quality and type of the film and of his collaborators, are no less annoying on that account. Unlike the director, who enjoys a considerable measure of independence and freedom in his dealings with the producer, the script-writer can only accept or refuse the task offered to him; but, once he has accepted it, he has no choice whatever in the matter of his collaborators: he is himself chosen, he does not choose. And so it comes about that, as a result of the personal likes and dislikes, the convenience, or the caprice of the producer, or simply as a result of chance, the script-writer finds himself forced to work with people he does not care for, people who are his inferiors in culture and breeding, who irritate him by features of character or behaviour that are offensive to him. Now, working together on a script is not like working together in an office, let us say, or a factory, where each man has his own job to do independently of his neighbour and where personal relations can be reduced to very little or even abolished altogether. Working together on a script means living together from morning to night, it means the marriage and fusion of one's own intelligence, one's own sensibility, one's own spirit, with those of the other collaborators; it means, in short, the creation, during the two or three months that the work lasts, of a fictitious, artificial intimacy whose only purpose is the making of the film, and thereby, in a last analysis (as I have already mentioned), the making of money. This intimacy, moreover, is of the worst possible kind – that is the most fatiguing, the most unnerving and the most cloying that can be imagined, since it is founded not on work that is done in silence, as might be that of scientists engaged together on some experiment, but on the spoken word. The director usually calls his collaborators together early in the morning, for this is necessitated by the shortness of the time allowed for the completion of the script; and from early morning until night-time the script-writers do nothing but talk, keeping to the work in hand most of the time, but often talking from sheer volubility or fatigue, wandering away together on the most varied subjects. One will tell dirty stories, one will expound his political ideas, one will psychologize about some common acquaintance, another talk about actors and actresses, another relieve his feelings by telling of his own personal circumstances; and in the meantime, in the room where they are working, the air is filled with cigarette-smoke, coffee-cups pile up on the tables amongst the pages of the script, and the script-writers themselves, who had come in in the morning well-groomed, tidy and with neatly-brushed hair, are to be seen in the evening rumpled and sweaty and untidy, in their shirt-sleeves, looking worse than if they had been trying to ravish a frigid, restive woman. And indeed the mechanical, stereotyped way in which scripts are fabricated strongly resembles a kind of rape of the intelligence, having its origin in determination and interest rather than in any sort of attraction or sympathy. Of course, it can also happen that the film is of superior quality, that the director and his collaborators were already, beforehand, bound together by mutual esteem and friendship, and that, in fact, the work is carried out in the ideal conditions that may occur in any human activity, however disagreeable; but these favourable combinations are rare – as, indeed, good films are rare.

It was after I had signed the contract for a second filmscript – this time not with Battista, but with another producer – that courage and determination suddenly abandoned me and I began, with increasing repugnance and annoyance, to resent all the disadvantages of which I have already spoken. Each day, from the time when I got up in the morning, seemed like an arid desert, with no oasis of meditation or leisure, dominated by the merciless sun of forced cinema inspiration. As soon as I entered the director's house and he welcomed me in his study with some remark such as 'Well, did you think about it last night? Did you find a solution?' I had a feeling of boredom and rebellion. Then, during our work, everything seemed to be infected with impatience and disgust – the divagations of every kind by which the director and the scriptwriters, as I have already mentioned, seek to alleviate the long hours of discussion; the incomprehension or obtuseness or simple divergence of opinion amongst my collaborators as the script was gradually written; even the director's praises for each of my inventions or decisions, praises which tasted bitter to me because I felt, as I have said, that I was giving the best of myself for something which did not fundamentally concern me and in which I was not participating willingly. This last disadvantage, in fact, appeared to me at that time to be the most intolerable of all; and, each time that the director, speaking in the demagogic, vulgar way that is common to so many of them, jumped up in his chair and exclaimed: 'Bravo!

42

You're a wow!' – I could not help thinking contemp-
tuously: 'I might have put that idea into some drama or
comedy of my own.' Furthermore, by some strange and
bitter contradiction, I could never manage, in spite of my
repugnance, to fail in my duty as a script-writer. Film-
scripts are rather like the old-fashioned four-in-hands, in
which there were some horses, stronger or more willing,
who did the pulling, and others who pretended to pull
while really they allowed themselves to be dragged along
by their companions. Well, in spite of all my impatience
and disgust, I was always the horse who did the pulling;
the other two, the director and my script-writer colleague,
when faced with any difficulty always waited – as I very
soon noticed – for me to come forward with my solution.
And I, though inwardly cursing both my conscientiousness
and my facility, did not hesitate, but, with some sudden
inspiration, provided the solution required. I was not
driven to do this from any spirit of rivalry, but merely
from a sense of honesty stronger than any contrary desire;
I was paid, therefore I had to work. But each time I was
ashamed of myself and had a feeling both of avarice and of
regret, as though, for a little money, I had ruined something beyond price, something of which I could, somehow
or other, have made an infinitely better use.

As I said, I did not become aware of all these disadvantages until two months after I had signed the first contract
with Battista. And at first I did not understand why they
had not been obvious to me from the beginning and why I
had taken such a long time to notice them. But, when the
feeling of repugnance and failure aroused in my mind by
the work I had once so ardently desired still persisted, I
could not help – very gradually, as often happens – coming to connect it in some way with my relations with
Emilia. And at last I realized that the work disgusted me

43

because Emilia no longer loved me, or at least gave an appearance of no longer loving me. And that I had faced the work with courage and confidence as long as I had been sure of Emilia's love. Now that I was no longer sure of it, courage and confidence had deserted me and the work seemed to me nothing better than slavery, waste of talent, and loss of time.

6

I began therefore to live like one who carries within him the infirmity of an impending disease but cannot make up his mind to go to the doctor; in other words, I tried not to reflect too much either upon Emilia's demeanour towards me, or upon my work. I knew that some day I should have to face this kind of reflection; but, just because I was aware that it was unavoidable, I sought to put it off for as long as possible: the little I had already suspected made me shy away from it, and also, albeit unconsciously, fear it. And so I went on having those relations with Emilia which at the beginning had seemed to me intolerable, and which now, when I feared the worst, I tried to persuade myself – without any success – were normal: during the day indifferent, casual, evasive conversations; at night, from time to time, love-making, with much embarrass-ment and a hint of cruelty on my side, and no real participation on hers. In the meantime I continued to work diligently, even furiously, though more and more unwillingly and with a more and more decided repugn-ance. If I had had the courage to acknowledge the situation to myself, at that moment, I should certainly have renounced my work and renounced love as well, for I should have been convinced, as I was later, that all life had gone out of both. But I did not have that courage; and perhaps I deluded myself into believing that time would take it upon itself to solve my problems, without any effort on my part. Time, in fact, did solve them, but not in the way I should have wished. And so the days passed, in a dull, dim atmosphere of expectancy, with Emilia denying herself to me and myself denying myself to my work.

The script I was writing for Battista was meanwhile nearing its end; and at the same time Battista mentioned a new undertaking to me, of much more serious importance than the first, in which he wanted me to have a share. Battista was a hurried, evasive sort of man, like all producers; and the very fleeting hints he gave me never went beyond such remarks as: 'Molteni, as soon as you've finished this script, we're going to start at once on another . . . a really important one'; or: 'Molteni, be prepared, one of these days . . . there's a proposal I've got to make to you'; or again, rather more explicitly: 'Don't sign any contracts, Molteni, because in a fortnight's time you're going to sign one with me.' So I knew that, after this first, comparatively unimportant script, Battista was preparing to give me another, more important one to do, for which, naturally, I should be far better paid. I must confess that, in spite of my growing distaste for this type of work, the first thing I thought of, instinctively, was the flat and the money that still had to be paid on it; and I was delighted at Battista's proposal. In any case, that is what film work is like: even when, as in my case, one is not in love with it, every new offer is agreeable, and if offers do not arrive, one becomes suspicious and fears that one is being excluded.

But I said nothing to Emilia of this new offer of Battista's, and that for two reasons: in the first place, because I did not yet know whether I should accept it; and also because I had by now realized that my work did not interest her and I preferred not to speak of it, so as not to provoke some further confirmation of her coldness and indifference, to which, however, I persisted in paying no importance. These two things, furthermore, were linked together in a manner of which I was vaguely conscious: I was not sure about accepting the job precisely because I felt Emilia no longer loved me; whereas if she had loved me I should have talked about it to her, and talking about it to her meant, really and truly, accepting it.

I went out one morning in order to go and see the director with whom I was working on script No. 1 for Battista. I knew it was the last time I should be going there, because there were now only a few pages left before the end, and this thought cheered me: at last this toil was on the point of finishing and I should again be my own master for at least half the day. Besides, as always happens with film-scripts, two months of work had sufficed to imbue me with a profound dislike for the characters and the story of the film. I knew that I should very soon find myself at grips with a set of characters and a story destined quickly to become, in their turn, no less intolerable; but in the meantime I was escaping from the first set, and the prospect of this was enough to bring me considerable relief.

My hope of approaching freedom caused me to work, that morning, with unusual facility and inventiveness. In order to complete the script, not more than two or three points, of little importance, required touching up; upon these, however, we had been hesitating, without result, for some days. But, carried away by my inspiration, I succeeded, from the very beginning, in guiding the discussion along the right lines and solving, one after the other, all the outstanding difficulties, so that, after barely a couple of hours, we realized that the script was really finished, this time beyond question. In the end – just as happens with a certain kind of interminable, unnerving mountain excursion, when the goal, by now despaired of,

47

appears suddenly at a bend in the path – I wrote down a sentence of dialogue and then exclaimed in surprise: 'Why, it can finish here!' The director, who was walking up and down his study while I was writing at the desk, came across to me; he looked over my shoulder at the page and then he too said, in a surprised, almost incredulous voice: 'You're right, it can finish there.' So I wrote the words 'The End' at the bottom of the page, closed the copybook and rose to my feet.

For a moment we said nothing, both of us looking at the desk upon which lay the portfolio, now closed, containing the completed script – indeed, rather like two almost exhausted mountain-climbers looking at the little lake or rock which has cost them so much toil to reach. Then the director said: 'We've done it.'

'Yes,' I repeated: 'we've done it!'

This director was called Pasetti and was a fairish young man, angular, thin, precise and clean-looking, with the appearance of a meticulous geometrician or accountant rather than of an artist. He was about the same age as myself; but, as always happens with script-writing, the relations between him and me were those of superior and inferior, for the director always has greater authority than any other of the collaborators. After a moment he resumed, with his characteristically cold, awkward pleasantness: 'I must say, Riccardo, I must say, you're just like a horse that smells its own stable . . . I was certain we'd have to work for at least four more days . . . and now we've polished it off in two hours. . . . It was the prospect of the cash, was it – that inspired you?'

I did not dislike Pasetti, in spite of his mediocrity and his almost unbelievable psychological obtuseness; and there had grown up between us a relationship that was in a way well-balanced, he being a man without imagination and without nerves, but conscious of his limitations and fundamentally modest, while I was all nerves and imagination, morbidly sensitive and complex. Adopting his facetious tone and joining in the joke, I answered: 'Of course, what you say is quite true – it was the prospect of the cash.'

Lighting a cigarette, he went on: 'But don't imagine the game is finished . . . All we've done is the main part of the job; we've got to revise the whole of the dialogue . . . You can't rest on your laurels yet.'

I could not help noticing, yet again, how he expressed himself almost entirely in commonplaces and ready-made phrases; and I looked discreetly at the clock. It was almost one. 'Don't worry,' I said, 'I shall be at your service for any touching-up that's needed.'

Shaking his head, he replied: 'I know my chickens . . . I shall tell Battista to hold up the last instalment of your pay until you can't hold out any longer.'

He had his own way, facetious yet authoritative, and surprising in one so young, of spurring on his collaborators by alternating praise with blame, flattery with reserve, entreaty with command; and in this sense he might even have been called a good director, since directing – two-thirds of it, anyhow – consists in having a shrewd knowledge of how to get others to do one's bidding. I answered, drawing him out, as usual: 'No; you get him to pay me the whole instalment and I promise you I'll be at your service for any touching-up that's needed.'

'But what d'you do with all this money?' he asked, awkwardly jocose. 'It's never enough for you . . . and yet you haven't any mistresses, you don't gamble, you haven't any children . . .'

'I have to pay the instalments on the flat,' I replied seriously, lowering my eyes, slightly annoyed at his indiscreetness.

'Have you much to pay still?'

'Almost the whole amount.'

'I bet it's your wife who bullies you until you get yourself paid what's owing to you . . . I can hear her saying: "Now, Riccardo, remember to make them pay you that last instalment!"'

'Yes, it's my wife,' I lied; 'but you know what women are . . . their homes are immensely important to them.'

'You're telling me!' He started talking about his wife, who very much resembled him and whom he, nevertheless – or so I gathered – considered to be a bizarre creature, full of caprices and all sorts of unexpected things – in fact, a woman. I listened with an attentive expression, though in point of fact I was thinking about something else. He concluded in an unforeseen manner: 'That's all very well . . . but I know what you script-writers are: you're all the same, the whole lot of you . . . After you once get your money, one's lucky to see you again . . . No, no, I shall tell Battista to keep back the last instalment!'

'Come on, Pasetti, do what I ask!'

'Well, well, I'll see . . . But don't count on it.'

I glanced stealthily at the clock again. Now I had given him the chance to flaunt his authority and he had taken it: so I could go away. I began: 'Well, well, I'm pleased to have finished the job – or rather, as you say, the main part of it . . . But now I think it's time for me to go.'

He exclaimed in his blundering, vivacious way: 'Not at all, not at all; we've got to drink to the success of the film . . . My goodness, of course we have . . . You're not going away like that, after finishing the script!'

I answered resignedly: 'If it's a question of a drink, I'm all for it.'

'Come this way, then . . . I think my wife would be pleased to have a drink with us.'

I followed him out of the study, and along a narrow passage, bare and white and smelling strongly of cooking and baby's garments. He preceded me into the sitting-room, calling out: 'Luisa, Molteni and I have finished the script. . . . Now we're going to drink to the success of the film.'

Signora Pasetti rose from her armchair and came forward to meet us. She was a small woman with a large head and two bands of smooth black hair framing her long, oval, very pale face. Her eyes were large, but light in colour and inexpressive, and they became animated only when her husband was present: and then she never took them off his face for one single moment, like an affectionate dog with its master. But when her husband was not there she kept them lowered, with an almost stubbornly modest air. Fragile and minute in figure, she had brought four children into the world in four years of matrimony. With his usual embarrassing cheerfulness, Pasetti now said: 'Today we have a drink . . . I'm going to make a cocktail.'

'Not for me, Gino,' Signora Pasetti warned him. 'You know I don't drink.'

'*We'll* drink then.'

I sat down in an armchair of sand-papered wood with a flowered cover, in front of a red-brick chimney-piece; and Signora Pasetti sat down on the other side of the fireplace, on another exactly similar chair. The sitting-room, I noticed when I looked around, was an accurate copy of its master: furnished with a 'suite' in sham rustic style, it was bright and clean and orderly but at the same time rather bleak – just like, in fact, the house of a meticulous accountant or bank clerk. I had nothing to do but look, for Signora Pasetti did not appear to feel any need to speak to me. She sat opposite me with eyes lowered, her hands in her lap, quite motionless. Meanwhile, Pasetti went over to the other end of the room, to an extremely ugly composite piece of furniture, a radio containing a bar; then he stooped down twice, on his thin legs, and, with precise, angular movements, took out two bottles, one of vermouth and one of gin, three glasses and a shaker. He placed them all on a tray and carried the tray over to a little table in front of the fireplace. I noticed that the bottles were both of them sealed and intact: it did not look as if Pasetti often allowed himself the drink he was now about to prepare for us. The shaker, too, was bright and shining and appeared quite new. He announced that he was going to fetch some ice and went out.

We sat a long time in silence, and then, in order to say something, I said: 'We've finished the script, at last!'

Without raising her eyes, Signora Pasetti replied: 'Yes; so Gino said.'

'I'm sure it will make a fine film.'

'I'm sure it will too; otherwise Gino would not have agreed to do it.'

'Do you know the story?'

'Yes; Gino told it me.'

'Do you like it?'

'Gino likes it, so I like it too.'

'Do you always agree, you two?'

'Gino and I? Yes; always.'

'Which of the two of you is in command?'

'Gino, of course.'

I noticed that she had contrived to repeat the name of Gino each time she had opened her mouth. I had spoken lightly and almost jokingly; she had answered me all the time with the utmost seriousness. Then Pasetti came in again with the ice-pail and called out to me: 'Your wife's on the telephone, Riccardo.'

For some unaccountable reason I felt my heart sink, with a sudden return of my usual unhappiness. Mechanically I rose and started towards the door. Pasetti added: 'The telephone's in the kitchen – but if you like you can answer it here . . . I've switched it through.'

The telephone was, in fact, on a cabinet beside the fireplace. I took off the receiver and heard Emilia's voice say to me: 'I'm sorry, but today you'll have to go out to lunch somewhere . . . I'm going to my mother's.'

'But why didn't you tell me before?'

'I didn't want to disturb you at your work.'

'All right,' I said. 'I'll go and eat at a restaurant.'

'We'll meet later; good-bye.'

She rang off and I turned towards Pasetti. 'Riccardo,' he asked at once, 'are you not lunching at home?'

'No; I'm going to a restaurant.'

'Well, stay and have lunch with us . . . pot-luck, of course . . . but we'd be very pleased.'

An inexplicable feeling of despondency had come over me at the thought of having lunch alone at a restaurant, probably because I had been looking forward with pleasure to announcing to Emilia that the script was finished. Perhaps I should not have done this after all, knowing, as I have said, that she was no longer interested in what I did; but at first I had yielded to the old habit of our past relationship. Pasetti's invitation gave me pleasure; and I accepted it with almost excessive gratitude. He, in the meantime, had uncorked the two bottles, and now, with gestures more like those of a chemist calculating a dose of medicine than of a drinker, he was pouring the gin and the vermouth into a measure and then transferring them into the shaker. Signora Pasetti, as usual, never took her eyes off her husband. At last, when Pasetti had throughly shaken the cocktail and was about to pour it out into the glasses; she said: 'Only just a drop for me, please . . . And you too, Gino, don't drink much; it might do you harm.'

'It isn't every day that one finishes a script!'

He filled our two glasses, and in the third put only a little of the cocktail, as his wife had requested. We all three took our glasses and raised them in a toast. 'To a hundred more scripts like this one!' said Pasetti, just wetting his lips and putting his glass down again on the table. I emptied mine at one draught. Signora Pasetti drank with little sips and then got up, saying: 'I'm going to the kitchen to see what the cook is doing . . . if you'll allow me.'

She went out. Pasetti took her place in the flowered armchair, and we started chattering. Or rather, *he* chattered, talking mostly about the script, and I listened, showing my approval by muttered words and nods of the head, and drinking. Pasetti's glass was always at the same point, not even half emptied; but I had already emptied mine three times. I now, for some reason, had an acute feeling of unhappiness, and I drank in the hope that tipsiness would drive it away. But I can stand a lot of alcohol and Pasetti's cocktails were light and much watered down. And so those three or four little glasses served no purpose except to increase my obscure sense of wretchedness. All at once I asked myself, 'Why do I feel so unhappy?' and then I remembered that the first stab of pain had come when, shortly before, I had heard Emilia's voice on the telephone, so cold, so reasonable, so indifferent; and above all so different from that of Signora Pasetti, whenever she pronounced the magic name of Gino. But I was unable to analyse my thoughts more closely, because, shortly afterwards, Signora Pasetti appeared in the door and told us we could come through into the dining-room.

Pasetti's dining-room resembled his study and sitting-room: neat, cheap, coquettish furniture of sand-papered wood; coloured earthenware crockery; glasses and bottles of thick green glass; tablecloth and napkins of unbleached hemp. We sat down in this tiny room which was almost entirely taken up by the table, so that the maid, when handing round the dishes, could not help disturbing first one, then another of the party; and then started eating apologetically and in silence. Soon the maid changed the plates, and I, to get the conversation going, asked Pasetti some question or other as to his plans for the future. He answered me in his usual cold, precise, undistinguished voice, in which modesty and lack of imagination seemed to be responsible not merely for the choice of words, but even for the slightest variation in tone. I was silent, finding nothing to say, for Pasetti's plans did not interest me and, even if they had, that monotonous, colourless voice of his would have made them tedious. But, as my bored glances wandered from one object to another without managing to find anything to detain them, they came to rest at last upon the face of Pasetti's wife who was also listening, her chin supported on her hand and her eyes fixed, as usual, upon her husband. Then, as I looked at her face, I was struck by the expression in her eyes – amorous, melting, a mixture of humble admiration, unlimited gratitude, physical infatuation and a sort of melancholy timidity. This expression astonished me, partly because the feeling behind it was, to me, utterly mysterious: Pasetti, so colourless, so thin, so mediocre, so obviously lacking in qualities that might please a woman, seemed an incredible object for attention of that kind. Then I said to myself that every man always ends by finding the woman who appreciates and loves him, and that to judge of other people's feelings on the basis of one's own is a mistake; and I had a feeling of sympathy for her, in her devotion to her man, and of satisfaction on Pasetti's behalf, for whom, as I have already said, I cherished, in spite of his mediocrity, a sort of ironical friendship. But, all of a sudden, just as I was losing interest and turning my eyes elsewhere, I was transfixed by a thought from I know not where, or rather, by a sudden perception: 'In those eyes is the whole love of this woman for her husband . . . and he is content with himself and with his own work because she loves him . . . But it is a long time since that feeling ceased to show itself in Emilia's eyes . . . Emilia does not love me; she will never love me again.'

At this thought, which revived in me a deep-seated pain, I had a sense almost of physical shock; so much so that I made a grimace, and Signora Pasetti asked me anxiously if by any chance the meat I was eating was tough. Meanwhile, though I still pretended to listen to Pasetti, who went on talking about his plans for the future, I tried to analyse that first sensation of pain, so acute and at the same time so obscure. Then I understood that, during the last month, I had been seeking all the time to accustom myself to an intolerable situation, but that I had not, in reality, succeeded: I could not endure to go on living in that way, what with Emilia who did not love me and my work which, owing to her not loving me, I could not love. And suddenly I said to myself: 'I can't go on like this . . . I must have an explanation with Emilia, once and for all . . . and, if necessary, part from her and give up my work as well.'

Nevertheless, although I thought of these things with despairing resolution, I realized that I could not bring myself wholly to believe in them: in reality I was not yet altogether convinced that Emilia no longer loved me, nor that I should find the strength to part from her, give up my film work and go back to living alone. In other words, I had a feeling almost of incredulity, of a painful kind quite new to me, at finding myself faced with a fact that in my mind I now held to be indubitable. Why did Emilia no longer love me, and how had she arrived at this state of indifference? With a feeling of anguish in my heart, I foresaw that this first general conclusion, already so painful, would demand an infinite number of further, minor proofs before I became completely convinced – proofs which, just because they were of lesser importance, would be more concrete and, if possible, still more painful. I was, in fact, now convinced that Emilia could no longer love me; but I did not know either why or how this had come about; and in order to be entirely persuaded of it I must have an explanation with her, I must seek out and examine, I must plunge the thin, ruthless blade of investigation into the wound which, hitherto, I had exerted myself to ignore. This thought frightened me; and yet I realized that only after carrying my investigation through to the bitter end should I have the courage to part from Emilia, as, at the first moment, the desperate impulse of my mind had suggested.

In the meantime, I went on eating and drinking and listening to Pasetti, but almost without noticing what I was doing. In due time, however, lunch came to an end. We went back into the sitting-room, and there I had to submit to all the various formalities of the bourgeois guest – coffee with one, or two, lumps of sugar; the offer of a liqueur, sweet or dry, received with the customary refusal; idle conversation to pass the time. Finally, when it seemed to me that I could take my leave without giving an impression of haste, I rose from my chair. But, just at that moment, the Pasettis' eldest little girl was brought into the

57

room by her nurse, to be displayed to her parents before her daily walk. She was a dark-haired, pale child with very large eyes, of a very ordinary type, insignificant – in fact, like her parents. I remember that, as I watched her letting herself be kissed and embraced by her mother, this thought crossed my mind: 'I shall never be happy like them . . . Emilia and I shall never have a child'; and immediately afterwards, as a result of this first thought, a second one, even more bitter: 'How shabby all this is, how ordinary, how unoriginal . . . I am following in the footsteps of all husbands who are not loved by their wives – envying a perfectly ordinary couple while they kiss and hug their offspring . . . exactly, indeed, like any ordinary husband who finds himself in my position.' This mortifying idea aroused in me a feeling of impatience at the affectionate scene I was witnessing. I declared, brusquely, that I must go. Pasetti accompanied me to the door, his pipe between his teeth. I had a feeling that my leave-taking had astonished and shocked his wife, who was perhaps expecting me to be touched at the edifying spectacle of her maternal love.

7

I had no engagement until four o'clock, so that I had an hour and a half to spare; and when I was in the street, I started off, more or less instinctively, towards home. I knew that Emilia could not be there, since she had gone to lunch with her mother; but, filled as I was with distress and bewilderment, I almost hoped that this might not be true and that I should find her there after all: in which case, I said to myself, I would pluck up courage to speak to her frankly, to insist on a decisive explanation. I was aware that upon this explanation depended not only my relations with Emilia, but also my work; but now, after so many pitiful shilly-shallyings and hypocrisies, I felt I preferred any kind of disaster to the prolongation of a situation that was becoming only too painfully clear and less and less tolerable. Perhaps I should be compelled to part from Emilia, to refuse Battista's second script; so much the better. The truth, whatever it might be, seemed to me now to be infinitely more desirable than my present obscure, degraded position, with falsehood on the one hand and self-pity on the other.

As I came into my own street, I was again seized with perplexity: Emilia was certainly not at home, and I, in that new flat which now seemed to me not so much strange as actively hostile, should feel more lost and miserable than I should in a public place. For a moment I was almost tempted to turn back and to go and spend that hour and a half in a café. Then, with a sudden providential reawakening of memory, I recalled that I had promised Battista, the previous day, to be at home at that time, so that he could telephone me and arrange an appointment. This would be an important appointment, because Battista was to speak to me at last about the new script, and to make concrete proposals and introduce me to the director; and so I had assured him that I would be at home at that time – as, indeed, I always was. It is true that I myself could have telephoned to Battista from a café; but, to begin with, I was not entirely sure of finding him at home, because Battista often lunched at a restaurant; and, in addition, as I said to myself, I needed some pretext, in my acute state of bewilderment, to go back home; and Battista's telephone call exactly provided me with such a pretext.

So I entered the hall, crossed to the lift, closed the doors and pressed the button for the top floor on which I lived. But, while the lift was going up, it suddenly came into my head that in reality I had no right to fix this appointment, inasmuch as I was not at all sure that I should accept Battista's new proposition. Everything depended upon my explanation with Emilia, and I knew that, if Emilia declared explicitly that she no longer loved me, not merely should I not write this new script, but I should never write any more film-scripts for the rest of my life. Emilia, however, would not be at home; and when Battista telephoned, I should not be in a position, honestly, to tell him whether I agreed to discuss his proposition or not. Now, amongst all the many absurd things in my life, one of the most absurd would be, I felt, to negotiate a deal and then back out of it. At this thought I was assailed by an almost hysterical impulse of rage and repugnance, and all at once I stopped the lift and then pressed the button to go down again to the ground floor. It was better, I said to myself, far better not to let Battista find me at home when he telephoned. Later on, that same evening, I would have my explanation with Emilia; and next day I would give the producer an answer in accordance with its result. In the meantime, the lift was going down and I was looking at all those floors going past one after another, behind the ground glass doors, with the desperate eye of a fish seeing the level of the water rapidly descending inside the tank in which it lives. At last the lift stopped and I was on the point of opening the doors. But then, suddenly, a new idea made me pause: it was true that my decision about the new job with Battista depended upon my explanation with Emilia; but if it would happen that Emilia, that same evening, made me a fresh avowal of her love, should I not be taking the risk of annoying Battista by not being at home when he telephoned, and thereby losing the job? Producers, as I knew from experience, were as capricious as so many petty tyrants; a hitch of this kind might be enough to make Battista change his mind and might induce him to choose another script-writer. These reflections pursued one another swiftly through my aching head, producing in me an obscure feeling of acute wretchedness: truly I was an unfortunate creature, I said to myself, torn between interest and affection, incapable of choice or decision. And I do not know how much longer I should have stayed there, hesitating and bewildered, inside the lift, if a young lady, her arms laden with parcels, had not suddenly thrown open the doors. She uttered a cry of fright on discovering me standing there, stock still, in front of her; then recovering herself, she too came into the lift and asked me which floor I wanted to go to, I told her. 'I go to the second,' she announced, and pressed the button. The lift started to ascend again.

Once on my own landing, I had a sense of profound

relief; and at the same time it occurred to me: 'What sort of a state am I in, to be behaving like this? How can I have descended so low? What point have I reached?' With these thoughts in my head I went into the flat, closed the door and went through into the living-room. And there, lying on the sofa, in a dressing-gown, reading a magazine, I saw Emilia. Beside the sofa was a small table upon which could be seen plates and the remains of lunch: Emilia had not gone out, she had not lunched with her mother; in short, she had lied to me.

I must have had a troubled expression on my face, for she, after looking at me, asked: 'What's the matter? . . . What's happened to you?'

'Weren't you going to have lunch with your mother?' I said in a stifled voice. 'How on earth d'you come to be at home? You told me you were out for lunch!'

'My mother telephoned afterwards to say that she couldn't,' she replied placidly.

'But why didn't you let me know?'

'My mother rang up at the last moment . . . I thought you'd have left the Pasettis'.'

Suddenly – why, I could not tell – I was certain she was lying. But, being incapable of producing any proof of it, not merely to her but even to myself, I was silent, and I too sat down on the sofa. After a moment, turning over the pages of the magazine, she asked without looking at me: 'And you – what did you do?'

'The Pasettis asked me to stay.'

At that moment the telephone-bell rang in the next room. I thought: 'It's Battista . . . Now I shall tell him I'm not going to do any more scripts . . . To hell with everything . . . it's perfectly clear that this woman doesn't feel the smallest crumb of affection for me.' Meanwhile, Emilia, with her usual indolence, was saying: 'Do just go and see who it is . . . It's sure to be for you.' I rose and went out.

The telephone was in the adjoining room, on the bedside table. Before taking up the receiver, I looked towards the bed, saw the solitary pillow lying at the head of it, in the middle, and felt my resolution harden: all was finished; I should refuse the script and then leave Emilia. I took off the receiver, but then, instead of Battista's voice, I heard that of my mother-in-law, who asked: 'Riccardo, is Emilia there?'

Almost without thinking, I answered: 'No; she's not here . . . She said she was lunching with you . . . She's out . . . I thought you were together.'

'Why, I telephoned her to say I couldn't manage it because my maid has her day off today! . . .' she began in astonishment. At that moment I looked up from the telephone and saw, through the door which had been left open, Emilia lying on the divan looking at me; and I noticed that her eyes, which were fixed upon me, were full not so much of wonder as of quiet aversion and cold contempt. I realized that between the two of us, now, it was I who had lied, and that she knew why I had lied. So I mumbled a few words of farewell, and then, suddenly, as though correcting myself, I cried: 'No . . . wait . . . Here's Emilia just coming in . . . I'll send her to you.' At the same time I beckoned to Emilia to come to the telephone.

She got up from the sofa, crossed the room with her head bent and took the receiver from my hand without thanking or looking at me. I walked away towards the living-room, and she made an impatient gesture as if to tell me to shut the door. I did so; and then, my mind filled with confusion, I sat down on the divan and waited.

Emilia was a long time at the telephone, and I, in my painful, apprehensive impatience, almost felt that she was doing it on purpose. But, of course, I kept on saying to myself, her telephone conversations with her mother were always very long: she had remained deeply attached to her mother, who was a widow and all alone, and had no one but her; and she seemed to have made her her confidante. At last the door opened and Emilia reappeared. I sat silent and still, fully conscious, from her unwontedly hard expression, that she was angry with me.

And indeed she said at once, as she started collecting the plates and forks on the little table: 'Are you crazy? . . . Why on earth did you go and tell Mother I was out?'

Hurt by her tone, I did not open my mouth. 'To see if I had told the truth?' she went on. 'To see if it was true that Mother had really told me she couldn't have me to lunch?'

I answered at last, with an effort: 'That may have been the reason.'

'Well, please never do such a thing again . . . I speak the truth . . . and I've nothing to hide from you . . . and I just can't endure that kind of thing.'

She spoke these words in a tone of finality and then took up the tray on which she had put together the plates and glasses and went out of the room.

Left alone, I had, for a moment, a bitter feeling of victory. It was true, then: Emilia no longer loved me. In the old days she certainly would not have spoken to me like that. She would have said to me, with a mixture of gentleness and amused surprise: 'Perhaps you really thought I had told you a lie?' and then she would have laughed, as if at some childish, easily forgivable error, and finally – yes, finally she would have even shown herself flattered: 'My goodness, you don't mean to say you're really jealous? . . . And don't you know I love nobody except you?' It would all have ended in an almost motherly kiss, and a caress of her long, large hands on my

64

brow, as though to chase away all thought and anxiety. But it was also true that in the old days I should never have thought of watching her, still less of doubting her word. Everything was changed: she in her love, I in mine. And everything seemed set for a steady change for the worse.

But man is always ready to hope, even when convinced that there is no hope. I had had a clear proof that Emilia no longer loved me, and yet there was still a doubt in my mind – or, rather, a hope – that I might have placed a rash interpretation upon an incident which, fundamentally, was devoid of importance. All at once I said to myself that I must not be precipitate; that I must make her tell me herself that she no longer loved me; that only she could provide me with the proofs that I still lacked . . . These thoughts pursued each other swiftly through my mind as I sat on the divan staring into vacancy. Then the door opened and Emilia came in again.

She came over to the sofa and lay down again, behind me, and took up the magazine. Then, without turning, I said: 'In a few moments Battista is going to telephone and make a proposal for me to do another script . . . a very important script.'

'Well, you must be pleased, aren't you?' she said in her calm voice.

'With this script,' I went on, 'I shall be able to earn a lot of money . . . anyhow, enough to pay two instalments on the lease.'

This time she said nothing. I continued: 'This script, moreover, is important for me because, if I do it, I shall have others to do afterwards . . . this is to be a big film.'

At last, in the detached voice of a person who is reading and who speaks without looking up from the page, she asked: 'What film is it?'

'I don't know,' I replied. I was silent for a moment, and

then, in a rather emphatic tone, I added: 'But I've decided to refuse this job.'

'And why?' Her voice was still quiet, indifferent.

I rose, walked round the sofa, and came and sat down in front of Emilia. She was holding the magazine in her hand, but when she saw me sit down opposite her, she lowered it and looked at me. 'Because,' I said with full sincerity, 'I, as you know, hate this work and do it only for love of you . . . in order to pay the instalments on this flat, which means so much to you or seems to mean so much to you . . . But now I know for certain that you no longer love me . . . and so all this is useless.'

She was looking at me with her eyes wide open, but she said nothing. 'You don't love me any longer,' I went on, 'and I shall not go on doing these jobs . . . As for the flat . . . well I shall mortgage it or sell the lease . . . The fact is, I can't go on like this any longer, and I feel that the moment has come to tell you so . . . So now you know . . . In a short time Battista will telephone and I shall tell him to go to the devil.'

Now I had said it, and the moment had therefore arrived for the explanation I had so long both feared and desired. At this thought I felt almost relieved, and I looked at Emilia with a new frankness as I awaited her reply. She was silent for a little time before she answered me. Obviously my forthright declaration had surprised her. In the end, indeed, rather cautiously and precisely as if she wanted to gain time, she asked: 'What makes you think I don't love you any more?'

'Everything,' I answered with passionate vehemence.

'For instance?'

'Tell me first of all whether it's true or not.'

She insisted, obstinately: 'No; you tell me what makes you think that.'

'Everything,' I repeated; 'your way of talking to me, of looking at me, the way you behave to me . . . Everything . . . A month ago you even insisted on our sleeping apart . . . You wouldn't have wanted that once upon a time!'

She looked at me, irresolute; and then, suddenly, I saw her eyes light up with rapid decision. She had, in that precise moment, I thought, determined upon the attitude to be taken with me, and now would not deviate from her decision, whatever I might say or do. At last she replied, quite gently: 'But I assure you, I swear to you . . . I cannot sleep with the shutters open . . . I need darkness and silence . . . I swear it.'

'But I offered to sleep with the shutters closed.'

'Well,' she hesitated, 'must I also tell you, then, that when you're asleep you're not silent?'

'What d'you mean?'

'You snore.' She smiled faintly and then went on: 'You used to wake me up every night . . . That's why I decided to sleep by myself.'

I was somewhat disconcerted at this detail of my snoring, of which I was ignorant and which, furthermore, I found it difficult to believe: I had slept with other women and none of them had ever told me that I snored. 'And then,' I said, 'I know you don't love me because a wife who loves' – I hesitated, slightly shamefaced – 'does not make love in the way you've been doing, for some time past, with me.'

She immediately protested, irritably and roughly: 'Really, I don't know what it is you want . . . We make love every time you wish to . . . And have I ever refused you?'

I knew that of the two of us, in this kind of confidential talk, it was always I who was the modest, the shamefaced, the embarrassed one. Emilia, usually so reserved and

67

proper, seemed, in intimacy, to lose all idea of modesty or embarrassment; in fact, in a way that vaguely astonished me every time and that I found attractive for some quality it had of natural innocence, she used to talk, before, during, and after our love-making, of that love-making itself, without the slightest veil of tenderness or reticence and with a disconcerting crudeness and freedom. 'No; not refused,' I muttered: 'no . . . but . . .'

She resumed, in a conclusive tone of voice: 'Every single time you've wanted to make love, we've done so . . . And you're not one to be contented with just the simple act . . . You're good at making love, you know . . .'

'D'you think so?' I asked, almost flattered.

'Yes,' she said dryly, without looking at me. 'But if I didn't love you, the very fact of your being good at making love would irritate me, and I should try to avoid it . . . and a woman can always find excuses for refusing, can't she?'

'All right,' I said. 'You do it, you've never refused me . . . but the way in which you do it is not the way of a person who loves.'

'Why, in what way do I do it?'

I ought to have answered her: 'You do it like a prostitute who submits to her client and wants only that the thing shall be quickly over . . . that's how you do it!' But, out of respect for her and for myself too, I preferred to remain silent. And in any case, what would have been the use of it? She would have replied that it was not true, and – quite probably – she would have reminded me, with crude, technical precision, of certain transports of sensuality on her own side, in which everything was included – skill, pursuit of pleasure, violent excitement, erotic fury – everything except tenderness and the indescribable abandonment of true surrender; and I should

68

not have known what to say to this; and, into the bargain, I should have offended her with that insulting comparison and thus have put myself in the wrong. And so, in despair, realizing that the explanation I had wanted to bring about had now dissolved into thin air, I said: 'Well, anyhow, whatever the reason, I'm convinced you don't love me any more – that's all.'

Again, before either answering or moving, she looked at me as if to calculate, from the expression of my face, what would be the most suitable attitude for her to take towards me. I noticed then a peculiarity which I already knew: her beautiful, dark, serene face, so harmonious, so symmetrical, so compact, underwent, through the irreso- lution that cleft her mind, a process almost, as it were, of decay: one cheek seemed to have grown thinner (but not the other), her mouth was no longer exactly in the middle of her face, her eyes, bewildered and dim, seemed to be disintegrating within their sockets as though within a circle of dark wax. I said that I already knew this peculiarity of hers; this same thing did in fact happen every time she had to face a decision which she disliked or towards which she did not feel herself naturally drawn. And then, with a sudden impulse of her whole body, she threw her arms round my neck, saying in a voice that sounded to me false: 'But, Riccardo, why do you say that? . . . I do love you . . . just as much as I did in the past.' Her breath was warm in my ear, and I felt her pass her hand over my forehead, my temples, my hair, and pull my head down against her breast, clasping it tightly between her arms.

But the idea came into my mind that she was embracing me like that so as not to show me the expression on her face, which was perhaps merely bored and at the same time diligent, the expression of a person who does some- thing in which his spirit has no share, purely from volition;

69

and as I pressed my face, in a desperate longing for love, against her breast, half-bared and rising and falling with her calm breathing, I could not help thinking: 'These are only gestures . . . but she is bound to give herself away by some remark or some intonation in her voice.' I waited a little, and then she ventured to say, cautiously: 'What would you do if I really had ceased to love you?'

So I was right, I thought in bitter triumph; she had betrayed herself. She wished to know what I would do if she had ceased to love me, so as to weigh up and estimate all the risks of complete frankness. Without moving, speaking into her soft, warm breast, I said: 'I've already told you . . . the first thing I'd do would be to refuse Battista's new job.' I should have liked to add: 'And I should part from you'; but I had not the courage to say it at that moment, with my cheek against her breast and her hand on my forehead. In reality I still hoped that she might love me, and I was afraid that this separation, even by the admission of its mere possibility, might really come to pass. Finally, I heard her say, while she still went on embracing me closely: 'But I do love you . . . and all this is absurd . . . Now, you know what you're going to do? As soon as Battista telephones, you must make an appointment with him and then you must go and accept the job.'

'But why should I do that, seeing that you've ceased to love me?' I cried in exasperation.

Her answer, this time, was given in a tone of reasonable reproof. 'I love you, but don't go on making me repeat it . . . and it means a lot to me to stay in this flat . . . If it doesn't suit you to take this job, I shall not make any objection . . . but if you don't want to take it because you think I've ceased to love you or because you think the flat doesn't mean anything to me, let me tell you you're quite wrong.'

I began almost to hope that she was not lying; and at the same time I realized that, at least for the moment, she had persuaded me. And yet, in desperation, I now wanted to know more, to be utterly sure, to have incontestable proofs. Then, as though she had an intuition of my desire, she loosened her hold of me all of a sudden and whispered: 'Kiss me – won't you?'

I raised myself up and looked at her for a moment before kissing her; I was struck by the air of fatigue, almost of exhaustion, that was visible in her face, now more disintegrated, more irresolute than ever. It was as though she had undergone a superhuman strain while she had been speaking to me and caressing and embracing me; and as though she were preparing to undergo another, even more painful, during the kiss. Nevertheless, I took her chin in my hand and was on the point of bringing my lips close to hers. At that moment the telephone rang. 'It's Battista,' she said, disengaging herself with obvious relief, and running into the next room. From the sofa, where I remained seated, I saw her, through the open door, take off the receiver and say: 'Yes . . . yes; he's here. I'll get him at once . . . How are you?'

A few words followed from the other end of the line. Then, with a gesture of understanding towards me from where she stood, she said: 'We were just talking about you and your new film . . .'

A few more mysterious remarks. In a calm voice, she said: 'Yes; we must meet as soon as possible . . . Now I'll get Riccardo for you.'

I got up, went into the other room and took the receiver. Battista told me, as I had foreseen, that he was expecting me next day, in the afternoon, at his office. I said I would come, and exchanged a few more words with him; then replaced the receiver. Only then did I become aware that Emilia had left the room while I was speaking. And I could not help thinking that she had gone away because she had succeeded in persuading me to agree to the appointment with Battista; there was now no further need either of her presence or of her caresses.

8

I went to my appointment next day, at the time arranged. Battista's offices occupied the entire first floor of an ancient palace, once the abode of a patrician family and now – as so often happens – the business premises of a number of commercial concerns. The great reception-rooms, with their frescoed, vaulted ceilings and stuccoed walls, had been divided by him, with simple wooden partitions, into a number of little rooms with utilitarian furniture; where once old paintings with mythological or sacred subjects had hung, there were now large, brightly coloured posters; pinned up everywhere were photographs of actors and actresses, pages torn out of picture papers, framed certificates of festival awards, and other similar adornments generally to be found in the offices of film companies. In the ante-room, against a background of faded sylvan frescoes, rose, throne-like, an enormous counter of green-painted metal, from behind which three or four female secretaries welcomed visitors. Battista, as a producer, was still young, and he had made good progress in recent years with films inferior in quality but commercially successful. His company, modestly called 'Triumph Films', was, at the moment, regarded as one of the best.

At that hour the ante-room was already thronged, and, with the experience of film types I had now acquired, I could classify all the visitors with certainty at the first glance: two or three script-writers, recognizable by their look of mingled fatigue and industriousness, by the copy-books they held under their arms, and by the style of their clothes, at the same time both smart and careless; one or two elderly cinema organizers or managers, looking exactly like country estate agents or cattle-brokers; two or three girls, aspiring actresses or rather walkers-on, young and pretty perhaps, but as it were spoilt in advance by their ambitions, with their studied expressions, their excessive make-up, and their way of dressing from which all simplicity was banished; and finally a few nondescript individuals such as are always to be found in producers' ante-rooms – out-of-work actors, suggestion-mongers, cadgers of various kinds. All these people were walking up and down on the dirty mosaic floor, or lounging on the high-backed, gilt chairs round the walls, yawning, smoking and chattering in loud voices. The secretaries, when they were not speaking on one of the numerous telephones, remained motionless behind the counter, staring into vacancy with eyes that, from sheer boredom and absence of thought, looked glassy and almost squinting. From time to time a bell rang with violent and unpleasant shrillness; and then the secretaries would rouse themselves, call out a name, and one of the visitors would jump up hastily and disappear through a white-and-gold double door.

I gave in my name and then went and sat down at the far end of the room. I was now in a state of mind just as desperate as the day before, but much calmer. Immediately after my conversation with Emilia, and on thinking it over, I had convinced myself once and for all that she had lied to me in saying that she loved me; but for the moment, partly from discouragement, partly from a punctilious wish to force her into the complete and sincere explanation which I had not yet obtained, I gave up the idea, provisionally at least, of acting in accordance with my conviction. I had therefore decided not to refuse

Battista's new job, although I knew, for certain, that – like all the rest of my life, indeed – it now served no purpose. Later on, I thought, as soon as I had managed to wrest the truth from Emilia, there would always be time to break off the job and throw up everything. In some ways, in fact, I preferred this second and more dramatic solution to the first. The scandal and loss would to some extent emphasize my desperation and, simultaneously, my absolute determination to be done with all hesitation and compromise.

As I say, I felt calm; but it was the calm of apathy and listlessness. An uncertain evil causes anxiety because, at the bottom of one's heart, one goes on hoping till the last moment that it may not be true; a certain evil, on the other hand, instils, for a time, a kind of dreary tranquillity. I felt tranquil, but I knew that soon I should no longer be so; the first phase, the phase of suspicion, was over – or so I thought; soon would begin the phase of pain and revolt and remorse. All this I knew, but I knew also that between these two phases there would be an interlude of deathly calm, just like the false, stifling calm that precedes the second and worse period of a thunderstorm.

Then, as I waited to be shown into Battista's room, it flashed across my mind that so far I had restricted myself to making certain of the existence, or non-existence, of Emilia's love. But now, it seemed to me, I knew for certain that she no longer loved me. Therefore, I thought, almost surprised at my new discovery, I could now turn my mind to a new problem – that of the reason why she had ceased to love me. Also, once I had divined the reason, it would be easier for me to force her to an explanation.

I must admit that, as soon as I had put the question to myself, I was struck by a sense of incredulity, almost of extravagance. It was too unlikely, too absurd: it was quite impossible that Emilia could have a reason for ceasing to love me. From what source I derived this assurance, I could not have said; just as, on the other hand, I could not have said why – since according to me she could have no reason for ceasing to love me – it was yet quite obvious that she did *not* love me. I reflected for a few moments, bewildered by this contradiction between my head and my heart. Finally, as one does with certain problems in geometry, I said to myself: 'Let us grant it absurd that there should be a reason, although there cannot but be a reason. And let us see what it can possibly be.'

I have noticed that, the more doubtful one feels, the more one clings to a false lucidity of mind, as though hoping to clarify by reason that which is darkened and obscured by feeling. It gave me pleasure, at that moment when instinct produced such contradictory replies, to have recourse to a reasoned investigation, like a detective in a crime story. Someone has been killed; the motive for which he may have been killed must be sought out; if the motive is discovered it will be easy to trace the criminal . . . I argued, then, that the motives might be of two kinds: the first depending upon Emilia, the second upon me. And the first, as I immediately realized, were all summed up in a single one: Emilia no longer loved me because she loved someone else.

It appeared to me, on first thinking about it, that this supposition could be rejected without more ado. Not merely had there been nothing in Emilia's behaviour in recent times to lead one to suspect the presence of another man in her life, but there had been actually the opposite – an increase both in the amount of time she spent alone and in her dependence upon me. Emilia, I knew, was almost always at home, where she spent her time reading a little or telephoning to her mother or attending to her household chores; and for her distractions, whether going to the cinema, or taking a walk, or dining at a restaurant, she depended almost entirely upon me. Certainly her life had been more varied, and, in its modest way, more sociable, immediately after our marriage, when she still retained a few friendships from the time when she was a girl. But the bonds of such friendships had very soon been loosened; and she had clung ever more tightly to me, depending on me, as I have already mentioned, more and more, to an extent that was sometimes, for me, positively embarrassing. This dependence, moreover, had not weakened in the least, with the weakening of her feeling for me; she had not sought, even in the most innocent way, to find a substitute for me nor in the slightest degree to prepare for such an eventuality: in the same way as before – except that the love had gone out of it – she would sit at home waiting for my return from work, and she still depended on me for her few amusements. There was, in fact, something pathetic and unhappy about this loveless dependence of hers; it was as if somebody, by nature faithful, went on being faithful even when the reasons for faithfulness had disappeared. In a word, although she no longer loved me, it was almost certain that she had no one but me in her life.

Furthermore, another observation I had made caused me to exclude the possibility that Emilia might be in love with some other man. I knew her, or thought I knew her, very well. And I knew that she was incapable of telling lies, in the first place because of a certain rough and intolerant frankness in her, owing to which all falsehood appeared to her, not so much repugnant, as tedious and laborious; and secondly because of her almost complete lack of imagination, which did not permit of her grasping anything that had not really happened or that did not exist in concrete form. In view of this characteristic, I was sure that, in the event of her having fallen in love with another man, she would have found it best to tell me at once; and, into the bargain, with all the brutality and unconscious cruelty of the more or less uneducated class to which she belonged. Of reticence and silence she was perhaps capable, as indeed she was now proving herself to be with regard to her change of feeling towards me; but it would have been very difficult, if not impossible, for her to invent a double life in order to conceal adultery – I mean, the appointments with dressmakers and milliners, the visits to relations or friends, the delays at entertainments or the traffic hold-ups to which women usually have recourse in similar circumstances. No, her coldness towards me did not mean warmth towards another. And if there was a reason, as indeed there must be, it was to be sought, not in her life, but in mine.

I was so deeply absorbed in these reflections that I did not notice that one of the secretaries was standing in front of me, smiling and repeating: 'Signor Molteni . . . Dr Battista is waiting for you.' Finally, I pulled myself together, and, interrupting my investigations for the time being, hurried off to the producer's office.

He was sitting at the far end of a spacious room with a frescoed ceiling and walls adorned with gilt plasterwork, behind a desk of green-painted metal, exactly like the secretaries' counter that encumbered the ante-room. I realize at this point that, though I have often spoken of him, I have not yet described him, and I think it may be expedient to do so. Battista, then, was the kind of man whom his collaborators and dependants, as soon as his back was turned, referred to with charming names such as 'the brute', 'the big ape', 'the great beast', 'the gorilla'. I cannot say that these epithets were undeserved, at least as regards Battista's physical appearance; however, partly owing to my dislike of calling anyone by a nickname, I had never succeeded in adopting them. This was also because these nicknames erred, in my opinion, in not taking into account one of Battista's highly important qualities – I mean his most unusual artfulness, not to say subtlety, which was always present, though concealed under an apparent brutishness. Certainly he was a coarse, animal-like man, endowed with a tenacious, exuberant vitality; but this vitality expressed itself not only in his many and various appetites, but also in an acuteness that was sometimes extremely delicate and calculating, especially in relation to the satisfaction of those appetites.

Battista was of medium height, but with very broad shoulders, a long body and short legs; whence the similarity to a large ape which had earned him the nicknames I have mentioned. His face, too, was a little like that of an ape: his hair, leaving the two sides of his forehead bare, came down rather lower in the middle; and he had thick eyebrows, with a sort of pensive mobility of their own; small eyes; a short, broad nose; and a large but lipless mouth, thin as a slit made by a knife and slightly protruding. His figure was characterized by a stomach rather than a paunch; by which I mean that he habitually thrust out his chest and the upper part of his abdomen. His hands were short and thick and covered with black hair which continued upwards beyond his wrists into his sleeves: once when we had been to the sea together I had noticed that his hair bristled on his shoulders and chest and came right down to his belly. This man who looked so brutish expressed himself in a gentle, insinuating, conciliatory voice, with a polished, almost foreign accent, for Battista was not a Roman. It was in this unforeseeable, surprising voice that I detected an indication of the astuteness and subtlety of which I have spoken.

Battista was not alone. In front of the desk was sitting someone whom he introduced to me by the name of Rheingold. I knew very well who he was, although this was the first time I had met him. Rheingold was a German director who, in the pre-Nazi film era, had directed, in Germany, various films of the 'colossal' type which had had a considerable success at the time. He was certainly not in the same class as the Pabsts and Langs; but, as a director, he was worthy of respect, not in the least commercial, and with ambitions with which one might not perhaps agree, but which were nevertheless serious. After the advent of Hitler, nothing had been heard of him. It was said that he was working in Hollywood, but no film under his signature had been shown in recent years in Italy. And now here he was, popping up strangely in Battista's office. While the latter was talking to us, I looked at Rheingold with curiosity. Have you ever, in some old print, seen the face of Goethe? Just so, just as noble, as regular, as Olympian, was the face of Rheingold; and, like that of Goethe, it was framed in a fringe of clean and shining silver hair. It was, in fact, the head of a great man; except that, on closer examination, I became aware that its majesty and nobility were lacking in substance; the features were slightly coarse and at the same time spongy, flimsy, as though made of cardboard, like those of a mask; giving, in fact, the impression that there was nothing behind them, like the faces of the enormous heads that are carried round by tiny little men at carnival times. Rheingold rose to shake me by the hand, giving a little bow with his head only, a slight click of the heels, in the stiff German manner; and then I realized that he was quite a small man, although his shoulders, as if to match the majesty of his face, were very wide. I noticed also that, as he greeted me, he smiled at me in an extremely affable manner, with a broad smile like a half-moon, showing two rows of very regular and altogether too-white teeth which I at once imagined, I don't know why, to be false. But immediately afterwards, when he sat down again, the smile disappeared in a flash, leaving no traces – just as the moon is obliterated in the sky by a cloud passing in front of it – and giving place to a very hard, unpleasant expression, both dictatorial and exacting.

Battista, following his usual method, started off in a roundabout way. Nodding towards Rheingold, he said: 'Rheingold and I were just talking about Capri . . . D'you know Capri, Molteni?'

'Yes; a little,' I answered.

'I possess a villa in Capri,' went on Battista, 'and I was just saying to Rheingold what an enchanting place Capri is. . . . It's a place where even a man like me, taken up as I am with business affairs, feels himself becoming a bit of a poet.'

It was one of Battista's favourite habits to profess an enthusiasm for fine and beautiful things, for the things, in fact, that belong to the sphere of the ideal; but what disconcerted me most was that this enthusiasm, to which he called attention in so sure a manner, was perfectly sincere, though always, somehow or other, connected with purposes that were not at all disinterested. After a moment, as it were moved by his own words, he resumed: 'Luxuriant nature, a marvellous sky, a sea that is always blue . . . and flowers, flowers everywhere. I think that if I were like you, Molteni, a writer, I should like to live in Capri and take my inspiration from it . . . It's strange that painters, instead of painting the Capri landscape, should give us all those ugly pictures that no one can understand

. . . In Capri, pictures are ready made, so to speak . . . All you have to do is to put yourself in front of the landscape and copy it . . .'

I said nothing; I looked at Rheingold out of the corner of my eye and saw him nod his approval, his smile hanging in the middle of his face like a sickle moon in a cloudless sky. Battista went on: 'I'm always intending to spend a few months there, away from business, without doing anything, but I never manage it . . . We in the city here lead a life that is altogether against nature . . . Man isn't made to live amongst files of papers, in an office . . . and the people of Capri do, in fact, look far happier than we do . . . You ought to see them in the evening, when they come out to take a walk – young men and girls, smiling, serene, attractive, gay . . . It's because they have a life made up of small things, with small ambitions, small interests, small troubles . . . My goodness, how lucky they are!'

There was silence again. Then Battista resumed: 'As I was saying, I have a villa in Capri and I'm never there, worse luck . . . I must have stayed there just about a couple of months altogether since I acquired it . . . I was just saying to Rheingold that the villa would be the best possible place for writing the script of the film . . . The landscape would inspire you . . . especially because, as I was pointing out to Rheingold, the landscape is in harmony with the subject of the film.'

'One can work anywhere, Signor Battista,' said Rheingold; 'certainly Capri might be useful . . . especially if, as I think, we take the exterior shots of the film in the Bay of Naples.'

'Exactly . . . Rheingold, however, says he would rather go to an hotel, because he has his own habits, and, besides, he likes to be alone at certain times and to think over the work by himself . . . But I think that you, Molteni, might stay at the villa, together with your wife . . . It would be a pleasure for me if at last there was someone living there . . . The villa has every convenience, and you would have no difficulty in finding a woman to look after you . . .'

At once I thought of Emilia, as always; and I felt that a stay in a lovely villa in Capri might perhaps solve many difficulties. What I am saying is true: all of a sudden, for no reason, I was absolutely certain that it would indeed solve them. It was therefore with genuine warmth that I thanked Battista. 'Thank you,' I said. 'I also think that Capri would be the best possible place for writing the script . . . and my wife and I would be delighted to stay at your villa.'

'Excellent; that's understood, then,' said Battista, holding up his hand with a gesture that vaguely offended me, as if to check a flood of gratitude which I really had no intention of letting loose. 'That's understood; you'll go to Capri and I'll come and join you there . . . And now let us talk a little about the film.'

'High time too!' I thought, and looked closely at Battista. I had, now, an obscure feeling of remorse at having accepted his invitation so promptly. I did not know why, but I guessed instinctively that Emilia would have disapproved of my hastiness. 'I ought to have told him I must think it over,' I said to myself with some irritation; 'that I must first consult my wife.' And the warmth with which I had accepted the invitation seemed to me misplaced, a thing to be almost ashamed of. Battista, meanwhile, was saying: 'We're all agreed that something new in the way of films has got to be found . . . The after-the-war period is now over, and people are feeling the need of a new formula . . . Everyone – just to give an example – is a little tired of neo-realism . . . Now, by analysing the reasons for which we have grown tired of the neo-realist film, we may perhaps arrive at an understanding of what the new formula might be.'

I knew, as I have already mentioned, that Battista's favourite way of attacking a subject was always an indirect one. He was not a cynical type of man, or at any rate he was determined not to appear so. Thus it was very difficult for him to speak openly, as did many other producers franker than he, about financial matters: the question of profit, no less important to him than to the others – in fact, perhaps even more important – remained always shrouded in a discreet obscurity; and if – let us suppose – the subject of a film did not seem to him sufficiently profitable, he would never say, like the others, 'This subject won't put a penny into the cash-box,' but rather, 'I don't like this subject for such and such a reason'; and the reasons were always of an aesthetic or moral order. Nevertheless, the question of profit was always the final touchstone; and the proof of this was to be seen when, after many discussions upon the beautiful and the good in the art of the film, after a good many of what I called Battista's smoke-screens, the choice fell, invariably, upon the solution that held the best commercial possibilities. Owing to this, I had for some time now lost all interest in the considerations, often extremely long and complicated, put forward by Battista on films beautiful or ugly, moral or immoral; and I waited patiently for him to reach the point where, always and inevitably, he came to a halt – the question of economic advantage. And this time I thought: 'He certainly won't say that producers are tired of the neo-realist film because it isn't profitable . . . Let's see what he will say.' Battista, in fact, went on, after a moment's reflection: 'In my opinion, everyone is rather tired of the neo-realist film mainly because it's not a healthy type of film.'

He stopped, and I looked sideways at Rheingold: he did not blink an eyelid. Battista, who had intended, by pausing, to stress the word 'healthy', now went on to explain it. 'When I say that the neo-realist film is not healthy, I mean that it is not a film that inspires people with courage to live, that increases their confidence in life . . . The neo-realist film is depressing, pessimistic, gloomy . . . Apart from the fact that it represents Italy as a country of ragamuffins – to the great joy of foreigners who have every sort of interest in believing that our country really *is* a country of ragamuffins – apart from this fact, which, after all, is of some considerable importance, it insists too much on the negative sides of life, on all that is ugliest, dirtiest, most abnormal in human existence . . . It is, in short, a pessimistic, unhealthy type of film, a film which reminds people of their difficulties instead of helping them to overcome them.'

I looked at Battista and once again I remained uncertain as to whether he really believed the things he was saying or only pretended to believe them. There was sincerity of a kind in what he said; perhaps it was only the sincerity of a man who easily convinces himself of the things that are useful to him; nevertheless, sincerity there was. Battista went on speaking, in that voice of strangely inhuman timbre, almost metallic even in its sweetness. 'Rheingold has made a suggestion which interested me . . . He has noticed that in recent times films with subjects taken from the Bible have been highly successful . . . They have been, in fact, the best money-makers,' he observed at this point, almost pensively, but as though opening a parenthesis to which he himself wished no importance to be paid. 'And why? . . . In my opinion,

85

because the Bible remains always the *healthiest* book that has ever been written in this world . . . And so Rheingold said to me, the Anglo-Saxon races have the Bible, and you Mediterranean peoples, on the other hand, have Homer . . . Isn't that so?' He interrupted himself and turned towards Rheingold, as if uncertain that he was quoting him correctly.

'That's it exactly,' confirmed Rheingold, not without an expression of slight anxiety on his smiling face.

'To you Mediterranean peoples,' continued Battista, still quoting Rheingold, 'Homer is what the Bible is to the Anglo-Saxons . . . And so why shouldn't we make a film from, for instance, the *Odyssey*?'

There was silence. Astonished, I wanted to gain time, and so I asked, with an effort: 'The whole *Odyssey*, or an episode from the *Odyssey*?'

'We've discussed the matter,' Battista answered promptly, 'and we've come to the conclusion that it will be best to take into consideration the *Odyssey* as a whole . . . But that doesn't matter . . . What matters most,' he went on, raising his voice, 'is that, in re-reading the *Odyssey*, I've at last understood what I've been looking for so long without realizing it . . . something that I felt could not be found in neo-realist films . . . something, for instance, that I've never found in the subjects that you, Molteni, have suggested to me from time to time recently . . . something that I, in fact, have been feeling – without being able to explain it to myself – have been feeling was needed in the cinema as it is needed in life – poetry.'

I looked again at Rheingold: he was still smiling, perhaps a little more broadly than before, and was nodding his approval. I hazarded, rather dryly: 'In the *Odyssey*, as one knows, there is plenty of poetry . . . The difficulty is to get it over into the film.'

86

'Quite right,' said Battista, taking up a ruler from the desk and pointing it at me; 'quite right . . . but to do that, there are you two, you and Rheingold . . . I know there's poetry in it . . . It's up to you to pull it out.'

I replied: 'The *Odyssey* is a world in itself . . . one can get out of it what one wants . . . it depends what point of view one brings to it.'

Battista seemed now to be disconcerted by my lack of enthusiasm, and was examining me with ponderous intentness, as though trying to guess what purposes I was concealing behind my coldness. At last he appeared to be postponing his scrutiny to a later occasion, for he rose to his feet and, making his way round the table, started walking up and down the room, his head held high, his hands thrust into the hip pockets of his trousers. We turned to look at him; and, still walking up and down, he resumed: 'What struck me above all in the *Odyssey* is that Homer's poetry is always spectacular . . . and when I say spectacular, I mean it has something in it that infallibly pleases the public . . . Take for example the Nausicaa episode . . . All those lovely girls dressed in nothing at all, splashing about in the water under the eyes of Ulysses, who is hiding behind a bush . . . There, with slight variations, you have a complete Bathing Beauties scene . . . Or take Polyphemus: a monster with only one eye, a giant, an ogre . . . why, it's King Kong, one of the greatest pre-war successes . . . Or take again Circe, in her castle . . . why, she's Antinea, in *Atlantis* . . . That's what I call spectacle . . . And this spectacle, as I said, is not merely spectacle, but poetry too . . . .' Much excited, Battista stopped in front of us and said solemnly: 'That's how I see a film of the *Odyssey* produced by Triumph Films.'

I said nothing. I realized that, to Battista, poetry meant something very different from what I understood by it;

and that, according to his conception of it, the *Odyssey* of Triumph Films would be a film based upon the big Biblical and costume films of Hollywood, with monsters, naked women, seduction scenes, eroticism and grandiloquence. Fundamentally, I told myself, Battista's taste was still that of the Italian producers of the time of D'Annunzio. How indeed could it have been otherwise? In the meantime, he had made his way back round the desk and sat down again, and was saying to me: 'Well, Molteni, what do you say to that?'

Anyone who knows the world of the cinema knows that there are films of which one can be certain, even before a single word of the script has been written, that they will be brought to a final conclusion; while there are others which, even after the contract has been signed and hundreds of pages of the screen-play completed, will equally surely never be finished. So now I, with the experienced flair of the professional script-writer, recognized immediately, even while Battista was speaking, that this *Odyssey* film was, precisely, one of those which are much discussed, but, in the end, never made. Why should this be so? I could not have said; perhaps it was because of the inordinate ambitiousness of the work, perhaps it was Rheingold's physical appearance, so majestic when he was seated, so meagre when he stood up. I felt that, like Rheingold, the film would have an imposing beginning and a paltry conclusion, thus justifying the well-known remark about the Siren: *desinit in piscem*, she ends up in a fish. And then, why did Battista want to make such a film? I knew that he was fundamentally very prudent, and determined to make money without taking risks. Probably, I thought, beneath his desire there lay the hope of obtaining solid financial support, perhaps even American support, by playing upon the great name of Homer – the

Bible, as Rheingold had remarked, of the Mediterranean peoples. But on the other hand I knew that Battista, no different from other producers in this respect, would find some pretext, supposing the film were never made, for refusing to give me any remuneration for my hard work. It always happened like that: if the film failed to come off, payments also failed to come off, and the producer, generally, suggested transferring the emolument for the already completed script to other work to be done in the future; and the poor script-writer, forced by necessity, did not dare to refuse. I said to myself, therefore, that I must in any case forearm myself by asking for a contract and, above all, an advance; and that to achieve this goal there was only one method: to place difficulties in the way, to set a high price upon my collaboration. So I answered, tartly: 'I think it's a very good idea.'

'You don't seem, however, to be very enthusiastic.'

I replied, with a sufficient show of sincerity: 'I am afraid it may not be my kind of film . . . it may be beyond my powers.'

'Why? . . .' Battista seemed irritated now. 'You've always said you wanted to work at a film of quality . . . and now that I give you the chance, you draw back.'

I tried to explain what I meant. 'You see, Battista, I feel myself to be cut out chiefly for psychological films . . . whereas this one, as far as I understand, is to be a purely spectacular film . . . of the type, in fact, of the American films taken from Biblical subjects.'

This time Battista had not time to answer me, for Rheingold, in a wholly unexpected manner, broke in. 'Signor Molteni,' he said, summoning back his usual half-moon smile on his face, rather like an actor, suddenly sticking on a pair of false moustaches; and leaning forward slightly, with an obsequious, almost fawning expression.

'Signor Battista has expressed himself very well and has given a perfect picture of the film I intend to realize with his help . . . Signor Battisa, however, was speaking as a producer, and was taking into account, more especially, the spectacular elements . . . But if you feel yourself cut out for psychological subjects you ought, without any possible doubt, to do this film . . . because this film is neither more nor less than a film on the psychological relationship between Ulysses and Penelope . . . I intend to make a film about a man who loves his wife and is not loved in return.'

I was disconcerted by this, all the more so because Rheingold's face, illuminated by his usual artificial smile, was very close to me and seemed to cut me off from any possible loophole of escape: I had to reply, and at once. And then, just as I was about to protest, 'But it's not true that Penelope does not love Ulysses,' the director's phrase, 'a man who loves his wife and is not loved in return,' brought me suddenly back to the problem of my relations with Emilia – the relations, precisely, of a man who loved his wife and was not loved in return; and at the same time, through some mysterious association of ideas, it brought to the surface of my memory a recollection which – as I immediately became aware – seemed to provide an answer to the question I had put to myself in the ante-room, while I was waiting to see Battista: Why did Emilia no longer love me?

The story I am now going to tell may seem lengthy: in reality, owing to the almost vision-like speed of the recollection, the whole thing lasted only an instant. Well, then, as Rheingold bent his smiling face towards me, I saw myself, in a flash, in my study at home, in the act of dictating a script. I had just reached the end of a dictation which had lasted several days, yet I still could not have

90

said whether the typist was pretty or not; and then a minute incident opened my eyes, so to speak. She was typing out some sentence or other when, bending down to look at the sheet of paper over her shoulder, I realized that I had made a mistake. I leant forward and tried to correct the error myself by tapping out the word with my finger on the keys. But, as I did so, without meaning to, I lightly touched her hand which, I noticed, was very large and strong and strangely in contrast with the slightness of her figure. As I touched her hand, I was conscious that she did not withdraw it; I composed a second word, and again, this time perhaps not without intention, touched her fingers. Then I looked into her face and saw that she was looking straight back at me, with an expression of expectation, almost of invitation. I also noticed with surprise, as if for the first time, that she was pretty, with her little, full mouth, her capricious nose, her big black eyes and her thick, curly, brushed-back hair. But her pale, delicate face wore a discontented, scornful, angry expression. One last detail: when she spoke, saying with a grimace, 'I'm sorry, I wasn't thinking,' I was struck by the dry, precise, decidedly disagreeable tone of her voice. I looked at her then, and saw that she sustained my regard perfectly well – in fact, she returned it in a manner that was positively aggressive. I must then have shown some sign of emotion and indeed have given a mute response, for from that moment, for several days, we never stopped looking at each other. Or rather, it was she who never stopped looking at me, impudently, with deliberate effrontery, at every opportunity, pursuing my eyes when they avoided hers, seeking to hold them when our eyes met, delving into them when they came to a halt. As always happens, these glances, at first, were few and far between; then they became more and more frequent; finally, not knowing how to escape them, I was reduced to walking up and down behind her as I dictated. But the tenacious coquette found a means of circumventing this obstacle by staring at me in a big mirror hanging on the wall opposite, so that, each time I raised my eyes, I found hers waiting there to meet them. In the end, the thing that she wanted to happen, happened: one day, when, as usual, I was leaning over from behind to correct a mistake, I looked up at her, our eyes met, and our mouths were joined for one moment in a swift kiss. The first thing she said, after the kiss, was characteristic: 'Oh, at last! . . . I was really beginning to think you'd never make up your mind.' Indeed, she now seemed sure that she held me in her clutches, so sure that, immediately after the kiss, she did not trouble to demand any more, but went back to her work. I was left with a feeling of confusion and remorse: I found the girl attractive, certainly, otherwise I should not have kissed her; but it was also certain that I was not in love with her and that the truth of the matter was that she had forced the kiss from me by working upon my male vanity with her petulant and, to me, flattering persistence. Now she went on typing without looking at me, her eyes lowered, prettier than ever with her round, pale face and her big mop of black hair. Then she made – on purpose, perhaps – another mistake, and I again leant over her, seeking to correct it. But she was watching my movements, and, as soon as my face was close to hers, she turned in a flash and threw her arm round my neck, seizing hold of me by one ear and pulling my mouth sideways against hers. At that moment the door opened and Emilia came in.

What happened then, I think it is hardly necessary to relate in detail. Emilia withdrew at once, and I, after saying very hurriedly to the girl, 'Signorina, that's enough

for today . . . you can go home now,' almost ran out of the
study and joined Emilia in the living-room. I expected a
scene of jealousy, but all Emilia said, as I came in, was:
'You might at least wipe the red off your lips.' I did so,
and then sat down beside her and tried to justify myself,
telling her the truth. She listened to me with an indefinable expression of suspicious, but fundamentally indul-
gent, mistrust, and at last remarked that, if I was truly in
love with the typist, I had only to say so and she would
agree to a separation forthwith. But she spoke these
words without harshness and with a kind of melancholy
gentleness, as though tacitly inviting me to contradict
them. Finally, after many explanations and much desperation on my part (I was positively terrified at the thought of
Emilia leaving me), she appeared to be convinced and,
with some show of reluctance, consented to forgive me.
That same afternoon, in the presence of Emilia, I telephoned to the typist to inform her that I should not need
her again. The girl tried to wrest an appointment from me
at some outside meeting-place; but I gave her an evasive
answer, and have never seen her since.

This recapitulation, as I said, may seem lengthy,
whereas in reality the scene flashed across my memory in
the form of a lightning-like image: Emilia opening the
door at the moment when I was kissing the typist. And I
was at once surprised at not having thought of it before.
There could be no doubt, I now felt, that things had taken
the following course. Emilia, at the time, had shown that
she paid no importance to the incident, whereas in reality,
perhaps unconsciously, she had been profoundly disturbed by it. Afterwards she had thought about it again,
weaving round that first memory an ever-thicker, ever-
tighter cocoon of increasing disillusionment; so that that
kiss, which for me had been nothing more than a passing

weakness, had produced in her mind a trauma (to use a psychiatrist's term) – that is, a wound which time, instead of healing, had increasingly exacerbated. While I was pondering these things there must be no doubt have been a very dreamy expression on my face, for all at once, through the kind of thick mist that enveloped me, I heard Rheingold's voice asking in alarm: 'But do you hear what I am saying, Signor Molteni?'

The mist dissolved in an instant, and I shook myself and saw the director's smiling face stretching out towards me. 'I'm sorry,' I said. 'My mind was wandering . . . I was thinking of what Rheingold said: a man who loves his wife and is not loved in return . . . but . . . but . . . ' Not knowing what to say, I made the objection that had come into my mind in the first place: 'But Ulysses in the poem *is* loved in return by Penelope . . . in fact, in a sense, the whole of the *Odyssey* hinges on this love of Penelope's for Ulysses.'

Rheingold, I saw, swept aside my objection with a smile.

'Loyalty, Signor Molteni, not love . . . Penelope is loyal to Ulysses, but we do not know how far she loved him . . . and as you know, people can sometimes be absolutely loyal without loving . . . In certain cases, in fact, loyalty is a form of vengeance, of blackmail, of recovering one's self-respect . . . Loyalty, not love.'

I was struck, once again, by what Rheingold said; and again I could not help thinking of Emilia, wondering whether, in place of loyalty and indifference, I would not perhaps have preferred betrayal and the consequent remorse. Yes, undoubtedly I should: if Emilia had betrayed me and had felt towards me, it would have been possible for me to face her with assurance. But I had now demonstrated to myself that Emilia was not betraying me;

that it had been I myself, in fact, who had betrayed her. As my mind was wandering in this new direction I was aroused by the voice of Battista saying: 'Well then, Molteni, it's agreed that you'll work with Rheingold.'

'Yes,' I answered with an effort; 'yes, it's agreed.'

'Excellent,' declared Battista with satisfaction. 'Then let us arrange it like this. Rheingold has to go to Paris tomorrow morning and will be there for a week. You, Molteni, during that week, will make me a summary of the *Odyssey* and bring it to me . . . and as soon as Rheingold comes back from Paris, you'll go together to Capri and start on the work at once.'

After this conclusive remark, Rheingold rose to his feet, and mechanically I rose also. I realized that I ought to speak about the contract and the advance, and that, if I did not do so, Battista would have got the better of me; but the thought of Emilia upset me and, even more, the strange resemblance between Rheingold's interpretation of Homer and my own personal affairs. I managed nevertheless to murmur, as we went off towards the door: 'And how about the contract?'

'The contract is ready,' said Battista in an entirely unexpected manner and in a casual, magnanimous tone of voice, 'and the advance is also ready, together with the contract . . . All you have to do, Molteni, is to go to my secretary, and to sign the one and take away the other.'

Surprise almost stunned me. I had expected, as had happened in the case of other film-scripts, that there would be the usual manoeuvres on the part of Battista to cut down my remuneration or delay its payment; yet here he was paying me at once, without any discussion. As we all three passed into the adjoining room, which was the manager's office, I could not help murmuring: 'Thank you, Battista . . . You know I need it.'

I bit my lip: in the first place it was not altogether true that I needed it – not urgently, anyhow, as my remark implied; and besides, I felt that I ought not to have spoken those words, though I did not quite know why. Battista's reply confirmed my regret. 'So I guessed, my dear boy,' he said, clapping me on the back with a protective, fatherly gesture, 'and I saw that you had what you wanted.' Then, to a secretary who was sitting at a desk, he added: 'This is Signor Molteni . . . for that contract and the advance.'

The secretary rose to his feet and at once opened a portfolio and took from it an already drawn-up contract to which was pinned a cheque. Battista, after shaking Rheingold by the hand, clapped me on the shoulder again, wishing me good luck with my new job, and then went back into his office. 'Signor Molteni,' said Rheingold, coming up to me in his turn and holding out his hand, 'we shall meet again on my return from Paris . . . In the meantime, you'll be making that summary of the *Odyssey* . . . and then taking it to Signor Battista and discussing it with him.'

'Very well,' I said, looking at him in some surprise because I had seen him give me a sort of understanding wink.

Rheingold noticed my look and, all of a sudden, took me by the arm and put his mouth close to my ear. 'Don't worry,' he whispered to me hurriedly; 'don't be afraid . . . Let Battista say what he likes . . . We'll make a psycho- logical film, a purely psychological film.' I noticed that he pronounced the word 'psychological' in the German way – *psüchologhical*; then he smiled at me, shook my hand with a brisk nod of the head and a click of the heels, and walked away. Watching him go, I started when I heard the secretary's voice saying to me: 'Well, Signor Molteni . . . will you be so good as to sign here? . . .'

9

It was only seven o'clock and, when I reached home, I called in vain to Emilia through the deserted flat: but she had gone out and would not be back till dinner-time. I was disappointed and even, in a way, felt positively bitter. I had counted on finding her and talking to her at once about the incident of the typist; I was sure that that kiss had been at the bottom of our difference, and, feeling myself full of a new boldness, was confident that I could dispel the misunderstanding with a few words and then tell her the good news of the afternoon – my contract for the *Odyssey*, the advance I had received, our departure to Capri. It is true that my explanation was postponed only for a couple of hours, yet, all the same, I had an irritating feeling of disappointment and almost of foreboding. At that moment I felt sure of my own case; but I wondered whether, in two hours' time, I should have the power to be equally convincing. It will be seen that, although I pretended to myself that I had at last found the key to the difficulty – that is, the true reason why Emilia had ceased to love me – fundamentally I was not at all sure of it. And this unfortunate absence on her part was quite enough to fill me with apprehension and ill-humour.

Listless, demoralized and perplexed, I went into my study and looked mechanically in the bookshelf for the translation of the *Odyssey*. Then I sat down at the desk, put a sheet of paper into my typewriter and, having lit a cigarette, prepared to write the summary. I thought that the work would soothe my anxiety or at least make me forget it: I had tried this remedy on other occasions. So I opened the book and read, slowly, the whole of the First Canto. Then at the top of the page I typed the title: *Synopsis of the Odyssey*, and, underneath it, began: 'The Trojan War has been over for some time. All the Greek heroes who took part in it have now gone home. All except Ulysses, who is still far from his own island and his dear ones.' At this point, however, a doubt as to whether or not it was suitable to introduce into my summary the Council of the Gods, in the course of which this same return of Ulysses to Ithaca was discussed, caused me to interrupt my work. This Council was important, it seemed to me, because it introduced into the poem the notion of Fate, and of the vanity and, at the same time, the nobility and heroism of human effort. Cutting out the Council meant cutting out the whole supramundane aspect of the poem, eliminating all divine intervention, suppressing the figures of the various divinities, so charming and poetical in themselves. But there was no doubt that Battista would not want to have anything to do with the gods, who would seem to him nothing more than incompetent chatterboxes who made a great fuss about deciding things that could perfectly well be decided by the protagonists. As for Rheingold, the ambiguous hint he had given of a 'psychological' film presaged no good towards the divinities; psychology obviously excludes Fate and divine intervention; at most, it discovers Fate in the depths of the human spirit, in the dark intricacies of the so-called subconscious. The gods, therefore, would be superfluous, because neither spectactular nor psychological . . . I thought about these things with ever-growing confusion and weariness; every now and then I looked at the typewriter and said to myself that I must get on with my work, but I could not bring myself to it and sat without moving a finger; and finally I fell into a profound but blank meditation, sitting there at the desk, my eyes staring into vacancy. In reality I was not so much meditating as stirring together in my mind the cold, acid flavours of the various feelings, all of them disagreeable, that agitated me; but, in my bewildered, weary, vaguely irritable state, I did not succeed in defining them to myself in any precise manner. Then, all at once, like an air-bubble that rises suddenly to the still surface of a pond afer remaining for who knows how long under water, this reflection forced its way into my mind: 'Now I shall have to submit the *Odyssey* to the usual massacre, to reduce it to a film . . . and once the script is finished, this book will go back into its shelf along with all the others that have served me for other screen-plays . . . And in a few years' time, when I am looking for another book to cut to pieces for another film, I shall come upon it and say: Ah yes, of course, that was when I was doing the script of the *Odyssey* with Rheingold . . . And then nothing was done about it . . . nothing was done, after talking for months, morning and evening, day in day out, about Ulysses and Penelope and the Cyclops and Circe and the Sirens . . . Nothing was done because . . . because there wasn't enough money.' At this thought I was conscious, yet again, of a feeling of profound disgust for the trade I was forced to follow. And again I was conscious, with acute pain, that this disgust was born of the certainty that Emilia no longer loved me. Hitherto I had worked for Emilia, and for Emilia only; since her love had failed me, my work had no further object.

I do not know how long I remained like that, hunched up motionless in my chair in front of the typewriter, with my eyes turned towards the window. At last I heard the front door bang at the other end of the flat, and then the sound of footsteps in the living-room, and I knew that Emilia had returned. I did not move, but remained where I was. Finally I heard the door of the study open behind me and Emilia's voice asking: 'Are you in here? What are you doing? Are you working?' Then I turned round.

She was standing in the doorway with her hat still on her head and a parcel in her hand. I said at once, with a spontaneity which astonishes me after so many doubts and apprehensions: 'No; I'm not working . . . I was just wondering whether I ought or ought not to accept this new script of Battista's.'

She closed the door and came and stood beside me, near the desk. 'Have you been to see Battista?'

'Yes.'

'But you haven't come to an agreement . . . Doesn't he offer you enough?'

'Yes; he offers enough . . . and we have come to an agreement.'

'Well, then . . . But perhaps you don't like the subject?'

'No; it's a good subject.'

'What is the subject?

I looked at her for a moment before replying: as usual she appeared absent-minded and indifferent, and one could see she was only speaking from duty. 'It's the *Odyssey*,' I answered briefly.

She put down the parcel on the desk, lifted her hand to her head and slowly took off her hat, shaking out her pressed-down hair. But her face was blank and inattentive: either she had not understood that I was speaking of the famous poem, or – which was more probable – the title, though not entirely unknown, conveyed nothing to her. 'Well,' she remarked at last, almost impatiently, 'don't you like it?'

'Yes. I told you I did!'

100

'Isn't the *Odyssey* the thing one learns in school? Why don't you want to do it?'

'Because I don't feel like doing it now.'

'But surely, only this morning, you had decided to accept the job?'

All of a sudden I realized that the moment had come for another, and this time really decisive, explanation. I jumped to my feet, took hold of her by the arm and said: 'Let's go in there, into the living-room; I must talk to you.'

She was frightened – more, perhaps, by the almost frenzied force with which I gripped her arm than by the tone of my voice. 'What's the matter with you? . . . Are you mad?'

'No; I'm not mad . . . Let's go in there and talk.'

Meanwhile, I was dragging her, forcibly, across the study. I opened the door and thrust her into the other room, in the direction of an armchair. 'Sit down there!' I myself sat down facing her, and said: 'Now let's talk.'

She looked at me dubiously, and still a little frightened. 'Well, talk then. I'm listening.'

I began in a cold and colourless voice: 'Yesterday – d'you remember? – I told you that I had no desire to do this script because I was not sure that you loved me . . . and you answered that you did love me and that I ought to do it . . . Isn't that so?'

'Yes; that's so.'

'Well,' I declared resolutely, 'I believe you were telling me a lie . . . I don't know why – perhaps because you were sorry for me, perhaps in order to serve your own interests . . .'

'What interests?' she interrupted me harshly.

'The interest you may have,' I explained, 'in remaining in this flat which you like so much.'

Her reaction was such that I was struck by its violence.

101

She sat straight up in her chair and said in a louder voice than usual: 'Who told you that? . . . This flat doesn't matter to me in the least, not in the very least . . . I'm perfectly ready to go back and live in a furnished room . . . It's quite obvious you don't know me . . . It means nothing to me.'

These words gave me a feeling of acute pain – pain such as a man might feel who sees some gift, for which he has faced bitter sacrifices, despised and insultingly spurned. After all, this home of ours, of which she spoke with such contempt, represented my life for the last two years; for this home I had abandoned the work I most wished to do, I had renounced my dearest ambitions. I asked in a thin, almost incredulous voice: 'It means nothing to you?'

'Nothing; absolutely nothing.' Her voice sounded flat and unmusical, from some unexplained passion of contempt. 'Nothing . . . D'you understand? . . . Nothing!'

'But yesterday you said you cared very much about staying in this flat.'

'I only said it to please you . . . because I thought it was you who cared!'

I was inwardly amazed: so it was I – I who had sacrificed my theatrical ambitions, I who had never held such things to be of great importance – it was I who cared about the flat! I saw that she had now entered, for some reason unknown to me, upon the path of deceit, and I told myself that it would serve no purpose to exasperate her by contradicting her and reminding her of how much she had once desired what she now made such a show of despising. In any case, the flat was a mere detail; what really mattered was something quite different. 'Never mind the flat,' I said, trying to control my voice and adopt a conciliating, sensible tone. 'It's not the flat I wanted to talk about, but your feeling towards me . . . You lied to

102

me yesterday when you said, for some reason or other, that you loved me . . . You lied to me, and that's why I have no further desire to work for the cinema . . . because I did it entirely for you, and if you no longer love me I have no reason for going on with it.'

'But what makes you think I lied to you?'

'Nothing and everything . . . We talked about that yesterday, too, and I don't want to begin all over again . . . There are things that can't be explained, but which one feels . . . and I feel you no longer love me . . .'

She showed, suddenly, a first impulse of sincerity. 'Why do you want to know these things?' she asked unexpectedly in a sad, tired voice, looking away towards the window. 'Why? . . . Let it alone . . . it will be better for us both.'

'Well, then,' I persisted, 'you admit that I may be right?'

'I admit nothing . . . I only want to be left in peace . . . Leave me in peace!' There was a hint of tears in these last words. Then she added: 'I'm going now . . . I want to change my clothes'; and she rose and went off towards the door. But I caught her as she went, seizing her by the wrist. I had made this gesture more than once before: when she had risen, saying she must leave me, and I, as she passed in front of my chair, had taken hold of her by her long, slender wrist. But formerly I had seized hold of her because I felt a sudden desire for her, and she knew it, and would stop immediately, awaiting my second gesture, which consisted in embracing her legs and burying my face in her lap, or in pulling her down on to my knees. All this would end in love-making – after a little resistance and a few caresses – just where we found ourselves, in the armchair or on the divan close by. This time, however, my intention was different, and I could not help being aware

103

of it with some bitterness. She did not resist, but remained standing close beside me, looking down at me from her great height. 'Really,' she said. 'What *do* you want, I should like to know?'

'I want the truth.'

'You want to insist on making trouble between us – that's what you want!'

'Then you admit that the truth would not please me?'

'I admit nothing.'

'But you said it yourself – making trouble between us . . .'

'Oh well, I had to say something . . . Now let me go!'

She did not struggle, however, nor did she move; she simply waited for me to release her. I felt I should have preferred violent rebellion to this cold, contemptuous patience; and as though hoping, by a renewal of the old gesture which once had been the prelude to love, to arouse in her a feeling of affection, I let go of her wrist and put my arms round her legs. She was wearing a long, very ample skirt, full of folds; and as I embraced her I felt it shrink and tighten round her fine, straight legs, hard and muscular, like the ample sails of a ship round the mast. And then I felt desire for her, in a way that was almost painful because of its suddenness and because of the sense of impotent despair that accompanied it. Looking up at her, I said: 'Emilia, what have you against me?'

'I haven't anything at all . . . And now let me go!'

I clasped her legs more tightly with my two arms, pressing my face into her lap. Generally, when I made this gesture, I would feel, after a moment or two, the big hand that I loved so much being laid on my head in a slow, tentative caress. This would be the signal of her emotional response and of her willingness to do my pleasure. But this time her hand remained dangling and inert. This attitude on her part, so different from her former one, smote deep into my heart. I released her, and taking her by the wrist again, cried: 'No; you shan't go . . . You've got to tell me the truth . . . this very minute . . . You shan't leave the room until you've told me the truth.'

She went on looking down at me from above: I could not see her, but I seemed to feel her hesitating gaze on my bowed head. At last she said: 'Well, you've asked for it . . . All I wanted was to go on as we are . . . It's you who've asked for it. It's true, I don't love you now . . . There's the truth for you!'

It is possible to picture the most disagreeable things and to picture them with the certainty that they are true. But the confirmation of such fancies, or rather, of such certainties, always comes unexpectedly and painfully, just as though one had not pictured anything beforehand. Really and truly I had known all the time that Emilia no longer loved me. But to hear her say it had, nevertheless, a chilling effect upon me. She did not love me now: those words, so often imagined, assumed, when pronounced by her lips, an entirely new significance. They were fact, not fancy, however mixed the latter might have been with certainty. They had a weight, a size, which they had never before had in my mind. I do not remember clearly how I received this declaration. Probably I gave a start, like someone who goes under an icy shower-bath knowing that it is icy, and yet when he feels it, gives a start just the same, as if he had never known at all. Then I tried to recover myself, to show myself, somehow, reasonable and objective. I said, as gently as I could: 'Come here . . . Sit down and explain to me why you don't love me.'

She obeyed and sat down again, this time on the divan. Then she said, rather irritably: 'There's nothing to explain

105

. . . I don't love you now, and that is absolutely all I have to say.'

I realized that, the more I sought to show myself reasonable, the more deeply did the thorn of my unspeakable pain sink into my flesh. My face was twisted into a forced smile as I answered: 'You must at least admit that you owe me an explanation . . . Even when one sacks a servant, one explains the reason.'

'I don't love you any more; that's all I have to say.'

'But why? . . . You did love me, didn't you?'

'Yes, I loved you . . . very much . . . but now I don't any more.'

'You loved me very much?'

'Yes, very much; but it's all over now.'

'But why? There must be a reason.'

'Perhaps there may be . . . but I don't know what it is; I only know that I don't love you.'

'Don't repeat it so often,' I exclaimed almost in spite of myself, and raising my voice a little.

'It's you who make me repeat it . ... You refuse to be convinced, and so I have to go on repeating it.'

'I'm convinced now.'

There was silence. Emilia had now lit a cigarette and was smoking it with downcast eyes. I was bending forward with my head between my hands. Finally, I said: 'If *I* tell you the reason – will you recognize it?'

'But I don't know it myself.'

'But if I tell it to you, perhaps you'll recognize it.'

'All right, then; come on . . . tell me.'

'Don't speak to me like that!' I wanted to cry to her, wounded by her curt, indifferent tone. But I restrained myself and, trying to maintain my reasonable air, began: 'Do you remember that girl who came here some months ago to type out a script for me . . . that typist? You caught

106

us kissing . . . It was a stupid weakness on my part . . . But there was only that one kiss, I swear; it was the first and the last . . . and I've never seen her since . . . Now tell me the truth – wasn't it perhaps that kiss that first came between us? Tell me the truth – wasn't that kiss the first thing that made you lose your love for me?'

As I spoke, I watched her carefully. Her first movement was one of surprise, and of consequent denial: it was as if my supposition seemed to her completely absurd. Then, as I saw clearly, a sudden idea made her change expression. She answered slowly: 'Well, suppose it *was* that kiss . . . Now that you know, does it make you feel any better?'

At once I was absolutely certain that it had not been the kiss, as she was now insisting that I should believe. It was quite clear: at first Emilia had been downright astonished at my supposition, so remote was it from the truth; then a sudden calculation had made her accept it. I could not but think that the true reason of her loss of love must be much more serious than that one kiss which had led to nothing. It was a reason, probably, that she did not wish to reveal because of some remaining regard for me. Emilia was not unkind, as I knew, and did not like hurting anyone. Evidently the real reason would be hurtful to me.

I said gently: 'It's not true. It wasn't the kiss.'

She was astonished. 'Why! But I've just told you it was.'

'No, it wasn't the kiss . . . it was something else.'

'I don't know what you mean.'

'You know perfectly well.'

'No, on my word of honour, I don't know.'

'And I tell you you do know.'

She became impatient, almost like a mother with a child.

'Why do you want to know so many things? . . . It's

typical of you . . . Why d'you want to pry into everything? . . . What does it matter to you?'

'Because I prefer the truth, whatever it is, to lies . . . And above all, if you don't tell me the truth, I might imagine anything . . . I might imagine something really nasty.'

She looked at me for a moment in silence, in a strange manner. 'What does it matter to you?' she went on then. 'You have a clear conscience, haven't you?'

'Yes; certainly I have.'

'Then how can the rest matter to you?'

'It's true, then,' I persisted. 'It really is something nasty.'

'I didn't say that . . . I only said that, if you have a clear conscience, all the rest ought not to matter to you.'

'It's true that I have a clear conscience . . . but that doesn't mean anything . . . Sometimes even one's conscience deceives one.'

'But not yours, surely?' she said with a faint irony that did not, however, escape me, and that seemed to me even more wounding than her indifference.

'Yes; even mine.'

'Well, well, I must go,' she said suddenly. 'Have you anything else to say to me?'

'No; you shan't go until you've told me the truth.'

'I've already told you the truth: I don't love you.'

What an effect they had upon me, those four words! I turned pale, and implored her, miserably: 'I asked you before not to say that again . . . it hurts too much!'

'It's you who compel me to repeat it . . . It certainly doesn't give me any pleasure to say it.'

'Why d'you want to make me believe it's because of that kiss that you've stopped loving me?' I pursued, following the train of my reflections. 'A kiss is nothing at all . . . That girl was a perfectly ordinary little fool and I've never seen her since . . . You know and understand all that . . . No: the truth is that you've stopped loving me' – now I was not so much speaking as spelling out my words carefully in an attempt to express my own difficulty and obscure intuition – 'because something has happened . . . something that has changed your feelings towards me . . . something, in fact, that has perhaps changed, first and foremost, the idea you had of me, and consequently your feelings as well.'

'It must be admitted that you're intelligent!' she said in a tone of genuine surprise, almost of praise.

'It's true, then?'

'I didn't say it was true . . . I only said you were intelligent.'

I sought about in my mind, feeling that the truth was, so to speak, on the tip of my tongue. 'To put it briefly,' I insisted, 'before a certain thing happened, you thought well of me . . . afterwards, you thought badly . . . and therefore ceased to love me.'

'It might possibly have happened like that.'

All of a sudden I had a horrible feeling: this reasonable tone of mine, I realized, was not false. I was not reasonable, I was suffering, in fact, acutely, I was desperate, furious, I was shattered; and why in the world should I keep up a reasonable tone? I don't know what happened to me at that moment. Before I knew what I was doing, I had jumped to my feet, shouting, 'Don't imagine I'm here just to keep up a bright conversation,' and had leapt on top of her and seized her by the throat and thrown her back on to the divan and was yelling in her face: 'Tell me the truth . . . tell it once and for all . . . Come on!'

Beneath me the big, perfect body that I loved so much was struggling this way and that, and she had grown red

109

and swollen in the face; I must have been squeezing her throat tightly, and I knew that, in my heart, I wanted to kill her. I kept on saying, 'Tell me the truth, once and for all,' and at the same time I squeezed with redoubled force and thought: 'I'm going to kill her . . . but better dead than my enemy!' Then I felt her trying to kick me in the belly with her knee, and indeed she succeeded in doing so, and with such violence that it took my breath away. This blow hurt me almost as much as the phrase, 'I don't love you'; and it was in truth the blow of an enemy, an enemy who seeks to harm his adversary as much as possible. At the same time my murderous hatred ebbed, I relaxed my grip somewhat, and she struggled free, giving me a push that almost threw me off the divan. Then, before I could recover myself, she cried out in a voice of exasperation: 'I despise you . . . that's the feeling I have for you and that's the reason why I've stopped loving you . . . I despise you and you disgust me every time you touch me . . . There's the truth for you . . . I despise you and you disgust me!'

I was standing up now. My eye, followed at once by my hand, moved towards a massive glass ash-tray that stood on the table. She certainly thought I intended to kill her, for she uttered a groan of fear and covered her face with her arm. But my guardian angel stood by me. I do not know how I managed to control myself; I put the ash-tray back on the table and went out of the room.

10

As I have already mentioned, Emilia had not had a good
education: she had attended only the first elementary
school and then, for a few years, the normal school; then
she had broken off her studies and had learned to do
typing and shorthand, and at sixteen was already
employed in a lawyer's office. She came, it is true, of what
is called a good family – that is, of a family which in the
past had been in easy circumstances, having owned property in the neighbourhood of Rome. But her grandfather
had dissipated his heritage in unsuccessful commercial
speculations, and her father, up to the day of his death,
had been merely a minor official in the Ministry of
Finance. So she had grown up in poverty, and, as regards
her education and manner of thinking, could almost be
described as belonging to the working class; and, like
many women of that class, she seemed to have nothing to
fall back upon except her common sense, which was so
solid as to appear sometimes like stupidity or, to say the
least, narrowness of ideas. Yet by virtue solely of this
common sense she sometimes succeeded in a wholly
unexpected and, to me, mysterious, manner, in formulating comments and appreciations that were extremely
acute; just as, indeed, happens with people of the working
class, who are closer to nature than others, and whose
consciousness is not obscured by any convention or pre-
judice. Certain things she said merely because she had
thought them over seriously, with sincerity and candour,
and indeed her words had the unmistakable ring of truth.

But, since she was not aware of her own candour, she felt no complacency about it; thus in a way confirming, by her very modesty, the genuineness of her judgement.

And so, that day, when she cried out, 'I despise you', I was immediately convinced that these words, which, in the mouth of another woman might have meant nothing, when pronounced by her meant exactly what they said: she really did despise me and now there was nothing more to be done. Even if I had known nothing of Emilia's character, the tone in which she had uttered the phrase would have left me in no doubt: it was the tone of the virgin word that springs directly from the thing itself, pronounced by someone who had perhaps never spoken that word before, and who, urged on by necessity, had fished it up from the ancestral depths of the language, without searching for it, almost involuntarily. So indeed may a peasant, amongst a number of mutilated, worn-out, dialect expressions, sometimes utter a remark that sparkles with crystal-clear moral wisdom – a remark which in a different mouth might not be surprising, but which, in his, is astonishing and appears almost unbelievable. 'I despise you': these three words, as I noticed with bitterness, held the same absolutely genuine tone as those other words, so very different, which she had spoken to me the first time she had confessed her love: 'I love you very much.'

I was so sure of the sincerity and truth of those three words that, once I was alone in my study, I started walking up and down without thinking of anything, my hands trembling, my eyes distraught, not knowing what to do. Emilia's three words seemed to be penetrating more deeply every minute into my sensibility, like three thorns, with sharp and increasing pain; but beyond this pain, of which I was precisely conscious, I was incapable of understanding anything. The thing that made me suffer most, of course, was the knowledge that I was now not merely not loved, but actually despised; and yet, utterly unable as I was to discover any reason at all, even the slightest, for this contempt, I had a violent feeling of injustice, and, at the same time, a fear that, in reality, there was no injustice about it, and that the contempt had an objective foundation of which I was myself unaware, though to others it was quite obvious. I had a respectable opinion of myself, mixed with just a dash of pity, as of a man who is not too fortunate, a man upon whom Fate has not smiled as she ought to have done; but not in any way contemptible, quite the contrary. And now, behold, those words of Emilia's were completely upsetting this idea, were making me suspect, for the first time, that I did not know myself or judge myself as I really was, and that I had flattered myself beyond all truth.

Finally, I went into the bathroom and put my head under the tap, and the jet of cold water did me good; my brain had seemed to be red hot, just as though Emilia's words had set fire to it, discovering in it a combustible quality hitherto unknown. I combed my hair, washed my face, re-tied my tie, then went back into the living-room. But the sight of the table ready laid in the window embrasure aroused in me a feeling of rebellion: it was impossible that we should sit down as we did every day and eat together, in that room which still echoed with the words that had so deeply affected me. At that very moment Emilia opened the door and looked in, her face now recomposed into its usual serene, placid expression. Without looking at her, I said: 'I don't want to dine at home this evening . . . tell the maid we're going out, and then get dressed at once . . . We'll go and dine out somewhere . . .'

She answered, in some surprise: 'Why it's all ready . . . the whole thing will have to be thrown away.'

A sudden rage swept over me, and I shouted: 'That's enough . . . Throw away anything you like, but go and get dressed, because we're going out.' Still I did not look at her, but I heard her murmur: 'What a way to behave!' Then she closed the door again.

A few minutes later we left the house. In the narrow street flanked on both sides by modern buildings like our own, with façades full of balconies and verandas, amongst all the big, expensive motor-cars, my own small, utilitarian car awaited us – a recent acquisition, which, like the flat, had still, to a great extent, to be paid for out of the earnings of future film-scripts. I had only had it for a few months, and I still had that feeling of slightly childish vanity which such a possession can at first inspire. But that evening, as we walked towards the car, side by side, not looking at each other, in silence and not touching each other, I could not help thinking: 'this car, like the flat, represents the sacrifice of my ambitions . . . and that sacrifice has been in vain.' And in truth, just for a moment, I had a sharp sense of the contrast between the luxurious street in which everything looked new and expensive, our flat which looked down upon us from the third floor, the car that awaited us a few yards farther on, and my own unhappiness which made all these advantages appear useless and wearisome.

When I had got into the car, I waited until Emilia was seated and then stretched out my arm to shut the door. Usually, in making this movement, I brushed against her knees, or, turning a little, gave her a light, quick kiss on the cheek. This time, however, almost spontaneously I avoided touching her. The door closed with a bang and for a moment we sat motionless and silent. Then Emilia asked: 'Where are we going? . . . ' I thought for a few seconds and replied at random: 'Let's go to the Via Appia.'

114

Slightly surprised, she said: 'But it's too early for the Via Appia . . . It'll be cold and there won't be anyone there.'

'Never mind . . . *we* shall be there.'

She was silent, and I drove off quickly towards the Appian Way. Coming down from our own quarter, we crossed the centre of the city and went out by the Via dei Trionfi and the Passeggiata Archeologica. We passed the ancient, mossy walls, the gardens and vegetable plots, the villas hidden in trees along the first part of the Appian Way. Then we came to the entrance to the Catacombs, lit by two feeble lamps. Emilia was right; it was still too early in the year for the Via Appia. In the restaurant with the archaeological name, when we came into the big sham-rustic room adorned with amphoras and broken columns, we found nothing but tables and a quantity of waiters. We were the only customers, and I could not help thinking that, in the chilly, deserted room, surrounded by the tiresome solicitude of too many attendants, we should have no hope of solving the problem of our relationship – on the contrary. I remembered that it was in that very restaurant, two years before, at the time of our deepest love, that we had constantly dined; and all at once I understood why, amongst so many, I had chosen it, so dismal at that season of the year, and so forlorn.

The waiter was standing, menu in hand, on one side, and on the other the wine waiter was bowing, with the wine-list. I began ordering our dinner, making suggestions one by one, to Emilia, and bending forward slightly towards her, like an attentive, gallant husband. She kept her eyes lowered and answered without looking up, in monosyllables: 'Yes', 'No', 'All right'. I also ordered a bottle of the choicest wine, although Emilia protested that she did not want to drink anything. 'I'll drink it,' I said.

The wine waiter gave me an understanding smile, and the two waiters went off together.

I do not wish to give a description here of our dinner in all its details, but merely to depict my own state of mind – a state of mind which was entirely new to me that evening but which was henceforth to become normal in my relations with Emilia. They say that if we manage to live without too great an effort, it is entirely owing to the automatism which makes us unconscious of a great part of our movements. In order to take one single step, it seems, we displace an infinite number of muscles, and yet, thanks to this automatism, we are unaware of it. The same thing happens in our relations with other people. As long as I believed myself to be loved by Emilia, a kind of happy automatism had presided over our relations; and only the final completion of any course of conduct on my part had been illuminated by the light of consciousness, all the rest remaining in the obscurity of affectionate and unnoticed habit. But now that the illusion of love had faded, I discovered myself to be conscious of every one of my actions, even the smallest. I offered her something to drink, I passed her the salt, I looked at her, I stopped looking at her: each gesture was accompanied by a painful, dull, impotent, exasperated consciousness. I felt myself completely shackled, completely numbed, completely paralysed; at each act, I found myself wondering: Am I doing right? Am I doing wrong? I had, in fact, lost all confidence. With complete strangers one can always hope to regain it. But with Emilia, it was an experience of the past, a thing defunct: I could have no hope whatever.

And so, between us, there was silence that was only broken from time to time by some unimportant remark: 'Will you have some more wine? Will you have some bread? Some more meat?' I should like to describe the

116

intimate quality of this silence because it was that evening that it was established for the first time between us, never to leave us again. It was, then, a silence that was intolerable because perfectly negative, a silence caused by the suppression of all the things I wanted to say and felt incapable of saying. To describe it as a hostile silence would be incorrect. In reality there was no hostility between us, at least, not on my side; merely impotence. I was conscious of wanting to speak, of having many things to say, and was at the same time conscious that there could now be no question of words, and that I should now be incapable of finding the right tone to adopt. With this conviction in my mind, I remained silent; not with the relaxed, serene sensation of one who feels no need to speak, but rather with the constraint of one who is bursting with things to say and is conscious of it, and runs up against this consciousness all the time, as against the iron bars of a prison. But there was a further complication: I felt that this silence, intolerable as it was, was nevertheless for me the most favourable condition possible. And that if I broke it, even in the most cautious, the most affectionate manner, I should provoke discussions even more intolerable, if possible, than the silence itself.

But I was not yet accustomed to keeping silent. We ate our first course, and then our second, still without speaking. At the fruit, I was unable to hold out any longer, and I asked: 'Why are you so quiet?'

She answered at once: 'Because I've nothing to say.'

She seemed neither sad nor hostile; and these words, too, held the accent of truth. I went on, in a didactic tone: 'A short time ago you said things that would need hours of explanation.'

Still in the same sincere tone, she said: 'Forget those things . . . Try and imagine I never said them.'

117

I asked hopefully: 'Why should I forget them? I should forget them only if I knew for certain that they are not true . . . if they were just words that escaped you in a moment of anger.'

This time she said nothing. And again I hoped. Perhaps it was true: it was as a reaction from my violence that she had said she despised me. Cautiously, I insisted: 'Now confess, those horrible things you said to me today were not true . . . and you said them because at that moment you thought you hated me and you wanted to hurt me.'

She looked at me and was again silent. I thought I detected – or was I wrong? – a faint glistening of tears in her big dark eyes. Encouraged, I put out my hand and took hers as it lay on the tablecloth, saying: 'Emilia . . . they weren't true, then?'

But now she pulled away her hand with unusual violence, drawing back not only her arm but, it seemed to me, her whole body. 'They *were* true.'

I was struck by her accent of complete, albeit disconsolate, sincerity as she answered. It was as though she were aware that, at any moment, a lie would have put everything to rights again, anyhow for some time, at least in appearance; and clearly, just for a second, she had been tempted to tell such a lie. Then, on reflection, she had rejected the idea. I felt a new and sharper stab of pain, and, bending my head, murmured through my clenched teeth: 'But do you realize there are certain things that can't be said to anyone, just like that, without any justification . . . not to anyone, least of all to your own husband?'

She said nothing; all she did was to gaze at me, with apprehension almost; and indeed, my face must have been distorted with rage. At last she replied: 'You asked for it and I told you.'

'But it's up to you to explain.'

'How d'you mean?'

'You've got to explain why . . . why you despise me.'

'Ah, that I shall never tell you . . . not even if I were on the point of death.'

I was struck by her unusually resolute tone. But my surprise did not last long. I was filled with a fury which now permitted no time for reflection. 'Tell me,' I insisted, and again I seized her hand, but this time in a far from caressing manner, 'tell me . . . why do you despise me?'

'I've already said I shall never tell you.'

'Tell me . . . if not, I shall hurt you.' Beside myself with rage, I twisted her fingers. She looked at me in surprise for a moment, then screwed up her mouth in a grimace of pain; and immediately afterwards, the contempt of which hitherto she had merely spoken, showed itself clearly in her expression. 'Stop it,' she said roughly. 'So you want to hurt me now as well.' I noticed this 'as well', in which there appeared to be an allusion to other severities that I wished to inflict upon her, and was left breathless. 'Stop it . . . Aren't you ashamed of yourself? . . . The waiters are watching us.'

'Tell me why you despise me.'

'Don't be a fool; leave me alone.'

'Tell me why you despise me.'

'Ow!' She wrenched her fingers away with a violent jerk that knocked a tumbler off the table. There was a sound of broken glass, and she jumped up and walked away towards the door, saying loudly: 'I'm going to wait for you in the car . . . while you pay the bill.'

She went out, and I was left sitting motionless where I was, humiliated, not so much from shame (it was true, as she had said, that all those idle waiters had been watching us the whole time and had not missed a single word or

119

gesture of our quarrel) as by the strangeness of her behaviour towards me. Never before had she spoken to me in that tone; never before had she abused me. The words 'as well' continued, moreover, to echo in my ears like a new and unpleasant enigma that had to be solved, amongst so many others: how and when had I inflicted those things upon her of which, with her 'as well', she was now complaining? At last I summoned the waiter, paid the bill, and followed her out.

Outside the restaurant, I found that the weather, which all day had been cloudy and uncertain, had turned to a thick drizzle. A little farther on, in the darkness of the open space, I could see the figure of Emilia standing beside the car: I had locked the doors, and she was waiting there, patiently, in the rain. I said, in a shaky voice: 'I'm sorry. I'd forgotten I had locked the car'; and heard her voice, quite quietly, answer: 'Never mind . . . It's raining so little.' Once again, at those forgiving words, hope of a reconciliation reawakened, crazily, in my heart; how was it possible to be filled with contempt, if one spoke in a voice so quiet, so kindly? I opened the door, got into the car, and she got in beside me. I started the engine, and said to her, in a voice that seemed to me, all of a sudden, strangely hilarious, almost jovial: 'Well, Emilia, where would you like to go?'

She answered without turning, looking straight ahead: 'I don't know . . . Wherever you like.'

Without waiting, I drove off. As I said, I now had a kind of jovial, carefree, hilarious feeling; it seemed almost as though, by turning the whole affair into a joke, by substituting lightness for seriousness and frivolity for passion, I might succeed in solving the problem of my relations with Emilia. I do not know what it was that possessed me at that moment: perhaps desperation, like

120

an over-potent wine, had gone to my head. I said, in an amused, deliberately playful tone: 'Let's go wherever luck takes us . . . We'll just see what happens.'

I felt absurdly awkward as I said these words; rather like a cripple trying to demonstrate a dance-step. But Emilia did not speak, and I abandoned myself to this new humour of mine which I imagined to be an inexhaustible stream, but which very soon turned out to be no more than a thin and timid trickle. I was now driving along the Via Appia, of whose cypresses and brick ruins and white marble statues and Roman pavement, with its big, irregular paving-stones, I caught a glimpse now and then by the light of the headlamps on the road in front, through the thousand glistening threads of the rain. I went straight on for a little and then said, in a tone of false elation: 'Let's forget, for once, who we are, and imagine we're two young students looking for a quiet corner, far away from indiscreet eyes, where they can make love in peace.'

Still she said nothing, and I, encouraged by her silence, went a short distance farther along the road and then brought the car suddenly to a stop. It was pouring with rain now; the arms of the windscreen-wiper, going backwards and forwards on the glass of the windscreen, did not move fast enough to sweep away the streams of water. 'We're two young students,' I said again in an uncertain voice: 'I'm called Mario and you're Maria . . . and we've at last found a quiet place though it's rather wet . . . But inside the car we're all right . . . Give me a kiss.' As I said this, with the decisiveness of a drunken man, I put my arm round her shoulders and tried to kiss her.

I don't know what I was hoping for: what had occurred in the restaurant should have made me understand what I ought to expect. At first Emilia tried to withdraw herself, with quite a good grace and in silence, from my embrace;

121

then, when I persisted and, taking her chin in my hand, tried to turn her face towards mine, she thrust me harshly away. 'Are you crazy?' she said. 'Or are you drunk?'

'No; I'm not drunk,' I murmured. 'Give me a kiss.'

'I shouldn't dream of it,' she answered with typically honest indignation, thrusting me away again. After a moment she went on: 'And then you wonder that I tell you I despise you . . . when you behave like this . . . after what has happened between us.'

'But I love you.'

'I don't love *you*.'

I felt ridiculous, but in a distressed kind of way, like someone who realizes he has been forced into a position which has the double disadvantage of being both comic and irreparable. But I was not yet disposed to consider myself beaten. 'You're going to give me a kiss; if you won't do it for love, I'll make you do it,' I muttered in a voice that was meant to be brutal and masculine. And I threw myself upon her.

She said nothing this time, but she opened the door, and I fell forward on to her empty seat. She had jumped out of the car and run away down the road, despite the rain which was now falling very heavily.

I paused for a moment in astonishment, confronted by this empty seat. Then I said to myself, 'I'm an idiot', and I too got out of the car.

It was raining really hard, and when I put my foot to the ground I felt myself plunge up to the ankle in a puddle. This irritated me violently, and gave me an acute feeling of wretchedness. Exasperated, I called out: 'Emilia . . . come on, come back here and don't worry . . . I won't touch you.'

From some point that was indistinguishable in the

darkness, but not very far off, she answered: 'Either you stop it, or I walk back into Rome.'

I said, in a voice that trembled: 'Come along, I promise anything you wish.'

It was still raining heavily; the water was running down between the collar of my coat and my shirt-collar, wetting the back of my neck in a disagreeable fashion, and I felt it trickling over my forehead and the sides of my head. The headlamps of the car lit up only a small stretch of the road, together with a fragment of ruined Roman brickwork and a tall, black cypress, truncated by the darkness; and, strain my eyes as I might, I was unable to see Emilia. Disheartened, I called again: 'Emilia . . . Emilia . . .' and my voice ended on an almost tearful note.

At last she came forward out of the darkness into the beam of the headlamps, and said: 'Then you promise you won't touch me?'

'Yes, I promise.'

She went over and got into the car, adding: 'What sort of a joke is this? . . . I'm soaked through now . . . and my head's dripping . . . Tomorrow morning I shall have to go to the hairdresser.'

I got into the car too, in silence, and we started off at once. She sneezed, then, a couple of times, very loudly, in a vindictive way, as if to let me see I had made her catch a cold. But I did not take up the challenge: I was driving now as though in a dream. An ugly dream, in which I was really called Riccardo and I had a wife who was called Emilia, and I loved her and she did not love me – in fact, she despised me.

11

I awoke next morning languid and aching, and with a deep and pervading sense of repugnance for what awaited me that day and the days following, whatever was destined to happen. Emilia was still asleep, in the bedroom; and I lay idle for a long time in the half-darkness, on the divan in the living-room, slowly and disgustedly regaining full consciousness of the reality which sleep had made me forget. Turning things over in my mind, I realized that I had to decide whether I would accept or refuse the *Odyssey* script; I had to know why it was that Emilia despised me; I had to find the way to win back Emilia's affections.

I have said that I was feeling exhausted, languid, inert; and this almost bureaucratic manner of summarizing the three vital questions of my life was, fundamentally, as I immediately realized, nothing more than an attempt to deceive myself with regard to an energy and a lucidity that I was very far from possessing. A general, a politician, a businessman will try, in this way, to get a close hold on the problems he has to solve, to reduce them to clear-cut objects, easily handled and lifeless. But I was not a man of that type; on the contrary. And, as for the energy and lucidity which I pretended to myself I possessed at that moment, I felt they would fail me completely once I passed from reflection to action.

I was well aware, however, of my insufficiency; and as I lay on my back on the divan with my eyes closed, I became conscious that, as soon as I attempted to formu-

124

late a reply to these three questions, my imagination no longer rested on the firm ground of reality, but soared away into the vacant heaven of aspiration. Thus in imagination I saw myself doing the *Odyssey* script as though it were nothing at all; reaching an explanation with Emilia and discovering that the whole story of her contempt for me, in appearance so terrible, sprang in reality from a childish misunderstanding; and finally being reconciled with her. But, as I thought of these things, I realized that all I had in view was the happy conclusions which I longed to achieve: between these conclusions and the present position lay a gaping void which I was totally unable to fill to fill, anyhow, with anything that had even the slightest quality of solidity and coherence. My ambition – to put it briefly – was to solve the problem of my present position in accordance with my highest desires, but I had not the least idea of how I should contrive to do it.

I dropped into a doze, no doubt, and at a certain moment fell fast asleep again. All of a sudden I awoke once more and caught a glimpse of Emilia sitting at the foot of the divan, in her dressing-gown. The living-room was still in semi-darkness, the shutters being lowered; but on the table close to the divan, a small lamp was burning. Emilia had come into the room, turned on the light and sat down near me without my noticing it.

Seeing her sitting there at the end of my bed, in a familiar attitude that reminded me of other, very different awakenings in happier times, I had a moment's illusion. Sitting up in bed, I stammered: 'Emilia, do you love me?'

She waited a little before answering; then she said: 'Listen. I've got to talk to you.'

I felt suddenly cold; and I was on the point of answering her that I didn't want to talk about anything, and would she leave me in peace because I wanted to go to sleep. But instead, I asked: 'Talk about what?'

'About us two.'

'But there's nothing to be said,' I replied, trying to overcome a sudden anxiety. 'You've ceased to love me – in fact, you despise me . . . That's all there is to it.'

'No; I wanted to say,' she announced slowly, 'that I'm going back to my mother's – today . . . I wanted to tell you before I telephoned . . . There, now you know.'

I had not at all foreseen this declaration, which, after all, considering what had happened the day before, was perfectly logical and to be expected. The idea that Emilia might leave me had never entered my mind, strange though that may seem; I thought that she had already reached the farthest limit of her hardness and cruelty towards me. And yet, here was that limit being passed at one bound, in a fashion that was, to me, totally unexpected. Scarcely understanding what she meant, I stammered: 'You mean to leave me?'

'Yes.'

For a moment I was silent; then, all at once, I felt an urgent need for action, driven on by the very sharpness of the pain that pierced me. I jumped from the divan and went, in pyjamas as I was, to the window, as though I intended to push up the shutters and let in the light; but then I turned back and shouted in a loud voice: 'You can't go away like that . . . I don't want you to go.'

'Don't talk like a child,' she said in a reasonable manner. 'We've got to separate; it's the only thing now for us to do . . . There's nothing left between us two – at least as far as I'm concerned . . . It'll be better for us both.'

I do not remember at all what I did after she had spoken these words: or rather, I remember only a few sentences, a few movements. As though in the grip of some kind of delirium, I must have said and done things then of which I was not in the least conscious. I believe I went round and round the room with long strides, in my pyjamas, my hair all untidy, at one moment beseeching Emilia not to leave me, at another, explaining my own position, and then simply addressing my remarks to the air, as if I had been alone. The *Odyssey* film-script, the flat, the instalments to be paid, my sacrificed theatrical ambitions, my love for Emilia, Battista, Rheingold, all the aspects of my life and all the people in it were jumbled up in my mouth, in a rapid, incoherent rush of words, like the little pieces of coloured glass at the bottom of a kaleidoscope when a violent hand shakes it. But at the same time I felt that this kaleidoscope was nothing but a poor, illusory thing – simply, in fact, a few bits of coloured glass with no order or design about them; and now the kaleidoscope was broken, and the pieces of glass lay scattered on the floor, under my eyes. I had at the same time a very precise feeling of abandonment and of fear of being abandoned, but beyond this feeling I could not go: it oppressed me and prevented me not merely from thinking, but almost from breathing. My whole self rebelled violently at the thought of the separation and of the loneliness that would follow; but I realized that, in spite of the sincerity of this feeling of rebellion, I was not speaking convincingly; on the contrary. And indeed every now and then there was a rent in the clouds of alarm and terror that enveloped me, and then I would see Emilia sitting on the divan, still in the same place, and calmly answering me: 'Riccardo, do be sensible: it's the only thing for us to do, now.'

'But I don't *want* you to go,' I repeated for the last time, stopping in front of her: 'I don't *want* you to.'

'Why don't you want me to? Be logical.'

I don't know what I said, and then I went to the far end

of the room again and thrust my hands into my hair and pulled it. Then I saw that, in the state I was in, I was quite incapable not merely of convincing Emilia, but even of expressing myself. I managed, with an effort, to control myself, and I went and sat down on the divan again and, bending forward and taking my head in my hands, asked: 'When d'you intend to go?'

'Today.'

After saying this, she rose to her feet and, taking no further notice of me as I sat hunched up with my head in my hands, went out of the room. I had not expected her to do this, just as hitherto I had not expected any of the things she had said and done; and for a moment I was astonished and almost incredulous. Then I looked round the room and felt a strange sensation, chilling in its exactness: the separation had already taken place and my loneliness had already begun. The room was the same as it had been a few minutes earlier, when Emilia was sitting on the divan; and yet, I realized, it was already quite different. It was, I could not help thinking, as though it had lost a dimension. The room was no longer the one I had been accustomed to see, knowing that Emilia was there; it was already the one I should be seeing for an unknown length of time, in the knowledge that Emilia was *not* there and never would be there again. There was a deserted look in the air, in the aspect of all the things, everywhere, and, strangely, this look did not go out from me towards the things but seemed to come from the things back towards me. I did not think all this so much as become aware of it in the depths of my dull, aching, dazed sensibility. Then I found I was crying, because I felt a sort of tickling sensation at the corner of my mouth, and, when I put up my finger, found my cheek was wet. I heaved a deep sigh and began

128

to weep openly, violently. In the meantime, I had risen and walked out of the room.

In the bedroom, in a light which to me, after the semi-darkness of the living-room, and being in pyjamas with my face bathed in tears, seemed dazzling and intolerable, Emilia was sitting on the untidy bed, listening at the telephone; and from a single word I knew that she was speaking to her mother. I thought I noticed that her face wore a perplexed, disconcerted expression; and then I sat down too, and, taking my face between my hands, went on sobbing. I did not very well know why I was crying like this: perhaps it was not only because my life was ruined, but because of some more ancient sorrow that had nothing to do with Emilia or with her decision to leave me. In the meantime Emilia was still listening at the telephone. Her mother was evidently making a long and complicated speech; and even through my tears, I saw a disappointed, angry, bitter expression, swift and dark as the shadow of a cloud over a landscape, pass across her face. Finally she said: 'All right, all right, I understand, we won't talk about it any more'; but she was interrupted by another long speech from her mother. This time, however, she had not the patience to listen right to the end and said suddenly: 'You've told me that already, all right, I understand, goodbye'. Her mother said something more, but Emilia repeated her 'goodbye' and hung up the receiver, although, as I could hear, her mother's voice was still audible through it. Then she raised her eyes in my direction, but without looking at me, as though dazed. With an instinctive movement I seized her hand, stammering: 'Don't go away, please don't . . . don't go.'

Children believe that tears have a decisive value as a form of sentimental persuasion; and so, in general, do women and persons of feeble and childish spirit. At that moment – like a child or a woman or other feeble creature – although I was weeping from genuine sorrow, I cherished some kind of hope that my tears would persuade Emilia not to leave me; and this illusion, if it comforted me a little, at the same time aroused in me a feeling almost of hypocrisy. It was just as if I were weeping on purpose, as if I intended to make use of my tears in order to blackmail Emilia. All at once I was ashamed; and, without waiting for Emilia's reply, I rose and left the room.

After a few minutes Emilia followed me. I had had time to recompose myself as best I could, to wipe my eyes, to put on a dressing-gown over my pyjamas. I had sat down in the armchair and was automatically lighting a cigarette which I did not want. She also sat down, and said at once: 'Don't worry . . . Don't be afraid . . . I'm not going away.' But she said it in a bitter, despairing, apathetic voice. I looked at her: she kept her eyes lowered and appeared to be reflecting; but I noticed that the corners of her mouth were trembling and that her hands were occupied in turning back the edge of her dressing-gown, a gesture that showed she was disturbed and perplexed. Then, in a suddenly exasperated voice, she added: 'My mother doesn't want me . . . She says she's let my room to a lodger . . . She had two already; now she has three and the whole house is full . . . She says she doesn't believe I'm really in earnest . . . that I ought to think it over . . . And so I don't know where to go . . . No one wants me . . . and I shall be compelled to stay with you.'

I was struck by this last phrase, so cruel in its sincerity; and I think I gave a violent start, as if I had been stabbed. I could not help exclaiming, in resentment: 'Why d'you talk to me like that? . . . "Compelled." . . . What have I done to you? . . . Why do you hate me so?'

Now it was she who was crying, as I perceived, although she was trying not to show it, by hiding part of her face with her hand. Then she shook her head and said: 'You didn't want me to go away . . . Well, I'm staying . . . You ought to be pleased, oughtn't you?'

I got up from the armchair, sat down beside her on the divan and took her in my arms, although I was conscious, at the first contact, that she withdrew and resisted me. 'Certainly I want you to stay,' I said, 'but not in that way, not "compelled" . . . What have I done to you, Emilia, that you speak to me like that?'

'If you like, I'll go away,' she answered. 'I'll take a room somewhere . . . and you won't have to help me except just for a short time . . . I'll get a job as a typist again . . . And as soon as I find work, I shan't ask anything more from you.'

'No, no,' I cried. 'I want you to stay . . . But, Emilia, not "compelled" to stay, not "compelled" . . .'

'It's not you who compel me,' she replied, still weeping. 'It's life.'

Once again, as I clasped her in my arms, I felt a temptation to ask her why it was that she had ceased to love me, why, in fact, she despised me, and what had happened, what I had done to her. But now, perhaps as a counterpoise to her tears and bewilderment, I had regained, partly, my composure. I said to myself that this was not the moment to ask certain questions; that probably, by such questions, I should gain no ground at all; and that perhaps, in order to get at the truth, I ought to have recourse to different, and less brusque, stratagems. I waited a little, while she went on weeping in silence, her face turned away from me. Then: 'Look,' I proposed, 'let's not have any more discussions or explanations . . . they serve no purpose except to make us hurt each other

131

. . '. There's nothing more I want to know from you, at any rate for the present . . . But just listen to me for a moment: I have agreed, after all, to do the *Odyssey* script . . . But Battista wants us to do it somewhere in the Bay of Naples, where most of the exteriors will be taken . . . so we've decided to go to Capri . . . I'll leave you to yourself there, I swear; in any case, I won't be able to help doing so, as I shall be working all day with the director, and I may or may not see you at meal-times . . . Capri is an extremely beautiful place, and soon it will be possible to start bathing . . . You can rest, and bathe, and go for walks; it'll be good for your nerves, and you can think it all over and decide at your leisure what you want to do . . . Your mother is really right, after all: you ought to think it over . . . Then, in four or five months' time, you can tell me what you've decided, and then – and not till then – we'll talk about it again.'

She kept her head turned sideways all the time, as if to avoid seeing me. Then she asked, in a somewhat comforted tone of voice: 'And when should we be going?'

'At once . . . that is, in about ten days . . . as soon as the director comes back from Paris.'

I was wondering now, as I held her against me and felt the roundness and softness of her breast against mine, whether I dared take the risk of kissing her. Actually, she was taking no sort of share in our embrace, but merely submitting to it. All the same, I deceived myself into thinking that this passivity was not entirely the result of indifference, and that it contained some element of interest. Then I heard her ask, still in the same comforted, yet at the same time reluctant, tone: 'Where shall we stay in Capri? In a hotel?'

I answered joyfully, thinking to give her pleasure: 'No; we shan't go to a hotel . . . hotels are so tiresome . . . I've

132

something better than a hotel; Battista is lending us his villa . . . We shall be able to use the villa the whole time I'm working at the script.'

I was immediately aware – as I had feared a few days before, when I had too hastily accepted Battista's offer – that Emilia, for some reason of her own, did not like this plan. In fact, she at once freed herself from my embrace and, drawing away to one corner of the divan, repeated: 'Battista's villa . . . and you've already accepted?'

'I thought you would be pleased,' said I, trying to justify myself. 'A villa is far better than a hotel.'

'You've already accepted?'

'Yes; I thought I was doing right.'

'And we shall be there with the director?'

'No; Rheingold is going to live at the hotel.'

'Will Battista come there?'

'Battista?' I replied, vaguely surprised by this question. 'I suppose he may come now and then . . . but only for a short time, a week-end, a day or two . . . just to see how our work is going.'

This time she said nothing: but she fumbled in the pocket of her dressing-gown, took out her handkerchief and blew her nose. As she did so, she pushed aside her dressing-gown, which fell wide open almost up to her waist, uncovering her belly and her legs. She kept her legs tightly crossed, as if from modesty, but the white, youthful, plump belly flowed over on to the crossed muscular thighs with a generous innocence that seemed more powerful than any rebuff. Looking at her then, as she seemed to be unconsciously offering herself, I felt a violent desire, of unparalleled spontaneity, which for a moment gave me the illusion that I might approach and possess her.

But I knew that, however great my longing might be, I

would not do so; and all I did was to watch her, almost furtively, while she blew her nose – as though I were afraid of being discovered in the act of looking at her, and put to shame. As soon as she had finished, however, she remarked that I had now reached the point of looking secretly at my wife's nudity, with the excitement with which one looks at forbidden things, like a boy peeping through a crack into a bathing-hut; and with a feeling of violent annoyance I put out my hand and pulled down the edge of her dressing-gown over her legs. She did not appear to be aware of my gesture but, putting her handkerchief back into her pocket, said in a voice that was now perfectly calm: 'I'll come to Capri, then . . . but on one condition . . .'

'Don't talk to me of conditions . . . I don't want to hear anything,' I cried all at once, unexpectedly. 'All right; we'll go . . . But I don't want to hear anything . . . And now go away.' There must have been some kind of fury in my voice, for she immediately got up, as though she were frightened, and hurriedly left the room.

12

The day arrived when we were to leave for Capri. Battista
had decided to accompany us to the island, to do us the
honours of his house, as he himself expressed it; and that
morning, when we came down into the street, we found
the producer's high-powered red motor-car standing beside my own unpretentious little machine. It was now the
beginning of June, but the weather was still unsettled,
cloudy and windy. Battista, wearing a leather wind-jacket
and flannel trousers, was standing beside the car talking to
Rheingold, who – like a good German, thinking of Italy
as the land of sunshine – had dressed very lightly for the
occasion, with a peaked cap of white cloth and a striped
linen suit of Colonial cut. Emilia and I came out of the
house followed by the porter and the maid carrying our
suitcases; the other two at once left the car and came to
meet us.

'Well, how shall we arrange ourselves?' asked Battista
after we had greeted each other. Then, without waiting
for an answer: 'I suggest that Signora Molteni comes with
me in my car, and Rheingold goes with you, Molteni . . .
Then you can begin talking about the film during the
journey . . . Because,' he concluded with a smile, but in a
serious voice, 'the real work begins today . . . and I want
to have the script in my hands in two months' time.'

I glanced, automatically, at Emilia, and noticed on her
face that curious look of disintegration of the features that
I had observed on other occasions – the sign, in her, of
perplexity and aversion. But I attached no importance to

it; nor did I in any way connect this expression with Battista's proposal, which was in any case quite reasonable. 'Very good idea,' I said, forcing myself to appear cheerful, as the happy circumstance of this trip to the seaside seemed to demand. 'Very good idea – Emilia will go with you and Rheingold with me . . . But I don't promise to talk about the script . . .'

'I'm frightened of going fast,' began Emilia, 'and you, in that car of yours – you always drive too fast . . .' But Battista, impulsively, took her by the arm, crying: 'No need to be frightened with me . . . Besides, what are you frightened of? I've got my own skin to think about, too'; and as he spoke he almost dragged her off towards his own car. I saw Emilia look at me with a bewildered, questioning air, and wondered whether I ought not to insist on taking her with me. But I thought Battista might take offence; motoring was a passion with him and, to tell the truth, he drove extremely well; and so I again said nothing. Emilia made one more feeble objection: 'But I should rather have gone in my husband's car'; and Battista protested, facetiously: 'Husband indeed! . . . Why, you spend the whole day with your husband . . . Come on, or I shall be offended.' In the meantime they had reached the car. Battista opened the door, Emilia got in and sat down, Battista was walking round the car to get in, himself, on the other side . . . Watching them in a rather dreamy way, I gave a start as Rheingold's voice said to me: 'Are we ready, then?' I roused myself, got into my own car, and started the engine.

Behind me I heard the roar of Battista's car as it started; then it passed us and went off swiftly down the hill. I had scarcely time to catch a glimpse, though the rear window, of the head and shoulders of Emilia and Battista side by side; then the car turned a corner and vanished.

Battista had suggested that we should talk about the script during our journey. The suggestion was superfluous: when we had traversed the whole length of the city and I had turned into the Formia road at the moderate speed allowed by my small car, Rheingold, who so far had been silent, began: 'Now, tell me honestly, Molteni, you were afraid, that day in Battista's office, weren't you, that you were going to be forced into making a *kolossal* film?' He stressed the German word with a smile.

'I'm still afraid of it,' I answered absent-mindedly, 'partly because that's the way things are going at present in the Italian studios.'

'Well, you're not to be afraid . . . We,' he said, assuming all at once a hard, authoritative tone, 'we are going to make a film that is psychological and only psychological . . . as indeed I said to you that day . . . I, my dear Molteni, am not accustomed to doing what the producers want, but what *I* want . . . On the set, it is *I* who am the master, and no one else . . . Otherwise I don't make the film . . . Quite simple, isn't it?'

I answered that it was, indeed, quite simple; and I spoke in a tone of sincere pleasure, because this assertion of autonomy made me hope that I would easily come to such terms with Rheingold as would result in the work being less tedious than usual. After a moment's silence, Rheingold resumed: 'And now I should like to explain some of my ideas to you . . . I presume you can drive and listen at the same time?'

'Of course,' I said; but at that same moment, as I turned very slightly towards him, a cart drawn by two oxen appeared out of a side road and I had to swerve suddenly. The car heeled over, zigzagged violently, and I had considerable difficulty in righting it, just in time to

137

avoid a tree, by a narrow margin. Rheingold started to laugh. 'One would say *not*,' he remarked.

'Don't bother about that,' I said, rather annoyed. 'It was quite impossible for me to have seen those oxen . . . Go on: I'm listening.'

Rheingold needed no persuading: 'You see, Molteni,' he went on, 'I've agreed to go to Capri . . . and in fact we shall certainly shoot the exteriors of the film in the Bay of Naples . . . But that will be only the background; for the rest we might as well stay in Rome . . . The drama of Ulysses, in fact, is not the drama of a sailor, or an explorer, or a war veteran . . . It is the drama of Everyman . . . the myth of Ulysses conceals the true story of a certain type of man.'

I remarked, at random: 'All the Greek myths depict human dramas – dramas without time or place, eternal.'

'Exactly . . . All the Greek myths, in other words, are figurative allegories of human life . . . Now, what ought we moderns to do in order to resuscitate such ancient and obscure myths? . . . First of all, to discover the significance which they can have for us of the modern world, and then to fathom that significance as deeply as we can, to interpret it, to illustrate it . . . but in a live, independent way, without allowing ourselves to be crushed by the masterpieces that Greek literature has drawn from these myths . . . Let us take an example . . . No doubt you know O'Neill's *Mourning Becomes Electra*, from which the film was also taken?'

'Yes; certainly I know it.'

'Well, O'Neill too understood this very simple truth – that the ancient myths have to be interpreted in a modern manner, including the *Oresteia* . . . But I don't care for *Mourning Becomes Electra* – d'you know why? Because O'Neill allowed himself to be intimidated by Aeschylus

138

. . . He thought, quite rightly, that the Orestes myth could be interpreted psychoanalytically; but, intimidated by the subject, he made too literal a transcription of the myth . . . Like a good schoolboy writing out an exercise in a book with ruled paper – you can see the lines, Molteni.' I heard Rheingold laughing to himself, pleased with his own criticism of O'Neill.

We were driving across the Roman *campagna* now, not far from the sea, between low hills, yellow with ripe corn, with an occasional leafy tree here and there. We must be far behind Battista, I thought; the road, as far as the eye could reach, was empty – empty in its long, straight tracts, empty, at every bend. At that moment Battista would be driving far ahead, at sixty miles an hour, perhaps more than thirty miles in front of us. I heard Rheingold's voice begin again; 'If O'Neill understood this truth, that the Greek myths must be interpreted in a modern manner, according to the latest psychological discoveries, he ought not to have respected his subject too much, but should have torn it to pieces, turned it inside out, put new life into it . . . This he did not do, and his *Mourning Becomes Electra* is tedious and cold . . . it's a school exercise.'

'I think it's rather fine,' I objected.

Rheingold disregarded the interruption and went on: 'We've now got to do with the *Odyssey* what O'Neill did not wish, or did not know how, to do with the *Oresteia* . . . that is, open it up, as a body is opened up on the dissecting table, examine its internal mechanism, take it to pieces and then put it together again according to our modern requirements.'

I was wondering what Rheingold was driving at. I said, rather distractedly: 'The mechanism of the *Odyssey* is well known: the contrast between the longing for home and family and fatherland, and the innumerable obstacles which stand in the way of a quick return to fatherland and home and family . . . Probably every prisoner of war, every war veteran who for some reason is detained far away from his own country after the end of a war, is, in his own way, a little Ulysses.'

Rheingold gave a laugh which sounded like the clucking of a hen. 'I was expecting that: the veteran, the prisoner . . . No, no; none of that, Molteni . . . You're going no farther than the externals, the facts . . . In that way the *Odyssey* film really does run the risk of being nothing more than a *kolossal* film, an adventure film, as Battista would like it to be . . . But Battista is the producer and it is right that he should think in that way . . . Not you, however, Molteni: you who are an intellectual . . . Molteni, you're intelligent and you must use your brain . . . Try to use it.'

'I *am* using it,' I said, rather irritated; 'that's exactly what I am doing.'

'No; you're not using it . . . Take a good look and think carefully and observe one fact before all others: the story of Ulysses is the story of Ulysses' relations with his wife.'

I said nothing this time. Rheingold continued: 'What is the thing that strikes us most in the *Odyssey*? It is the slowness of Ulysses' return, the fact that he takes ten years to get home . . . and that, during those ten years, in spite of his much-proclaimed love for Penelope, he does, in reality, betray her every time he gets a chance . . . Homer tells us that Ulysses thought only of Penelope, that the one thing he desired was to be reunited with Penelope . . . but ought we to believe him, Molteni?'

'If we don't believe Homer,' I said more or less jokingly, 'I really don't see who we are to believe.'

'Why, ourselves, men of the modern world, who know how to see right through the myth . . . Molteni, after reading and re-reading the *Odyssey* several times, I've come to the conclusion that, really and truly – and of course without realizing it – Ulysses did not *want* to get home, did not *want* to be reunited to Penelope . . . that's my conclusion, Molteni.'

I said nothing, and again Rheingold, emboldened by my silence, resumed. 'Ulysses, in reality, is a man who is afraid of returning to his wife – and we shall see later why – and, with this fear in his heart, seeks, in his subconscious mind, to create obstacles in his own path . . . That famous spirit of adventure is really no more than an unconscious desire to slow down his journey, frittering away the time in adventures that delay him and take him out of his way . . . It is not Scylla and Charybdis, Calypso and the Phaeacians, Polyphemus, Circe and the gods who are opposed to the return of Ulysses; it is Ulysses' own subconscious which, step by step, creates good excuses for him to stay a year here, two years there, and so on.'

So this was what Rheingold was driving at – this classic Freudian interpretation of the *Odyssey*. I was only surprised that I had not thought of it before: Rheingold was a German, he had started his career in Berlin, at the time of Freud's first successes, he had spent some time in the United States, where psychoanalysis was held in great esteem; it was only natural that he should seek to apply its methods even to that hero who was, *par excellence*, devoid of complexes, Ulysses. I said dryly: 'Very ingenious . . . But I still don't see how . . .,

'One moment, Molteni, one moment . . . It is therefore clear, in the light of my interpretation – which is the only correct one in accordance with the latest discoveries of modern psychology – that the *Odyssey* is merely the inside story of what I may call a conjugal repugnance . . . This conjugal repugnance is debated and examined at

141

great length by Ulysses, and it is only after ten years of struggle with himself that he finally succeeds in overcoming it and dominating it by accepting precisely the situation that had caused it . . . In other words, Ulysses, for ten years, invents for himself every possible kind of delay, makes every possible kind of excuse for not returning to the conjugal roof . . . he actually thinks, more than once, of binding himself to another woman . . . At last, however, he does succeed in gaining command over himself, and he goes home . . . And this return home of Ulysses amounts precisely to an acceptance of the situation owing to which he went away and did not want to come back.'

'What situation?' I asked, genuinely stupid this time. 'Didn't Ulysses go away simply in order to take part in the Trojan War?'

'Externals, externals . . . ' repeated Rheingold with impatience. 'But as to the situation at Ithaca before Ulysses' departure to the War, the Suitors and all the rest of it, I will speak about that when I explain the reasons for which Ulysses did not wish to return to Ithaca and was afraid to go back to his wife . . . In the meantime, however, I should like to stress first one important point: the *Odyssey* is not an extended adventure through geographical space, as Homer would have us believe . . . It is, on the contrary, the wholly interior drama of Ulysses . . . and everything that happens in it is a symbol of Ulysses' subconscious . . . Of course, you know your Freud, Molteni?'

'Yes; a little.'

'Well, Freud will serve us as a guide through this interior landscape of Ulysses, not Berard with his maps and his philology which explains nothing . . . and, instead of the Mediterranean, we shall explore the mind of Ulysses – or, rather, his subconscious.'

Vaguely irritated, I said, with perhaps excessive violence: 'What's the point of going to Capri, then, for a boudoir drama? . . . We might just as well work in a furnished room in a modern quarter of Rome.'

As I spoke, I saw Rheingold throw me a glance of mingled surprise and resentment; he then laughed disagreeably, as though he preferred to make a joke of a discussion that threatened to end badly. 'We'd better resume this conversation, calmly, at Capri,' he said, and then went on: 'You can't drive and discuss the *Odyssey* with me both at the same time, Molteni . . . Now you had better devote yourself to driving, and I, for my part, will admire this extremely beautiful landscape.'

I did not dare contradict him; and for almost an hour we went on in silence. We passed through the region of the ancient Pontine Marshes, with the thick, sluggish water of the canal on our right and the green expanse of the reclaimed plain on our left; we passed through Cisterna; we came to Terracina. After this latter town, the road started to run close beside the sea, being sheltered on its other side by rocky, sunscorched mountains of moderate height. The sea was not calm; it could be seen beyond the yellow and black dunes, and was of an opaque green, a colour that one guessed to be produced by the large quantity of sand stirred up from the bottom by a recent storm. Massive waves rose languidly, and their white water, like soap-suds, invaded the brief stretch of beach. Farther off, the sea was in movement, but there were no waves, and the green colour changed into an almost violet-blue, over which, driven by the wind, appearing and disappearing, white curls of foam ran swiftly. The same capricious, lively disorder reigned in the sky: there were white clouds travelling in all directions; vast blue spaces swept by radiant, blinding light; sea-birds turning and swooping and hovering, as though taking care to follow, with their flight, the gusts and eddies of the wind. I drove with my eyes upon this seascape; and, all of a sudden, as if in reaction against the remorse aroused in me by Rheingold's surprised, offended look when I described his interpretation of the *Odyssey* as a 'boudoir drama', there flashed into my mind the thought that, after all, I had not been wrong: upon that bright-coloured sea, beneath that luminous sky, along that deserted shore, it would not have been difficult to imagine the black ships of Ulysses outlined between one wave and another, sailing towards the then virgin and unknown lands of the Mediterranean. And Homer had wished to represent a sea just like this, beneath a similar sky, along a similar coast, with characters that resembled this landscape and had about them its ancient simplicity, its agreeable moderation. Everything was here, and there was nothing else. And now Rheingold was wanting to make this bright and luminous world, enlivened by the winds, glowing with sunshine, populated by quick-witted, lively beings, into a kind of dark, visceral recess, bereft of colour and form, sunless, airless: the subconscious mind of Ulysses. And so the *Odyssey* was no longer that marvellous adventure, the discovery of the Mediterranean, in humanity's fantastic infancy, but had become the interior drama of a modern man entangled in the contradictions of a psychosis. I said to myself, as a kind of conclusion to these reflections, that, in a sense, I could hardly have happened upon a more unfortunate script: to the usual tendency of the cinema to change everything for the worse which had no need to be changed at all, there was added, in this case, the particular gloom, entirely mechanical and abstract in quality, of psychoanalysis – applied, into the bargain, to a work of art as untrammelled and concrete as the *Odyssey*. We were passing along, at that moment, very close to the sea: beside the road were the green sprays of an exuberant vineyard planted almost in the sand, and beyond it a brief tract of shore, black with debris, upon which the big waves broke heavily from time to time. I pulled up suddenly and said dryly: 'I simply must stretch my legs.'

We got out of the car, and I immediately started off down a path that led through the vineyard to the beach. I explained to Rheingold: 'I've been shut up indoors for eight months . . . I haven't seen the sea since last summer . . . Let's go down to the beach for a moment.'

He followed me in silence; perhaps he was still offended, and still cross with me. The path wound through the vineyard for not much more than fifty yards and then petered out in the sand of the beach. The dull, mechanical sound of the engine had now been replaced by the irregular, echoing roar – to me a delicious sound – of waves piled upon each other and breaking in disorder. I walked a short distance, now going down on to the shimmering, wet sand and now withdrawing again, according as the waves advanced or retired; finally, I stopped and stood still for a long time on top of a sand- dune, my eyes turned towards the horizon. I felt I had offended Rheingold, that I ought to resume the conversation again in some more courteous manner, and that he was expecting me to do so. So, although it irritated me very much to be forced to interrupt my rapt contemplation of the far-off spaces of the sea, I finally made up my mind. 'I'm sorry, Rheingold,' I said all at once; 'perhaps I didn't express myself very well just now . . . But, to tell you the truth, your interpretation didn't entirely convince me . . . If you like, I'll tell you why.'

He answered at once, solicitously: 'Tell me . . . tell me . . . Discussion is part of our work, isn't it?'

'Well,' I resumed, without looking at him, 'I am not

145

entirely convinced, though I'm not saying that the *Odyssey* may not have that significance too. But the distinctive quality of the Homeric poems and, in general, of classical art is to conceal such a significance and a thousand other meanings, too, that may occur to us moderns, in a conclusive, and what I may call a profound, form . . . What I mean is,' I added with sudden, inexplicable irritation, 'the beauty of the *Odyssey* consists precisely in the belief in reality as it is and as it presents itself objectively . . . in this same form, in fact, which allows of no analysis or dissection and which is exactly what it is: take it or leave it . . . In other words,' I concluded, still looking not at Rheingold, but at the sea, 'the world of Homer is a real world . . . Homer belonged to a civilization which had developed in accordance with, not in antagonism to, nature . . . That is why Homer believed in the reality of the perceptible world and saw it in a direct way, as he represented it, and that is why we too should accept it as it is, believing in it as Homer believed in it, literally, without going out of our way to look for hidden meanings.'

I paused, but my attempt at clarification, far from calming me had strangely exasperated me, as though it had been an effort that I knew perfectly well to be useless. And indeed, almost immediately, came Rheingold's reply, accompanied by a burst of laughter, this time triumphant: 'Extrovert, extrovert . . . You, Molteni, like all Mediterranean people, are an extrovert, and you don't understand anyone who is an introvert . . . But, of course, there's no harm in that . . . I am an introvert and you are an extrovert . . . it was precisely for that that I chose you . . . You, with your extrovert character, will counterbalance my introvert character . . . Our collaboration will work marvellously well, as you'll see . . .'

I was on the point of answering him; and I think my answer would have been such as to offend him again, for I again felt violently irritated at his pig-headed obtuseness; when a well-known voice suddenly reached me from behind: 'Rheingold, Molteni . . . what are you doing here? . . . Taking the sea air?'

I turned and saw, clear-cut in the strong morning light, the two figures of Battista and Emilia, at the point where the dunes were highest. Battista was coming quickly down towards us, waving his hand in greeting, and Emilia was following more slowly, looking down at the ground. Battista's whole bearing showed a cheerfulness and an assurance even greater than usual; while that of Emilia seemed to me to exude discontent, perplexity and an indefinable disgust.

Rather surprised, I said at once to Battista: 'We thought you were far ahead . . . at Formia, at least, or even farther.'

Battista answered, in a self-possessed voice: 'We went a long way round . . . I wanted to show your wife a property of mine near Rome where I'm building a villa . . . then we found a couple of level-crossings closed.' He turned towards Rheingold and asked: 'Everything all right, Rheingold? . . . Been talking about the *Odyssey*?'

'Everything all right,' replied Rheingold in the same telegraphic style, from beneath the peak of his cloth cap. Obviously Battista's arrival annoyed him, and he would have preferred to continue the discussion with me.

'Splendid! That's wonderful'; and Battista took us both confidentially by the arm and moved away, drawing us towards Emilia, who had stopped at a little distance along the beach. 'And now,' he went on with a gallantry that seemed to me insufferable, 'now, fair signora, it's up to you to decide . . . Shall we lunch at Naples, or shall we lunch at Formia? . . . You must choose.'

147

Emilia gave a start and said: 'You three must choose
. . . it's all the same to me.'

'No, no. Goodness gracious! It's the ladies who have to
decide.'

'Well, then, let's lunch at Naples; I'm not hungry now.'

'All right; Naples let it be . . . Fish soup with *sughillo*
. . . A band playing *O sole mio* . . .' There could be no
doubt of Battista's cheerfulness.

'What time does the steamer leave for Capri?' asked
Rheingold.

'At half past two . . . We'd better get on,' replied
Battista. He left us and went off towards the road.

Rheingold followed and, catching him up, walked beside him. Emilia, on the other hand, remained where she
was for a moment, pretending to look at the sea, as
though to allow them to go on ahead of us. But, as soon as
I came up to her, she took me by the arm and said in a low
voice: 'I'm coming in your car now . . . and please don't
contradict me.'

I was struck by her tone of urgency. 'Why, what's
happened?'

'Nothing . . . only that Battista drives too fast.'

We walked up the path in silence. When we reached the
road, near the two stationary cars, Emilia moved in a
determined manner towards mine.

'Hi!' cried Battista. 'Isn't the signora coming with me?'

I turned: Battista was standing beside the open door of
his car, in the sun-filled road. Rheingold remained in
uncertainty between the two cars, looking at us. Emilia,
without raising her voice, said quietly: 'I'm going with my
husband now . . . We'll all meet at Naples.'

I expected Battista to give in without any more ado.
But, to my slight surprise, he came running over to us.
'Signora, you're going to be with your husband for two

148

months, at Capri . . . and I,' he added in a low voice, so as not to be overheard by the director, 'I've had just a bit too much of Rheingold in Rome, and I assure you he's not amusing . . . Surely your husband doesn't mind your coming with me. Do you, Molteni?'

I could not but answer, although it was an effort to me: 'No, not at all . . . But Emilia says you drive too fast.'

'I'll go at a snail's pace,' promised Battista facetiously, but with warmth. 'But I do beg of you not to leave me alone with Rheingold.' He lowered his voice again. 'If you knew what a bore he is . . . He talks of nothing but films.'

I don't know what came over me at that moment. Perhaps I thought it was not worth while annoying Battista for so frivolous a reason. Without giving myself time to reflect, I said: 'Come on, Emilia . . . Won't you do this to please Battista? . . . He's quite right, anyhow,' I added with a smile, 'there's nothing you can talk about to Rheingold except films.'

'Exactly,' confirmed Battista, satisfied. Then he took Emilia by the arm – very high up, right under the armpit – saying: 'Come along, fair signora, don't be unkind . . . I promise you I'll go at walking pace.'

Emilia threw me a glance which, at the time, I was quite unable to account for; then she answered slowly: 'Very well, if you say so.' She turned with sudden decision, and adding, 'Let's go, then,' walked off with Battista, who still kept a tight grip on her arm, as if he feared she might escape. I was left standing in uncertainty beside my own car, gazing at Emilia and Battista as they moved away. Beside Battista, thick-set and shorter than herself, she walked indolently, slowly, with an air of discontent that was yet full of an intense, mysterious sensuality. She seemed to me at that moment, extremely beautiful; not the middle-class 'fair signora' to whom Battista alluded, in that greedy, metallic voice of his; but truly very beautiful like some creature outside time or place, in harmony with the sparkling sea and the luminous sky against which her figure was outlined. And her beauty had about it a look of subjection, of reluctance, the cause of which I was at a loss to identify. Then, as I looked at her, I was struck by this thought: 'Idiot . . . Perhaps she wanted to be left alone with you . . . Perhaps she wanted to talk to you, to explain things once and for all, to confide in you . . . Perhaps she wanted to tell you that she loves you . . . And you forced her to go off with Battista.' This idea brought me a feeling of sharp regret, and I lifted my arm as though to call her. But by now it was too late: she was getting into Battista's car and Battista was getting in beside her and Rheingold was walking towards me. So I got into my car, and Rheingold took the seat beside me. At that same moment Battista's car went past us, grew rapidly smaller in the distance, and disappeared.

Perhaps Rheingold had become aware of the violent ill-humour that overcame me at that moment; for instead of resuming – as I feared he would – our conversation about the *Odyssey*, he pulled his cap down over his eyes, settled down into his seat, and was very soon asleep. I drove on in silence, therefore, urging my far from powerful little car to its greatest possible speed; and all the time, in an uncontrollable, frantic manner, my ill-humour increased. The road had turned away from the sea, and was now crossing a prosperous countryside, golden in the sunshine. At any other time I should have rejoiced in these luxuriant trees which, here and there, met over my head, forming a living gallery of rustling, leafy branches; in these grey olives scattered, as far as the eye could reach, over the red hillsides; in these orange groves laden with glossy, dark foliage in the midst of which shone the round, golden fruit; in these old blackened farm buildings guarded by two or three tawny haystacks. But I saw nothing; I drove on and on, and as time passed my wretched ill-humour increased more and more. I did not try to discover the reason for it, which undoubtedly went far beyond simple regret at not having insisted upon taking Emilia with me; even if I had wished to do so, my mind was so obscured by anger that I should have been incapable of it. But, like some kind of uncontrollable nervous convulsion which lasts as long as it is due to last and then, by successive phases, gradually dies down and ceases, leaving its victim all aching and dizzy, so my ill-humour gradually reached its highest point as we passed through fields and woods, plains and mountains, then decreased, and finally, as we came near Naples, vanished altogether. Now we were going swiftly down the hill towards the sea, in sight of the blue waters of the bay, amongst pines and magnolias; and I was feeling dull and torpid – just like, in fact, an epileptic who has been shaken, body and soul, by a convulsion of irresistible violence.

13

Battista's villa, as we learned on our arrival in Capri, was a long way from the main *piazza*, at a lonely point on the coast in the direction of the Sorrento Peninsula. After we had accompanied Rheingold to his hotel, Battista, Emilia and I went off towards the villa along the narrow lane.

At first our road took us along the sheltered walk that runs round the island, half-way up the mountainside. It was almost sunset, and only a few people passed, slowly and in silence, along the brick-paved walk in the shadow of the flowering oleanders or between the walls of the luxuriant gardens. Now and again, through the foliage of pines and carob-trees, one caught a glimpse of the distant sea, a sea of a hard and peerless blue, shot with the glittering, cold rays of the declining sun. I was walking behind Battista and Emilia, stopping from time to time to observe the beauties of the place, and, almost to my surprise, for the first time after a long period, I felt, if not exactly joyful, at least calm and composed. We traversed the whole length of the walk; then we turned off along another, narrower path. Suddenly, at a bend, the Faraglioni became visible, and I was pleased to hear Emilia utter a cry of astonishment and admiration; it was the first time she had been to Capri and so far she had not opened her mouth. From that height the two great, red rocks were surprising in their strangeness, lying on the surface of the sea like two meteorites fallen from heaven on to a mirror. Elated at the sight, I told Emilia that there was a race of lizards on the Faraglioni that existed nowhere else in the world – bright blue because they lived between the blue sky and the blue sea. She listened to my explanation with curiosity, as though for a moment she had forgotten her hostility towards me; so that I could not but conceive a fresh hope of reconciliation, and in my mind the blue lizard, which I described nestling in the cavities of the two rocks, suddenly became the symbol of what we ourselves might become, if we stayed a long time on the island. We too should be of a pure blue within our hearts, from which the clear calm of our sojourn by the sea would gradually wash away the sooty blackness of gloomy town thoughts – blue and with a blue light within us, like the lizards, like the sea, like the sky, like everything that is bright and gay and pure.

After we had passed the Faraglioni, the path started to wind amongst rocky precipices, and there were no more villas or gardens. At last, on a lonely point, there appeared a long, low, white building, with a big terrace jutting out above the sea; this was Battista's villa.

It was not a large villa: apart from a living-room that opened on to the terrace, there were only three other rooms. Battista, who walked in front of us as though to display his pride of ownership, explained that he had never lived in it, and that it was scarcely a year since he had come into possession of it as part payment of a debt. He drew our attention to the way in which he had had all preparations made for our arrival: there were vases of flowers in the living-room; the glossy floor emitted a pungent smell of wax polish; when we looked into the kitchen, we saw the caretaker's wife busy in front of the cooking-stove, preparing our dinner. Battista, who made a special point of displaying all the conveniences of the villa to us, insisted on our examining every nook and corner of it; he carried his politeness even to the extent of

153

opening the cupboards and asking Emilia if there were enough coat-hangers. Then we went back into the living-room. Emilia said she was going to change her clothes, and went out. I should have liked to follow her example; but Battista sat down in an armchair and invited me to do the same, thus preventing me. He lit a cigarette and then, without any preamble, asked, in a wholly unexpected manner: 'Well, Molteni, what d'you think of Rheingold?'

I answered in some astonishment: 'Really, I don't know . . . I've seen too little of him to be able to judge . . . He seems to be a very serious sort of person . . . He's said to be an extremely good director.'

Battista reflected for a moment and then went on: 'You see, Molteni . . . I don't know him at all well either, but I know, more or less, what he thinks and what he wants . . . In the first place, he's a German, isn't he? Whereas you and I are Italians . . . Two worlds, two conceptions of life, two different sensibilities. . . .'

I said nothing. As usual, Battista was taking a round-about course and keeping away from all material concerns: so I waited to see what he was getting at. 'You see, Molteni,' he resumed, 'I wanted to put you, an Italian, to work beside Rheingold, just because I feel him to be so different from us. . . . I trust you, Molteni, and before I go away – I ought to leave here as soon as possible – I want to give you a few words of advice.'

'Go on,' I remarked coldly.

'I've been watching Rheingold,' said Battista, 'during our discussions about the film; either he agrees with me or he says nothing . . . but I know too much about people, by this time, to believe in that kind of attitude . . . You intellectuals, Molteni, all of you, all of you without exception, you think, more or less, that producers are simply business-men, and that's all there is to it . . . Don't

154

deny it, Molteni; that's what you think, and of course Rheingold thinks just the same . . . .Now, up to a point, it's true. . . . Rheingold perhaps thinks he can fool me by this passive attitude of his . . . but I'm wide awake . . . very wide awake, Molteni!'

'The fact of the matter is,' I said brutally, 'you don't trust Rheingold?'

'I trust him and I don't trust him . . . I trust him as a technician, as a professional. . . . I don't trust him as a German, as a man of another world, different from our world. . . . Now' – and Battista put down his cigarette in the ashtray and looked me straight in the eyes – 'now, Molteni, let it be quite clear that what I want is a film as much like Homer's *Odyssey* as possible. . . . And what was Homer's intention with the *Odyssey*? He intended to tell an adventure story which would keep the reader in suspense the whole time . . . a story which would be, so to speak, spectacular. . . . That's what Homer wanted to do. . . . And I want you two to stick faithfully to Homer. . . . Homer put giants, prodigies, storms, witches and monsters into the *Odyssey* – and I want you to put giants, prodigies, storms, witches and monsters into the film . . . .'

'But of course we shall put them in!' I said, somewhat surprised.

'Yes, you'll put them in, you'll put them in . . . ' cried Battista in sudden, unexpected anger. 'Perhaps you think I'm a fool, Molteni? . . . But I'm not a fool.' He had raised his voice and was staring at me with a furious look in his eyes. I was astonished at this sudden rage; and, even more, by the vitality of Battista who, after driving a car all day long and crossing from Naples to Capri, instead of resting when he arrived, as I should have done in his place, still had a desire to discuss Rheingold's intentions. I said, softly: 'But what makes you imagine that I think you're a . . . a fool?'

'Your attitude, the attitude of both of you, Molteni.'

'Please explain.'

Slightly calmer now, Battista took up his cigarette again and went on: 'You remember, that day when you met Rheingold for the first time, in my office . . . you said then, that you didn't feel you were cut out for a spectacular film, didn't you?'

'Yes, I think I did.'

'And what did Rheingold say to you, to reassure you?'

'I don't quite remember . . . '

'I will refresh your memory . . . Rheingold told you not to worry . . . he intended to make a psychological film – a film about the conjugal relations of Ulysses and Penelope . . . . Isn't that so?'

Again I was astonished: Battista, under that coarse, animal-like mask, was sharper than I had believed. 'Yes,' I admitted. 'I think he did say something of the kind.'

'Now, seeing that the script hasn't yet been started and that nothing has yet been done, it is just as well that I should inform you with the utmost seriousness that, for me, the *Odyssey* is not a matter of the conjugal relations of Ulysses and Penelope.'

I said nothing, and Battista, after a pause, went on: 'If I wanted to make a film about relations between husband and wife, I should take a modern novel, I should stay in Rome, and I should shoot the film in the bedrooms and drawing-rooms of the Parioli quarter . . . I shouldn't bother about Homer and the *Odyssey* . . . D'you see, Molteni?'

'Yes, yes, I see.'

'Relations between husbands and wives don't interest me – d'you see, Molteni? . . . The *Odyssey* is the story of

156

the adventures of Ulysses on his journey back to Ithaca, and what I want is a film of the adventures of Ulysses . . . and in order that there should be no more doubts on the matter, I want a spectactular film, Molteni – spec-tac-ular – d'you see, Molteni?'

'You need have no doubts about it,' I said, rather irritated; 'you shall have a spectacular film.'

Battista threw away his cigarette and, in his normal voice, endorsed what I had said. 'I don't doubt it,' he said, 'seeing that, after all, it's I who pay for it. . . . You must understand that I have said all this to you, Molteni, so as to avoid unpleasant misunderstandings. . . . You begin work tomorrow morning, and I wanted to warn you in time, in your own interest too. . . . I trust you, Molteni, and I want you to be my mouthpiece, so to speak, with Rheingold. . . . You must remind Rheingold, whenever it may become necessary, that the *Odyssey* gave pleasure, and has always given pleasure, because it is a work of poetry . . . and I want that poetry to get over, complete, into the film, exactly as it is!'

I realized that Battista was now really calm again: he was, in fact, no longer talking about the spectacular film that he insisted upon our producing, but rather about poetry. After a brief incursion into the earthy depths of box-office success, we had now returned to the airy regions of art and the spirit. With a painful grimace which was meant to be a smile, I said: 'Have no doubts about it, Battista. . . . You shall have all Homer's poetry . . . or anyhow all the poetry we're capable of finding in him.'

'Splendid, splendid; let's not talk of it any more.' Battista rose from his armchair, stretching himself, looked at his wrist-watch, said abruptly that he was going to wash before dinner and went out. I was left alone.

I also had previously thought of retiring to my room and

getting ready for dinner. But the discussion with Battista had distracted and excited me, and I started walking up and down the room, almost without knowing what I was doing. The truth was that the things Battista had said to me had, for the first time, given me a glimpse of the difficulty of a task which I had undertaken rather light-heartedly and thinking only of material advantage: and now I felt that I was succumbing in advance to the fatigue from which I should be suffering by the time the script was finished. 'Why all this?' I said to myself. 'Why should I subject myself to this disagreeable effort, to the discussions that will doubtless take place between ourselves and Battista, to say nothing of those that will crop up between me and Rheingold, to the compromises that are bound to follow, to the bitterness of putting my name to a production that is false and commercial? . . . Why all this?' My visit to Capri, which had seemed to me so attractive when I looked down upon the Faraglioni from the high path, a short time before, now appeared as it were discoloured by the dreariness of a thankless and questionable under-taking – that of reconciling the demands of an honest man of letters such as myself with the wholly different demands of a producer. I was once again conscious, in a painfully precise manner, that Battista was the master and I the servant, and that a servant must do anything rather than disobey his master; that any methods of cunning or flattery by which he may seek to evade his master's authority are in themselves more humiliating than com-plete obedience; that, in brief, by appending my signature to the contract, I had sold my soul to a devil who, like all devils, was at the same time both exacting and mean. Battista had said quite clearly, in a burst of sincerity: 'It's I who pay!' I, certainly, had no need of all that amount of sincerity to say to myself: 'And it's I who am paid!' This phrase sounded continually in my ears, every time I turned my mind to the film-script. Suddenly these thoughts gave me a feeling of suffocation. I felt a strong desire to escape from the very air that Battista breathed. I went over to the french window, opened it and stepped out on to the terrace.

14

Night had fallen, by now; and the terrace was gently illuminated by the indirect, but already intense, brilliance which a still invisible moon spread across the sky. A flight of steps led from the terrace to the path that ran round the island. I hesitated a moment, wondering whether to descend these steps and go for a walk, but it was late and the path was too dark. I decided to stay on the terrace. I stood looking over the balustrade and lit a cigarette.

Above me, black and sharp against the clear, starry sky, rose the rocks of the island. Other rocks could be dimly discerned on the precipice below. The silence was profound: if I listened, I could just hear the brief rustling sound of a wave breaking, from time to time, on the pebbly beach in the inlet far below, and then retreating again. Or perhaps I was wrong, and there was no rustling sound, but only the breathing of the calm sea swelling and spreading with the movement of the tide. The air was still and windless; raising my eyes towards the horizon, I could see, in the distance, the little white light of the Punta Campanella lighthouse on the mainland, ceaselessly turning, now flashing out, now extinguished again, and this light, scarcely perceptible as it was, and lost in the vastness of the night, was the only sign of life I could see all around me.

I felt myself growing quickly calmer under the influence of this calm night; and yet I was aware, with complete lucidity, that all the beauty in the world could produce only a fleeting interruption in the sequence of my troubles. And indeed, after I had stood for some time motionless and thinking of nothing, staring into the darkness, my mind, almost against my will, came back to the thought that dominated it, the thought of Emilia; but this time, perhaps as a result of my conversations with Battista and Rheingold and of the place I was in, so similar to places described in Homer's poem, it was strangely mingled and bound up with the thought of the *Odyssey* script. Suddenly, from some unknown spring of memory, there rose in my mind a passage from the last canto of the *Odyssey*, in which Ulysses, in order to prove his true identity, gives a minute description of his marriage bed; and so, at last, Penelope recognizes her husband and turns pale and almost faints, and, then, weeping, throws her arms round his neck and speaks words which I had learned by heart from having so very often re-read and repeated them to myself: 'Ah, Ulysses, be not angry, thou who in every event didst always show thyself the wisest of men. The gods condemned us to misfortune, being unwilling that we should enjoy the green and flourishing years side by side, and then see, each of us, the other's hair grow white.' Alas, I did not know Greek; but I was aware that the translation could not be a truly faithful one, if only because it failed to reproduce the beautiful naturalness of the Homeric original. Nevertheless, I had always taken a singular pleasure in these lines, because of the feeling that shone through them, even in so formal an expression; and, as I read them, it had so happened that I had compared them with Petrarch's lines in the sonnet that begins:

Tranquillo porto avea mostrato amore

and ends with the triplet:

Et ella avrebbe a me forse risposto
Qualche santa parola, sospirando,
Cangiati i volti e l'una e l'altra chioma.

What had struck me at the time, both in Homer and in Petrarch, was the feeling of a constant, unshakeable love, which nothing could undermine and nothing could cool, even old age. Why did those lines come back now into my mind? I saw that the recollection arose from my relations with Emilia, so different from those of Ulysses with Penelope or of Petrarch with Laura, relations which were in peril not after thirty or forty years of marriage, but after a few months, relations to which the comforting expectation of ending our lives together was certainly denied, or of remaining lovers always, as on the very first day, notwithstanding that 'our faces were changed and the hair of both of us'. And I – I who had so ardently wished that our relations might be such as to justify the hope of this expectation – was left with a feeling of astonishment and terror in face of the rupture – to me incomprehensible – that was preventing my dream from coming true. Why? Almost as though I were seeking a reply from the villa which in one of its rooms enclosed the person of Emilia, I switched round towards the window, turning my back on the sea.

I happened to be standing at one corner of the terrace, in such a way that I could see, albeit slantwise, right into the living-room, without myself being seen. As I looked up, I saw that Battista and Emilia were both in the room. Emilia, who was wearing the same low-necked, black evening dress that she had worn on the occasion of our first meeting with Battista, was standing close beside a little movable bar; and Battista, bending over the bar, was preparing some alcoholic mixture in a large crystal glass. I was suddenly struck by something unnatural in Emilia's demeanour – a look of mingled perplexity and impudence, something between embarrassment and temptation: she stood waiting for Battista to hand her the glass, and in the meantime was looking round her with an uneasy expression in which I recognized that look of disintegration that was caused, in her, by doubt and bewilderment. Then Battista finished mixing the drinks, carefully filled two glasses, and held one out to Emilia as he rose; she started, as though awakening from a fit of deep abstraction, and slowly put out her hand to take the glass. My eyes were upon her at that moment, as, standing in front of Battista, leaning slightly backwards, she raised one hand with the glass in it and supported herself with the other on the back of the armchair; and I could not help noticing that she seemed, as it were, to be offering her whole body as she thrust forward her bosom and her belly beneath the tight glossy material of her dress. This gesture of offering, however, did not betray itself in any way in her face, which preserved its same expression of uncertainty. Finally, as though to break an embarrassing silence, she said something, turning her head towards a group of armchairs at the far end of the room, round the fireplace; and then, cautiously, so as not to spill her brimming glass, she walked towards them. And then the thing happened, which by now, in reality, I was expecting: Battista caught up with her in the middle of the room and put his arm round her waist, bringing his face close to hers, over her shoulder. She immediately protested, with no severity in her manner, but with a vivacity that was imploring and perhaps even playful, as, with her eyes, she indicated the glass which she was now holding tightly between her fingers in mid-air. Battista laughed, shook his head and drew her more closely towards him, with a movement so abrupt that as she had feared, the glass was

163

upset. 'Now he's going to kiss her on the mouth,' I
thought; but I failed to take into account Battista's
character, Battista's brutality. He did not in fact kiss her,
but, grasping the edge of her dress on her shoulder in his
fist, with a strange, cruel violence, twisted and pulled it
roughly downwards. One of Emilia's shoulders was now
completely bare, and Battista's head was bending over it
so that he might press his mouth against it; and she was
standing upright and still, as though waiting patiently for
him to have finished; but I had time to see that her face
and her eyes, even during the kiss, remained perplexed
and uneasy, as before. Then she looked in the direction of
the window, and it seemed to me that our eyes met; I saw
her making a gesture of disdain and then, holding up the
torn shoulder-strap with one hand, leave the room hurriedly. I turned and walked back along the terrace.

My chief sensation at the moment was one of confusion
and astonishment, because it seemed to me that what I
had seen was in complete contradiction with what I knew
and had hitherto thought. Emilia, who no longer loved me
and who, in her own words, despised me, was in reality,
then, deceiving me with Battista. And so the situation
between us was now reversed: from being vaguely in the
wrong I had become clearly in the right; after seeing
myself despised for no reason, it was I, now, who had full
justification for despising; and the whole mystery of
Emilia's conduct towards me resolved itself into a perfectly ordinary intrigue. It may be that this first harsh yet
logical reflection, dictated largely by my own personal
pride, prevented me, at the moment, from being conscious of any pain caused by the discovery of Emilia's
unfaithfulness (or what appeared to me to be unfaithfulness). But as I approached the balustrade at the edge of
the terrace, feeling irresolute and half-stunned, I became

suddenly aware of the pain, and, recoiling to the opposite extreme, was certain that what I had seen was not, could not be, the truth. Certainly, I said to myself, Emilia had let herself be kissed by Battista; but, in some mysterious way, my own guilt did not on that account disappear, nor, as I realized, did I now have the right to despise her in my turn; in fact – why, I did not know – it seemed to me that she still retained this right towards me in spite of the kiss I had seen. And so, really and truly, I was making a mistake: she was not being unfaithful to me; or, at most, her unfaithfulness was merely apparent; and the essential truth of this unfaithfulness still had to be discovered, lying, as it did, right outside mere appearances.

I remembered that she had always shown a determined and, to me, inexplicable, aversion for Battista; and that, no longer ago than that very day, that very morning, she had twice besought me not to leave her alone, during the journey, with the producer. How could I reconcile this behaviour on her part with the recent kiss? There could be no doubt that this kiss had been the first: Battista, in all probability, had managed to take advantage of a favourable moment which, before this evening, had never occurred. Nothing, therefore, was yet lost; I might still come to know why in the world it was that Emilia had let herself be kissed by Battista; and why, above all, I felt, in an obscure but unmistakable way, that in spite of the kiss our relations were not changed, but that – as before and no less than before – she still had the right to refuse me her love and to despise me.

It may be thought that this was not the moment for such reflections, and that my first and solitary impulse should have been to burst into the sitting-room and reveal my presence to the two lovers. But I had been pondering too long over Emilia's demeanour towards me to give way to a

165

candid, unprepared outburst of that kind; and, further-more, what mattered most to me was not so much to put Emilia in the wrong as to shed new light upon our relationship. By bursting into the room, I should have precluded, once and for all, every possibility either of getting to know the truth or of winning back Emilia. Instead, I told myself, I must act with all possible reason-ableness, with all the prudence and circumspection im-posed upon me by circumstances which were at the same time both delicate and ambiguous.

There was another consideration which kept me from crossing the threshold of the living-room, this one, perhaps, of a more selfish kind: I saw that I now had a good reason for throwing over the *Odyssey* script, for ridding myself of a task that disgusted me and returning to my beloved theatre. This consideration had the quality of being good for all three of us – for Emilia, for Battista, and for myself. The kiss I had witnessed marked, in reality, the culminating point of the falsity against which my whole life was contending, both in my relations with Emilia and in my work. At last I saw the possibility of clearing away this falsity, once and for all.

All this passed through my mind with the swiftness with which, if a window is suddenly thrown open, a blast of wind rushes into the room, bearing with it leaves and dust and all kinds of rubbish. And just as, if the window is closed again, there is a sudden silence and stillness within the room, so my mind, in the end, became all at once empty and silent, and I found myself standing there in astonishment, staring into the darkness, with no more thought or feeling in me. In this stupefied condition, and almost without knowing what I was doing, I left the balustrade and went over to the french window; I opened it and went into the living-room. How long had I remained on the terrace after coming unawares upon Battista embracing Emilia? Longer than I had thought, certainly, for I found Battista and Emilia already seated at table, half-way through dinner. I noticed that Emilia had taken off the dress which Battista had torn and had again put on the one she had worn for the journey; and this detail, for some reason, troubled me deeply, as a particularly cruel and eloquent proof of her infidelity. 'We thought you must have gone for a nocturnal swim,' said Battista jovially. 'Where the devil have you been hiding yourself?'

'I was just outside there,' I answered in a low voice. I saw Emilia raise her eyes in my direction, look at me for a moment and then lower them again; and I was quite sure she had seen me watching their embrace from the terrace, and that she knew that I knew she had seen me.

15

Emilia was silent during dinner, but without any visible embarrassment, which surprised me, because I thought she ought to be troubled and I had always, hitherto, considered her incapable of dissimulation. Battista, on the other hand, did not conceal his jubilant, victorious state of mind and never stopped talking, uninterruptedly, while at the same time eating with a good appetite and drinking with a freedom that was perhaps excessive. What did Battista talk about that evening? Many things, but I noticed, mainly about himself, whether directly or indirectly. The word 'I' boomed aggressively from his mouth, with a frequency that irritated me; and I was no less disgusted by the way in which he contrived to make use of even the most far-fetched pretexts to descend by degrees to his own self. I realized, however, that this self-applause was due not so much to simple vanity as to a wholly masculine wish to glorify himself before Emilia, and possibly to humiliate me: he was convinced that he had made a conquest of Emilia, and now, very naturally, was taking pleasure in strutting like a peacock and showing off his most brilliant plumes in front of his victim. I am bound to admit, at this point, that Battista was no fool; and that, even during this display of masculine vanity, he still kept his feet on the ground and said things that were, for the most part, interesting; as when, at the end of dinner, he told us, in a lively manner but also with seriousness of judgement, of his recent trip to America and of a visit he had paid to the studios of Hollywood. But this did not prevent his arrogant, self-centred, indiscreet tone from becoming intolerable to me; and I imagined, somewhat ingenuously, that the same must be true of Emilia, whom I still, for some reason, held to be hostile to him, in spite of what I had seen and knew. But once again I was wrong: Emilia was not hostile to Battista – on the contrary; more than once while he was speaking I seemed to catch in her eyes a look which, if not exactly love-sick, at least showed a serious interest and was even, at moments, full of a wondering esteem. This look was as disconcerting and bitter to me as Battista's male vanity – if not more so; and it recalled to my memory another, similar look; but where I had noticed it, I could not at first remember. Then, suddenly, at the end of dinner, it came back to me: it was the same look – or anyhow, not far different – as the one I had caught, not very long ago, in the eyes of the wife of the film director Pasetti, when I had had lunch with them at their home. Pasetti – pallid, insignificant, precise – was talking; and his wife gazed at him with spellbound eyes in which could be read, simultaneously, love, awe, admiration and self-surrender. Certainly Emilia had not yet reached that point with Battista, but it seemed to me that her look already held the germ of the feelings that Signora Pasetti cherished for her husband. Battista, in fact, did quite right to show off; Emilia, inexplicably, was already partly subjugated, and would soon be wholly so. At this thought I felt myself transfixed by a feeling of pain even sharper, perhaps, than the pain I had felt shortly before, when I had seen them kissing. And I could not prevent the expression on my face from becoming visibly more gloomy. Battista must have noticed this change, for he threw me a penetrating glance and then suddenly asked: 'What's the matter, Molteni? . . . Aren't you pleased to be at Capri? Is there something wrong?'

'Why?'

'Because,' he said, pouring himself out some wine, 'you look gloomy . . . not to say ill-humoured.'

This was his method of attack: perhaps because he knew that the best way to be on the defensive is to be offensive. I answered with a promptness that surprised me: 'I started feeling ill-humoured out on the terrace looking at the sea.'

He raised his eyebrows and looked at me questioningly but with no sign of agitation. 'Oh, really . . . why?'

I looked at Emilia: she did not appear to be worried either. They were both of them incredibly sure of themselves. Yet Emilia had certainly seen me, and in all probability had told Battista. Suddenly these unpremeditated words issued from my mouth: 'Battista, may I talk to you frankly?'

Again I wondered at his imperturbability. 'Frankly?' he asked. 'But of course! . . . I always like people to talk to me frankly.'

'You see,' I went on, 'when I was looking at the sea, I imagined for a moment that I was here working on my own account . . . My ambition, as you know, is to write for the theatre . . . And so I thought how this would be the ideal spot, as they say, to devote myself to my work: beauty, silence, peace, my wife with me, nothing to worry about . . . Then I remembered that I was here, in this place which is so lovely and so favourable in every way, not for *that* purpose, but – I'm sorry, but you wanted me to be frank – in order to spend my time writing a film-script which will certainly be good, but which, in fact, really and truly doesn't concern me . . . I shall give of my very best to Rheingold, and Rheingold will make whatever use of it he likes, and in the end I shall be given a cheque . . . and I shall have wasted three or four months

170

of the best and most creative time of my life . . . I know I shouldn't say such things to you, nor to any other producer . . . but you wanted me to be frank . . . Now you know why I'm in a bad temper.'

Why had I said these things instead of the others that were on the tip of my tongue and that concerned the conduct of Battista towards my wife? I did not know; perhaps owing to a sudden weariness of overstrained nerves; perhaps because in this way I expressed, indirectly, my desperation at Emilia's unfaithfulness which I felt to be somehow connected with the commercial and subordinate character of my work. But, just as Battista and Emilia had remained untroubled by my ominous preamble, so now they failed to show any relief at all at the wretched confession of weakness that had followed it. Battista said seriously: 'But I'm sure, Molteni, you'll write a very fine script.'

Having started out on the wrong track, I was now committed to it to the bitter end. I answered in a tone of exasperation: 'I am afraid I didn't make myself clear . . . I am a writer for the theatre, Battista, not one of the large number of professional writers of film-scripts . . . and this script, however fine, however perfect it is, will be, for me, merely a script . . . a thing – allow me to say frankly – that I do simply in order to earn money . . . Now at the age of twenty-seven one has what are commonly called ideals – and my ideal is to write for the theatre! . . . Why am I unable to do so? Because the world today is so constructed that no one can do what he would like to do, and he is forced, instead, to do what others wish him to do . . . Because the question of money always intrudes – into what we do, into what we are, into what we wish to become, into our work, into our highest aspirations, even into our relations with the people we love!'

I realized that I had become over-excited and that my eyes had actually filled with tears. And I was ashamed and in my heart I cursed my excess of feeling which encouraged me to make confidences of this kind to the man who, a few moments earlier, had successfully tried to entice my wife away from me. But Battista was not put out of countenance for so small a matter. 'You know, Molteni,' he said, 'hearing you talk, I seem to see myself again at the time when I was your age.'

'Oh, really?' I stammered, disconcerted.

'Yes. I was extremely poor,' pursued Battista, helping himself to more wine, 'and I also had, as you say, ideals . . . What those ideals were, I could not now say, and perhaps I did not know even then . . . but I had them nevertheless . . . or perhaps I did not have this or that ideal, but Ideals with a capital I . . . Then I met a man to whom I owe a very great deal, if only for having taught me certain things.' Battista paused a moment, with characteristic, heavy solemnity, and I could not help calling to mind, almost involuntarily, that the man to whom he was alluding was without doubt a certain film producer, forgotten now, but famous in the days of the early Italian cinema, with whom, and under whose orders, Battista had indeed started out upon his prosperous career; a man who, however, as far as I knew, was to be admired for nothing except his capacity for making money. 'To that man,' Battista went on, 'I made more or less the same speech as you've made to me this evening . . . You know what he answered me? That ideals, until one knows exactly what one wants, are best forgotten and put aside . . . but, as soon as one has planted one's foot on solid ground, then one should remember them, and *that* should become one's ideal . . . the first thousand-lire note one earns – *that's* the best ideal!. . . Then, as he said to me,

172

one's ideal develops and becomes a film studio, a theatre, films that have been made and that are going to be made – one's everyday work, in fact . . . That's what he said to me . . . and I did as he told me and everything turned out well . . . But you – you have the great advantage of knowing what your ideal is – to write plays . . . Well, you *will* write them!'

'I *will* write them?' I could not help asking, feeling doubtful but, at the same time, already somewhat comforted.

'Yes; you will write them,' Battista affirmed; 'you will write them if you really want to, even if you *are* working for money, even if you *are* making scripts for Triumph Films . . . D'you want to know what the secret of success is, Molteni?'

'What is it?'

'Get into the queue, in life, just as you get into the queue at the booking-office, at the station . . . Our moment always comes, if we have patience and don't change queues . . . Our moment always comes, and the booking-office clerk gives each person his ticket . . . each person according to his merits, of course . . . anyone who is going a long way, and is capable of doing so, may even be given a ticket for Australia . . . Others who are not going so far are given tickets for shorter journeys – for Capri, possibly!'He laughed, pleased with this ambiguous allusion to our journey, and then added: 'I hope you yourself may receive a ticket for a very far-off destination . . . How about America?'

I looked at Battista, who was smiling at me in a fatherly manner, then I looked at Emilia and saw that she too was smiling; it was a very faint smile, it is true, but no less sincere on that account – at least so it seemed to me. And I realized once again that Battista, that day, had somehow

173

managed to change her aversion into a feeling that was almost one of liking for him. At this thought I was overwhelmed anew by the sadness that had assailed me when it seemed to me that I detected Signora Pasetti's look in the eyes of Emilia. I said sadness, rather than jealousy: in reality I was extremely tired, owing both to the journey and to the various events of the day, and weariness was intermingled with all my feelings, even the most violent, deadening them and changing them into an impotent, despairing melancholy.

Dinner came to an end in unexpected fashion. After listening sympathetically to Battista, Emilia appeared suddenly to remember me – or rather, to remember my existence – in a manner that once again confirmed my uneasiness. To an insignificant remark from me: 'We might go out on the terrace . . . the moon should have risen by now,' she replied dryly: 'I don't want to go out on the terrace . . . I'm going to bed . . . I'm tired'; and without more ado she got up, said goodnight to us, and went out. Battista did not appear to be surprised at this abrupt departure; in fact – or so it seemed to me – he looked almost pleased at it, as a flattering indication of the havoc he had contrived to create in Emilia's mind. But I felt my uneasiness to be doubled. And although, as I said, I felt exhausted, although I was well aware that it would have been better to postpone all explanations till next day, in the end I could no longer contain myself. With the excuse that I felt sleepy, I too said good night to Battista and left the room.

16

My bedroom communicated with Emilia's by means of an inside door. Without any delay, I went to this door and knocked. Emilia called to me to come in.

She was sitting on the bed, quite still, in a thoughtful attitude. When she saw me, she at once asked, in a weary, irritable voice: 'What more d'you want of me?'

'Nothing at all,' I answered coldly, for I felt perfectly calm and lucid now, also less tired. 'Just to wish you a good night.'

'Or is it that you want to know what I think of the conversation you had this evening with Battista . . . Well, if you want to know, I'll tell you at once: it was not only inopportune, but ridiculous as well.'

I took a chair and sat down, then asked: 'Why?'

'I don't understand you,' she said, annoyed; 'really I don't understand you . . . You set so much store by this script, and then you go and tell the producer that you're working simply to make money, that you don't like the work, that your ideal would be to write for the theatre, and so on . . . But don't you realize that although, out of politeness, he gave in to you this evening, tomorrow he'll think it over, and he'll take good care not to give you any more work? Can't you possibly understand a thing as simple as that?'

So she launched her attack. And although I knew she was doing it in order to conceal other, more important, anxieties from me, I still could not help noticing a certain sincerity in her voice, however painful and humiliating it

175

might be for me. I had promised myself that I would keep calm. But her tone of utter contempt made me flare up in spite of myself. 'But it's the truth,' I cried all of a sudden; 'I don't like this job, I've never liked it . . . And it's by no means certain that I'm going to do it.'

'Of course you're going to do it.' Never had she despised me so much as at this moment.

I set my teeth and tried to control myself. 'Perhaps I may not do it,' I said in a normal voice. 'I had intended to do it even as late as this morning . . . but certain things have happened during the course of today which will cause me, in all probability, to announce to Battista, not later than tomorrow, that I'm giving it up.'

I uttered this sibylline remark deliberately, with a feeling almost of vindictiveness. She had tortured me so much, and now I wanted to torture her by alluding to what I had seen through the window, without, however, speaking of it directly or precisely. She looked at me fixedly, and then asked in a quiet voice: 'What things have happened?'

'Plenty of things.'

'But what?'

She was insistent: it seemed to me that she sincerely desired me to accuse her, to reprove her for her unfaithfulness. But I continued to be evasive. 'They're things to do with the film . . . things between myself and Battista . . . there's no need to mention them.'

'Why don't you want to mention them?'

'Because they wouldn't interest you.'

'Possibly; but you won't have the courage to give up the job. You'll do it all right.'

I could not quite make out whether this remark showed merely the usual contempt, or whether it contained an unspecified hope. I asked, cautiously; 'Why d'you think so?'

'Because I know you.' She paused a moment and then sought to gloss over what she had said. 'It's always like that with film-scripts, anyhow . . . How many times have I known you to declare that you wouldn't do this or that job, and then you've done it! . . . The difficulties in scripts always get smoothed out in the end.'

'That may be, but this time the difficulty is not in the script.'

'Where is it, then?'

'In myself.'

'What d'you mean by that?'

'Battista kissing you,' I should have liked to reply. But I restrained myself: our relationship had never been clarified right down to the bare truth, it had always been carried on by means of allusions. Before we reached the truth, there were so many other things that would have to be said. I bent forward slightly and declared with the greatest seriousness. 'Emilia, you already know the reason; as I said at dinner, it's because I'm tired of working for other people and want at last to work for myself.'

'And who's preventing you?'

'You,' I said emphatically; then, seeing at once that she started to make a gesture of protest: 'Not you directly . . . but your presence in my life . . . Our relations are, unfortunately – what they are: don't let's speak of them . . . but all the same you are my wife, and I, as I've told you before, take on these jobs mainly because of you . . . If it wasn't for you, I wouldn't accept them . . . To put it briefly – you know it perfectly well and there's no need for me to repeat it – we have a great many debts, we still have several instalments to pay on the flat, even the car hasn't yet been completely paid for . . . that's why I do these film-scripts . . . Now, however, I want to make you a suggestion . . .'

'What?'

I imagined myself to be very calm, very lucid, very reasonable; and yet at the same time a faint feeling of uneasiness warned me that there was a certain falsity – a worse than falsity, an absurdity – in my calm, in my lucidity, in my reasonableness. After all, I had seen her in Battista's arms: and that alone was what should have mattered. I went on, nevertheless: 'The suggestion I want to make to you is as follows: that you yourself should decide whether I am to do this script or not . . . I promise you that if you tell me not to do it, I'll go and tell Battista so, first thing tomorrow morning – and we'll leave Capri by the first boat.'

She did not raise her head, but appeared to be meditating. 'You're very cunning,' she said at last.

'Why?'

'Because, if you regret it afterwards, you'll always be able to say it was my fault!'

'I shan't say anything of the kind . . . considering it's I myself who am asking you to decide.'

She was now, obviously, reflecting upon the answer that she should give me. And I saw that her answer would provide an implicit corroboration of her feeling for me, whatever it might be. If she told me to do the script, it would mean that she now despised me to the point of considering that my work could continue, in spite of everything; if her answer, on the other hand, was in the negative, it would imply that she still retained some respect for me and did not want me to be dependent on her lover for my work. And so, after all, I came back again to the usual question; whether she despised me and why she despised me. At last she said: 'These are things that one can't allow other people to decide for one!'

'But I'm asking you to decide.'

178

'Then remember you insisted on my deciding,' she said all at once, with sudden solemnity.

'Yes; I shall remember.'

'Well, I think that, since you've taken on the job, you ought not to give it up . . . You yourself, in any case, have said that to me many times . . . Battista might be annoyed and never give you any more work . . . I think you should certainly do this job.'

I thought of that kiss, and said, in an almost hostile manner: 'Very well, then . . . But don't tell me later on that you gave me this advice because you'd realized that, really and truly, I wanted to do the job . . . like that day when I had to sign the contract . . . Let it be quite clear that I *don't* want to do it.'

'Ugh, you've exhausted me,' she said carelessly, getting up from the bed and going over to the wardrobe. 'That's my advice anyhow . . . but of course you can do what you like . . .'

She had reassumed her tone of contempt, thus confirming my suppositions. And quite suddenly I experienced the same pain that I had felt that first time in Rome, when she had flung her aversion in my face. I could not help exclaiming: 'Emilia, why all this? . . . Why are we so hostile to each other?'

She had opened the wardrobe and was looking at herself in the mirror on the door. She said, in an absent-minded way: 'Well, well, it's life, I suppose!'

Her words took my breath away, leaving me rigid and silent. Emilia had never spoken to me in that way, with such indifference and apathy and in so conventional a phrase. I knew I could have reversed the situation again by telling her I had seen her with Battista, as she herself knew perfectly well; that, in asking her to decide for me about the film-script, I had simply wished to put her to the test – which was true; and that, in short, the question between her and me was still the same as ever. But I had not the courage, or rather, the strength, to say these things: I felt utterly tired, and quite unable to start all over again. So, instead, I said, almost timidly: 'And what will you do all the time we're in Capri, while I'm working on the film?'

'Nothing special . . . I'll go for walks . . . and swim, and sun-bathe . . . the same as everyone does.'

'All alone?'

'Yes; all alone.'

'Won't you be bored, alone?'

'I'm never bored . . . I've plenty of things to think about!'

'D'you sometimes think about me?'

'Yes; of course I do.'

'And what d'you think?' I too had risen, and had gone over to her and taken her hand.

'We've talked about that so many times already.' She resisted my hold, yet without disengaging her hand.

'D'you still think about me in the same way?'

This time she pulled herself away from me and said brusquely: 'Now listen. You'd better go to bed . . . I know there are certain things you don't like, and indeed it's quite natural . . . On the other hand, I can only repeat what I've said before . . . What's the point of talking about them again?'

'But I *do* want to talk about them again.'

'Why . . . I should only have to say again, all the things I've already said so many times . . . I haven't changed my mind just because I've come to Capri: on the contrary.'

'What d'you mean by "on the contrary"?'

'When I said "on the contrary",' she explained rather confusedly, 'I meant that I haven't changed – that's all.'

'You still have the same . . . the same feeling about me, in fact? Isn't that so?'

Unexpectedly, and in an almost tearful voice, she protested. 'Why d'you torment me like this? . . . D'you think it gives me any pleasure to say these things to you? . . . I dislike them more than you do!'

I was moved by the pain which I seemed to detect in her voice. Taking her hand again, I said: 'Anyhow, *I* think a great deal of *you* . . . and I always shall,' I added, as though to make her see that I forgave her for her unfaithfulness, which indeed was true, 'whatever happens.'

She said nothing. She looked away, and seemed to be waiting. But at the same time I felt her trying to disengage her hand from mine, with a sly but persistent and obstinately hostile movement. And so I abruptly bade her goodnight and left the room. It was with a sharp renewal of pain that I heard the key, almost at once, being turned in the lock.

17

Next morning I rose early, and, without taking steps to find out where Battista and Emilia were, left – or rather, made my escape from – the house. After the night's rest, the happenings of the previous day and, above all, my own behaviour, appeared in an unpleasant light, as a series of absurdities which had been confronted in an equally absurd fashion; now I wanted to think calmly over what I ought to do, without compromising my own freedom of action by some hurried and irreparable decision. So I left the house, went back over the path I had traversed the evening before, and made my way to the hotel where Rheingold was staying. I inquired for him and was told he was in the garden. I followed; and at the far end of an avenue caught sight of the slender parapet of a belvedere bathed in the brilliant light of the calm, sun-filled sea and sky. A few chairs and a small table were arranged in front of the parapet, and as I appeared someone rose to his feet with a gesture of greeting. It was Rheingold, all dressed up like a naval captain, in a white cap with a gold anchor on it, a blue jacket with gold buttons, and white trousers. On the table was a tray with the remains of breakfast; also a portfolio and writing materials.

Rheingold seemed extremely cheerful. He immediately asked me: 'I say, Molteni – what d'you think of a morning like this?'

'I think it's an exquisitely beautiful morning.'

'What would you say, Molteni,' he went on, taking me

by the arm and turning with me towards the parapet, 'what would you say to letting our work go hang, hiring a boat and rowing slowly all around the island? . . . Don't you think it would be better, infinitely better?'

I answered him without conviction, thinking in my heart that an excursion of that kind in the company of Rheingold would lose a good deal of its charm. 'Yes,' I said; 'in a sense it would be better.'

'You've said it, Molteni!' he exclaimed triumphantly. 'In a sense . . . But in what sense? Not in the sense in which *we* understand life . . . for us life means duty – doesn't it, Molteni? . . . Duty, first and foremost; and so, Molteni, to work!' He left the parapet and sat down again at the table; then, leaning towards me and looking into my eyes, said, with a certain solemnity: 'Sit down here, opposite me . . . this morning we'll just talk . . . I have a great many things to say to you . . .'

I sat down. Rheingold adjusted his cap over his eyes and resumed: 'You will remember, Molteni, that I was explaining my interpretation of the *Odyssey* to you during our drive from Rome to Naples . . . but this explanation was interrupted by the appearance of Battista . . . Then, for the rest of the journey I was asleep, and so the explanation was postponed . . . You remember, Molteni?'

'Yes; certainly I do.'

'You will also remember that I gave you the key to the *Odyssey* – in this way: Ulysses takes ten years to return home because really, in his subconscious mind, he does not *want* to return.'

'Yes, indeed.'

'I will now reveal to you, then, the reason why, according to my idea, Ulysses does not want to return home,' said Rheingold. He paused for a moment as if to

183

mark the beginning of the revelation, and then, wrinkling his eyebrows and gazing at me with characteristic dictatorial seriousness, he went on: 'Ulysses, in his subconscious mind, does not wish to return to Ithaca because in reality his relations with Penelope are unsatisfactory . . . that's the reason, Molteni . . . And these relations had been unsatisfactory even before the departure of Ulysses to the war . . . in fact, really Ulysses had gone off to the war because he was unhappy at home . . . and he was unhappy at home precisely because of his unsatisfactory relations with his wife!'

Rheingold was silent for a moment, but without ceasing to frown in that half-dictatorial, half-didactic manner; and I took advantage of the pause to turn my chair so that I did not have the sun in my eyes. Then he continued: 'If his relations with Penelope had been good, Ulysses would not have gone off to the war . . . Ulysses was not a swaggerer or a warmonger . . . Ulysses was a prudent, wise, wary kind of man . . . If his relations with his wife had been good, Ulysses, simply in order to prove to Menelaus that he supported him, would perhaps just have sent an expeditionary force under the command of some man he trusted . . . instead of which he went off himself, taking advantage of the war to leave home and thus escape from his wife.'

'Very logical.'

'Very psychological, you mean, Molteni,' corrected Rheingold, having noticed, perhaps, a touch of irony in my tone, 'very psychological . . . And remember that everything depends upon psychology; without psychology there is no character, without character there is no story . . . Now, what is the psychology of Ulysses and Penelope? . . . This is it: Penelope is the traditional feminine figure of archaic, feudal, aristocratic Greece, she is virtuous, noble, proud, religious, a good housewife, a good mother, a good wife . . . Ulysses, on the other hand, anticipates, in character, the men of a later Greece, the Greece of the sophists, and the philosophers . . . Ulysses is a man without prejudices, and, if necessary, without scruples, subtle, reasonable, intelligent, irreligious, sceptical, sometimes even cynical.'

'It seems to me,' I objected, 'that you're blackening the character of Ulysses . . . in reality, in the *Odyssey* . . .'

But he interrupted me impatiently. 'We're not going to worry ourselves in the least about the *Odyssey* . . . or rather we're going to interpret, to develop the *Odyssey* . . . We're making a film, Moltenl . . . The *Odyssey* is already written . . . the film is yet to be made!'

I was silent again, and he resumed: 'The reason for the bad relations between Ulysses and Penelope must therefore be sought in the difference between their characters . . . Before the Trojan War, Ulysses had done something to displease Penelope . . . What? . . . This is where the Suitors come in . . . In the *Odyssey*, we know that they aspire to the hand of Penelope and in the meantime live extravagantly at Ulysses' expense, in his house . . . We've got to reverse the situation.'

I gazed at him open-mouthed. 'Don't you understand?' he asked. 'Well, I'll explain it to you at once . . . As for the Suitors, it may perhaps be convenient for us to reduce them to one person, Antinous, for instance . . . The Suitors, then, have been in love with Penelope since before the Trojan War . . . and, being in love, they shower presents upon her, according to Greek custom . . . Penelope, being proud and dignified, in the antique manner, would like to refuse their presents, would, above all things, like her husband to turn the Suitors out . . . but Ulysses, for some reason that we don't yet know but that

185

we shall easily find, does not wish to offend the Suitors
. . . As a reasonable man, he does not attach much
importance to their courting of his wife, since he knows
she is faithful; nor does he attribute much significance to
their gifts, which perhaps do not really displease him at all
. . . Remember that all Greeks were greedy for presents,
Molteni . . . Naturally, Ulysses does not for a moment
advise Penelope to yield to the Suitors' desires, but merely
not to offend them because he does not consider it worth
while . . . Ulysses wants a quiet life, and he hates scandals
. . . Penelope, who was expecting anything rather than
this passive attitude on Ulysses' part, is disgusted, almost
incredulous . . . She protests, she rebels . . . but Ulysses
is not to be shaken, there seems to him no cause for
indignation . . . so he again advises Penelope to accept the
presents, to behave kindly – what does it cost her, after
all? . . . and Penelope, in the end, follows her husband's
advice . . . but at the same time conceives a deep contempt for him . . . She feels she no longer loves him, and
tells him so . . . Ulysses then realizes, too late, that by his
prudence, he has destroyed Penelope's love . . . Ulysses
then tries to remedy matters, to win his wife back again,
but he is unsuccessful . . . His life at Ithaca becomes a hell
. . . Finally, in desperation, he seizes the opportunity of
the Trojan War to leave home . . . After seven years, the
War ends and he puts to sea again to return to Ithaca . . .
but he knows he is awaited at home by a woman who no
longer loves him, who, in fact, despises him . . . and
therefore, unconsciously, he welcomes any excuse for
putting off this unpleasant, this dreaded, return . . . and
yet, sooner or later, return he must . . . But, on his
return, the same thing happens to him as happened to the
knight in the legend of the dragon – d'you remember,
Molteni? . . . The princess demanded that the knight

should kill the dragon if he wished to be worthy of her love . . . so the knight killed the dragon and then the princess loved him . . . In the same way, Penelope, at Ulysses' return, after proving that she had been faithful to him, gave him to understand that her faithfulness did not mean love, but merely virtue: she would recover her love for him on one, and only one condition – that he would slay the Suitors . . . Ulysses, as we know, was not in the least bloodthirsty or vindictive . . . he would perhaps have preferred to dismiss the Suitors by gentler means, by persuasion . . . But this time he made up his mind, knowing, in fact, that upon the killing of the Suitors depends the esteem of Penelope and consequently her love also . . . So he kills them . . . Then, and only then, does Penelope cease to despise him, only then does she love him again . . . And so Ulysses and Penelope are again in love, after all those years of separation . . . and they celebrate their true marriage – their "Bluthochzeit", their blood-marriage . . . Well, d'you understand, Molteni? Now, to sum up . . . Point one: Penelope despises Ulysses for not having reacted like a man, like a husband, and like a king, to the indiscreet behaviour of the Suitors . . . Point two: her contempt causes the departure of Ulysses to the Trojan War . . . Point three: Ulysses, knowing that he is awaited at home by a woman who despises him, delays his return as long as he can . . . Point four: in order to regain Penelope's esteem and love, Ulysses slays the Suitors . . . d'you understand, Molteni?'

I said I understood. All this was not, really, very difficult to understand. But now, the feeling of aversion I had had for Rheingold's interpretation, from the very beginning, sprang up in me again, stronger than ever; and it made me perplexed and bemused. In the meantime Rheingold was explaining pedantically: 'D'you know how

I arrived at this key to the whole situation? . . . By means of a simple consideration of the slaughter of the Suitors, as it is told in the *Odyssey* . . . I observed that this slaughter, brutal, ferocious, ruthless, as it was, was in absolute contrast to the character of Ulysses as hitherto presented to us: cunning, flexible, subtle, reasonable, cautious . . . and I said to myself: "Ulysses might very well have politely shown the Suitors the door . . . he had the possibility of doing this; being in his own house, and being king, all he had to do was to show himself as such . . . As he doesn't do it, it is a sign that he has some good reason for not doing it . . . What reason? . . . Obviously Ulysses wishes to prove that not only is he cunning, flexible, subtle, reasonable, cautious, but also, if necessary, as violent as Ajax, as unreasonable as Achilles, as ruthless as Agamemnon . . . And to whom does he want to prove this? . . . Obviously to Penelope – and so: eureka!"'

I said nothing. Rheingold's argument was very nicely worked out, and fitted in perfectly with his inclination to transform the *Odyssey* into a psychoanalytical case-history. But, precisely because of that, it gave me a feeling of profound repugnance, as though I were confronted with a kind of profanation. In Homer, everything was simple, pure, noble, ingenuous, even the astuteness of Ulysses, poetically contained as it was within the limits of an intellectual superiority. In Rheingold's interpretation, on the other hand, everything was debased to the level of a modern play, full of moralizings and psychologizings. In the meantime Rheingold, extremely pleased with his own exposition, was concluding: 'As you see, Molteni, the film's already there, in all its details . . . all we have to do is to write it down.'

I broke in, almost violently: 'Look here, Rheingold, I don't care for this interpretation of yours at all!'

He opened his eyes very wide, more astonished, one would have said, by my boldness than by my disagreement. 'You don't care for it, my dear Molteni? And why don't you care for it?'

I answered with an effort, but with an assurance that grew steadily as I spoke: 'I don't care for it because your interpretation implies a complete falsification of the original character of Ulysses . . . In the *Odyssey* Ulysses is described, certainly, as a man who is subtle, reasonable, astute if you like, but always within the bounds of honour and dignity . . . He never ceases to be a hero – that is, a brave warrior, a king, an upright husband . . . Your interpretation – if you will allow me to say so, my dear Rheingold – runs the risk of making him into a man without dignity, without honour, without decency . . . apart from the fact that it's much too far removed from the *Odyssey* . . . '

As I spoke, I saw Rheingold's half-moon smile grow narrower and narrower till it faded away altogether. Then he said, in a harsh tone and putting into his voice a Teutonic accent which he generally managed to conceal: 'My dear Molteni, allow me to say that, as usual, you have understood nothing at all!'

'As usual?' I repeated, hurt, with ironical emphasis.

'Yes, as usual,' asserted Rheingold; 'and I say so at once because . . . now listen to me carefully, Molteni.'

'I'm listening, you can be sure of that.'

'I do not wish to make Ulysses, as you seem to imagine, into a man without dignity, or decency, or honour . . . I merely want to make him into the man who appears in the *Odyssey* . . . Who is Ulysses in the *Odyssey*, what does he represent? Ulysses in the *Odyssey* is, simply, civilized man, he represents civilization . . . Amongst all the other heroes who are, to be precise, *non*-civilized men, Ulysses is the only one who *is* civilized . . . And in what does Ulysses' civilized quality consist? It consists in not having prejudices, in always making use of reason, at all costs, even in questions – as you say – of decency, of dignity, of honour . . . in being intelligent, objective, I would almost say scientific . . . Naturally,' Rheingold went on, 'civilization has its inconveniences . . . It forgets, for instance, very easily, the importance that so-called questions of honour have for people who are not civilized . . . Penelope is not a civilized woman, she is a woman of tradition . . . she does not understand reason, she only understands instinct, blood, pride . . . Now listen carefully, Molteni, and try to understand me . . . Civilization, to all those who are not civilized, may appear – in fact often does appear – to be corruption, immorality, lack of principles, cynicism . . . That, for instance, was the complaint that Hitler, a man who was certainly not civilized, had to make against civilization . . . and he too talked a great deal about honour . . . but we know now what Hitler was and what honour meant to *him* . . . In the *Odyssey* – to put it briefly – Penelope represents barbarism and Ulysses civilization . . . D'you know, Molteni, that you, whom I thought to be civilized like Ulysses, argue just like the barbarian Penelope?'

These last words were uttered with a broad and brilliant smile: obviously Rheingold was extremely well pleased with his bright idea of comparing me to Penelope. But I felt this comparison, for some unknown reason, to be quite particularly distasteful. In fact I believe I turned pale with anger, and I said, in a voice that trembled: 'If by civilization you mean that a husband should give a helping hand to the man who is courting his wife, well, my dear Rheingold, in that case I am, and I feel, a barbarian.'

This time, however, much to my surprise, Rheingold

did not lose his temper. 'One moment,' he said, raising his hand; 'you're not being reasonable this morning, Molteni . . . Just like Penelope . . . Now let's do this . . . You go off and have a bathe now, and think it over . . . Then tomorrow morning, come back here and tell me the result of your reflections . . . Is that all right?'

Disconcerted, I answered: 'Yes; that's all right . . . but I doubt if I shall change my mind.'

'You go and think it over,' repeated Rheingold, rising and holding out his hand.

I, too, rose to my feet. Rheingold added serenely: 'I'm sure that tomorrow, when you've thought it over, you'll agree with me.'

'I don't think so,' I replied. And I walked away, down the path towards the hotel.

18

I had not been with Rheingold for more than an hour: the discussion about the *Odyssey* had lasted about that length of time. I had, therefore, the whole day in front of me to 'think it over', as he had expressed it, to make up my mind, in fact, as to whether I accepted his interpretation or not. To tell the truth, as soon as I came out of the hotel, my first thought was by no means to meditate over Rheingold's ideas but rather to chase away even the very memory of them and enjoy the beauty of the day. On the other hand I felt that there was something in Rheingold's ideas that went right outside the limits of film production; something I could not yet define, but which had been revealed to me by my excessively strong reaction. And so, after all, I really should have to 'think it over'. I recalled that, when I left the villa that morning, I had caught a glimpse of a small, lonely cove down below the house, so I decided to go there: there I should be able to take the director's advice and 'think it over'; or, if I preferred, not think about it at all but simply take a swim in the sea.

I took the same path as before, therefore, the path that runs round the island. It was still early, and I met scarcely anyone along the shady track – a few boys whose bare feet, in the surrounding silence, made a soft sound on the brick paving; a couple of little girls who walked along with arms round each other's shoulders, chattering in low voices; two or three old ladies taking their dogs for a walk.

At the lowest point of the path I turned off down the narrow lane that winds along the loneliest and most precipitous part of the island. I walked a little farther and found myself confronted by a fork: a smaller path branched off from the lane, leading to a belvedere perched at the edge of a precipice. I turned into this path and, when I reached the belvedere, looked down. The sea, three hundred feet below, trembled and sparkled in the sun, shifting and changing colour according to the wind, blue in one place, almost violet in another, green farther away. From this remote, silent sea, the perpendicular rocks of the island seemed to be flying to meet me, to be coming upward in swarms, like arrows, their bare points flashing in the sun. Then, all at once, a kind of suicidal exaltation came over me, and I felt I had no further desire to live; and I said to myself that if at that moment I suddenly launched myself into that luminous immensity I should perhaps die in a manner not altogether unworthy of the better part of myself. Yes, I should be killing myself to attain, in death, the purity which in life I had failed to achieve.

The temptation to suicide was genuine, and perhaps, for a moment, my life was really in danger. Then, almost instinctively, I thought of Emilia, wondering how she would receive the news of my death, and suddenly I said to myself: 'You wouldn't be killing yourself because you're tired of life . . . you're not tired of life . . . You would be killing yourself for Emilia!' I was disconcerted by this idea, which, almost maliciously, it seemed, robbed my exaltation of all quality of disinterestedness. Then I went on to ask myself: 'Because of Emilia or for the sake of Emilia? . . . the distinction is important'; and immediately I answered my own question: 'For the sake of Emilia . . . in order to regain her esteem, even in a posthumous way . . . in order to leave her with the remorse of having unjustly despised you.'

No sooner had I formulated this thought, than – as in a children's puzzle, when a number of disordered pieces are put together to form a single design – the picture of my present situation was, in part, completed by this new idea: 'You reacted to Rheingold's theories in that violent manner because in reality it seemed to you that, when he was explaining the relations between Ulysses and Penelope, he was alluding, though he did not know it, to the relations between you and Emilia . . . When Rheingold spoke of Penelope's contempt for Ulysses, you thought of Emilia's contempt for you . . . The truth, in short, annoyed you, and it was against the truth that you protested.'

The picture was still not complete; but now a few more considerations put the last, final touches to it. 'You thought of killing yourself because you're not clear in your own mind . . . in reality, if you want to regain Emilia's esteem, it's not in the least necessary for you to kill yourself . . . much less than that will suffice . . . Rheingold indicated what you ought to do . . . Ulysses, in order to regain Penelope's love, killed the Suitors . . . In theory, you ought to kill Battista . . . but we live in a less violent and uncompromising world than that of the *Odyssey* . . . All you need to do is to throw up the script, break off all relations with Rheingold, and leave again for Rome tomorrow morning . . . Emilia advised you not to throw up the job because, in reality, she *wants* to despise you and wants you, by your behaviour, to confirm her in her contempt . . . but you mustn't take any notice of her advice; you must act, instead, just as – according to Rheingold – Ulysses acted.'

This was, in truth, the whole matter: I had examined my situation from beginning to end, ruthlessly and with complete sincerity. It seemed to me clear that there was now no further need to 'think it over', as Rheingold had advised; I could go straight back to him and announce what was now my immovable decision. But next moment I said to myself that, just because there was now no necessity to 'think it over', I must not do things in a hurry, and so give a wrong impression of rashness and obstinacy. I would go during the afternoon, quite calmly, to Rheingold and tell him what I had decided. When I returned home I would, in the same calm manner, ask Emilia to pack her bags. As for Battista, I decided to say nothing to him; in the morning, when we left, I would leave him a short note, attributing my decision to the fact that my ideas and those of Rheingold were incompatible – which was, indeed, true. Battista was a shrewd man: he would understand, and I should not see him again.

With these thoughts in my mind, and almost without realizing where I was going, I turned into the lane, went along it until I was below the villa, and then started running down a steep, crumbling path towards the little lonely cove of which I had had a glimpse when I came out that morning. I was out of breath when I reached it, and, to recover myself, I stood still for a moment on a rock, looking round. The brief stretch of stony beach was all surrounded by great irregular masses of rock which looked as if they had that very moment come rolling down from the heights above; two rocky promontories closed it in, rising sheer from the green, transparent water which was penetrated by rays of sunlight that showed up the white, pebbly bottom. Then I noticed a black rock, all crannied and corroded and half submerged in sand and water, and thought I would go and lie down behind it to be sheltered from the sun which was already very strong. But no sooner had I walked round it than I caught sight of Emilia lying, quite naked, on the shingle.

To tell the truth, I did not at once recognize her, for her face was hidden by a big straw hat; in fact my first impulse was to retreat, as I thought I had come upon some unknown sun-bather. Then my eye fell on the arm which was stretched out on the pebbles, and, following the arm down to the hand, I recognized on the forefinger a ring in the shape of two little hardstone acorns set in golden husks which I had given Emilia some time before as a birthday present.

I was right behind Emilia and saw her foreshortened. She was naked, as I said, and her clothes were lying beside her on the shingle, a little pile of coloured garments; it seemed impossible that they could have covered that large body. The thing that struck me most, indeed, about Emilia's nudity, from the very first glance, was not this or that detail, but, in general, the size and powerfulness of her body. I knew, of course, that Emilia was no larger than a great many other women; but at that moment her nudity seemed to me immense, as though the sea and sky had lent her some of their vastness. As she was lying flat on her back, her breasts were only vaguely defined by the slight swelling of the stretched-out muscle, but to my eyes they seemed very large, both in outline and in volume and in the rosy circles of the nipples; so did also her hips, spread out over the shingle in strong, comfortable amplitude; so also her belly, that seemed to gather all the light of the sun into its circle of flesh; and so her legs, which, lower than the rest of her body on account of the slope, looked as though they were being pulled downwards by their weight and their length. All of a sudden I wondered what could be the source of this feeling in me of this sense of largeness and power, so profound and so disturbing, and then I realized that it arose from the desire that had been reawakened in me at this unexpected moment. It was a desire which, in its immediacy and urgency, was not so much physical as spiritual, a desire to be united with her, but not with her body, not inside her body; rather, through the medium of her body. I was, to put it briefly, hungry for her; yet the satisfaction of this hunger did not depend on me but only on her, on an act of consent on her part that would reach out to meet my hunger. And I felt that she refused me this consent, although, naked as she was, she appeared by an illusion of the eye to be offering herself to me.

But I could not remain in indefinite contemplation of this forbidden nakedness. I at last took a step forward and said clearly, amid the surrounding silence: 'Emilia!'

She made a rapid, double movement. She threw off her hat, stretched out her hand and snatched a chemise from the pile of clothes, as if to cover herself with it; and at the same time sat up and twisted herself round to look behind her. But when I added, 'It's me, Riccardo,' she at last saw me, and then she dropped the chemise on the shingle. Meanwhile, she remained twisted round in order to see me better. She was afraid first of all, I supposed, that I might be a stranger; but then, seeing that it was I, she judged it no longer necessary to cover herself – as though she were in the presence of someone who actually did not exist. I record this thought, fundamentally absurd though it was, so as to give an exact idea of my state of mind at that moment. It never entered my head that she did not cover herself merely because I was not a stranger, but her husband. I was convinced that I no longer existed for her, at any rate from the sexual point of view, and in that ambiguous gesture of hers I naturally recognized a confirmation of my own non-existence. I said in a low voice: 'I've been standing here looking at you for at least five minutes . . . d'you know, I felt I was seeing you for the first time?'

She said nothing; all she did was to turn a little farther round towards me so as to see me better, at the same time adjusting her dark glasses on her nose with a gesture of indifferent curiosity. I went on: 'D'you mind my staying here, or would you rather I went away?'

I saw her considering me; then, with a calm movement, she stretched herself out in the sun again, saying: 'Stay if you like, as far as I'm concerned – As long as you don't take the sun off me!'

So she really did consider me to be non-existent – nothing but an opaque body that might put itself between the sun and her own, naked body, which, according to my desire, ought on the other hand to have felt itself in relationship with mine and have revealed this relationship in some way, whether by a show of modesty or of alarm. Her indifference disconcerted me in a most painful way; I felt my mouth grow suddenly dry, as though with fear; and I was aware that my face was assuming, against my will, an expression of uneasiness, of bewilderment, of false, distressing assurance. 'It's very pleasant here,' I said; 'I shall take a sunbath too . . .' And, in order to put a good face on it, I sat down at a little distance from her, leaning my back against one of the great lumps of rock.

There followed a very long silence. Endless waves of golden light, gently burning and dazzling, enveloped me, and I could not help half-closing my eyes, with a deep sense of well-being and peace. But I could not pretend to myself that I was there simply for the sun; I felt I could never enjoy it fully unless Emilia loved me. Almost as if I were thinking aloud, I said: 'This place seems purposely made for people who love each other.'

'Yes; doesn't it!' she echoed, without stirring, from under the straw hat which hid her face.

'Not for us, who no longer love each other!'

This time she said nothing. And I remained with my eyes fixed upon her, feeling, at the sight of her, a return of all the desire that had troubled me shortly before, when I had emerged from between the rocks and seen her for the first time.

Intense feelings have in them the virtue of making us pass from feeling to action in a wholly spontaneous fashion, without the concurrence of the will, almost unconsciously. All at once, without my knowing how it had happened, I found myself no longer sitting apart by myself, with my back against a rock, but kneeling beside Emilia, bending over her with my face held close to hers, while she lay motionless and asleep. I don't know how, but I had already removed the hat that hid her face, and, as I prepared to kiss her, I was looking at her mouth as one sometimes looks at a fruit before putting one's teeth into it. It was a large, very full mouth, and the redness of the lipstick upon it looked parched and cracked as though it had been dried up, not by the sun, but by some interior heat. I said to myself that that mouth had not kissed me for a very long time, and that the savour of the kiss, if it was returned by her as she lay thus between waking and sleeping, would be as intoxicating as that of some old, potent liquor. I think I must have gazed at her mouth for at least a minute; then, gradually, I lowered my lips to hers. But I did not immediately kiss her: I paused for a moment with my lips very close to her. I felt the light, quiet breath that came from her nostrils; and also, it seemed to me, the warmth of her burning lips. I knew that behind those lips, inside her mouth – like frozen snow preserved in a fold of sun-scorched earth – lay the coolness of her saliva, as surprising, as refreshing as such snow would be. While I was relishing this foretaste, my lips came truly into contact with Emilia's. The touch did not appear to awaken her, nor to surprise her. I pressed my lips against her, first softly, then more and more strongly; then, seeing that she remained perfectly still, I ventured upon a profounder kiss. This time I felt her mouth slowly opening, as I had hoped – like a shellfish whose valves open at the pulsating movement of some living creature wet with cool sea-water. Slowly, slowly it opened, the lips drawing back over the gums; and at the same time I felt an arm encircling my neck . . .

With a violent jolt, I started and awoke from what must evidently have been a kind of trance induced by the silence and the heat of the sun. In front of me, Emilia was lying on the shingle as before; and her face was still hidden by the straw hat. I realized that I had dreamed the kiss, or, rather, had actually experienced it in that state of delirious hankering which constantly replaces dreary reality with some more attractive illusion. I had kissed her and she had returned my kiss; but the one who had kissed and the one who had returned the kiss were merely a couple of phantoms evoked by desire and entirely dissociated from our two persons as we lay motionless and apart. I looked at Emilia and wondered suddenly: 'Suppose I now tried really to kiss her?' And I answered myself: 'No, you won't try . . . you're paralysed by timidity and by the conscious-ness of her contempt for you.' All at once I said, in a loud voice: 'Emilia!'

'What is it?'

'I fell asleep and dreamed I was kissing you.'

She said nothing. Frightened by her silence, I was anxious to change the subject, so I went on, at random: 'Where's Battista?'

She answered in a quiet voice, from underneath the hat: 'I don't know where he is . . . By the way, he won't be at lunch with us today . . . he's lunching with Rheingold at the beach.'

Before I knew what I was saying, I blurted out: 'Emilia, I saw you yesterday evening, when Battista kissed you in the living-room!'

'I knew you'd seen me . . . I saw you too.' Her voice was quite normal, though slightly muffled by the brim of the hat.

I was disconcerted by the manner in which she received my disclosure; and also, to some extent, by the way in which I myself had made it. The truth of the matter, I thought, was that the stupefying sunshine and the silence of the sea reduced and neutralized our quarrel in a general feeling of vanity and indifference. However, with a great effort, I went on: 'Emilia, you and I must have a talk.'

'Not now . . . I want to lie in the sun and be quiet.'

'This afternoon, then.'

'All right; this afternoon.'

I rose to my feet, and without looking back, walked off towards the path that led to the villa.

19

At lunch we scarcely spoke. Silence seemed to penetrate
inside the villa together with the strong light of noon; the
sky and sea that filled the big windows dazzled us and gave
us a feeling of remoteness, as though all this blueness were
a substantial thing, like a depth of water, and we two were
sitting at the bottom of the sea, separated by luminous,
fluctuating liquid and unable to speak. Moreover, I made
it a point of duty not to embark upon the explanation with
Emilia until the afternoon, as I myself had proposed. It
might be imagined that, in such circumstances, two people
who find themselves sitting face to face with an important
argument hanging between them, do not think of anything
else. But this was certainly not the case with us: I was not
thinking at all of Battista's kiss or of our rleationship; and
I was sure that Emilia was not thinking of them either.
There was, in a sort of way, a continuation of the
suspense, of the torpor, of the indifference that had
prompted me, on the beach that morning, to put off all
explanations till later.

After lunch, Emilia rose and said she was going to rest,
and went out. Left alone, I sat still for a while, looking
through the windows at the clear, luminous line of the
horizon, where the harder blue of the sea joined the deep
blue of the sky. A ship, small and black, was advancing
along this line, like a fly on a taut thread, and I followed it
with my eyes, thinking, absurdly, for some reason, of all
the things that were going on at that moment on board
that ship – sailors polishing brasses or washing the decks;

the cook washing up dishes in his galley; the officers still, perhaps, sitting at table; and, down in the engine-room, half-naked stokers throwing shovelfuls of coal into the furnaces. It was a small ship, and to me, as I looked at it, it was nothing but a black speck; but from close by it was a large object filled with human beings and human destinies. And, conversely, I thought of the people over there looking from their ship at the coast of Capri; their eyes would perhaps be brought to an unwilling halt by an isolated white spot on the coast, and they would not even suspect that that white spot was the villa and that I was inside it and with me was Emilia and we two did not love each other and Emilia despised me and I did not know how to regain her esteem and her love . . .

I became conscious that I was dozing off, and, with an abrupt burst of energy, decided to put into effect the first part of my plan: to go and inform Rheingold that I had 'thought it over' and that, as a result, I would not be collaborating in the script of the film. This decision had the effect upon me of a bucketful of fresh water. Wide awake now, I jumped to my feet and went out of the house.

Half an hour later, having walked rapidly along the path that ran round the island, I entered the hall of the hotel. I sent in my name and went and sat down in an armchair. I felt that my mind was exceedingly lucid, even though with a feverish and somewhat agitated lucidity. But judging from my growing sense of relief – my joy, almost – at the thought of what I was about to do, I knew that I had at last set out upon the right road. After a few minutes Rheingold entered the hall and came over to me with a clouded, surprised expression in which wonder at my having called at that hour appeared to be mingled with the suspicion that he was about to hear some unpleasant news. For politeness' sake, I asked him: 'Perhaps you were asleep, Rheingold . . . and I've woken you up?'

'No, no,' he assured me. 'I wasn't asleep, I never sleep in the afternoon . . . But come this way, Molteni; let's go into the bar.'

I followed him into the bar, which at that hour was deserted. Rheingold, as though anxious to delay the discussion he anticipated, asked me if I would like something to drink – coffee, a liqueur. He made this suggestion with an air of gloom and reserve, like a miser who is forced to provide expensive hospitality against his will. But I knew that the reason was quite a different one: he would have preferred me not to come at all. Anyhow, I refused; and, after a few polite remarks, I embarked without more ado on the main subject. 'You may perhaps be surprised,' I said, 'that I've come back so soon . . . I had a whole day to consider it . . . But there seemed no point in waiting till tomorrow . . . I've thought about it long enough . . . and I came to tell you the result of my reflections.'

'And what is that result?'

'That I cannot collaborate in this film-script . . . in fact, that I am throwing up the job.'

Rheingold did not receive this declaration with any surprise: he was evidently expecting it. But he appeared to be thrown into a kind of agitation. He said at once, in a changed voice: 'Molteni, you and I must speak plainly.'

'It seems to me I have already spoken extremely plainly: I am not going to do the script of the *Odyssey*.'

'And why? . . . Please tell me.'

'Because I do not agree with your interpretation of the subject.'

'In that case,' he retorted, quickly and unexpectedly, 'you agree with Battista!'

204

I do not know why I, in my turn, was irritated by this unforeseen accusation. It had not occurred to me that not to be in agreement with Rheingold meant to be in agreement with Battista! I said angrily: 'What's Battista got to do with it? . . . I don't agree with Battista either . . . But I tell you frankly, Rheingold, if I had to choose between the two, I should prefer Battista every time . . . I'm sorry, Rheingold: as far as I'm concerned, either one does the *Odyssey* of Homer or else one doesn't do it at all.'

'A masquerade in Technicolor with naked women, King Kong, stomach dances, brassières, cardboard monsters, model sets!'

'I didn't say that: I said the *Odyssey* of Homer!'

'But the *Odyssey* of Homer is *mine*,' he said with profound conviction, bending forwards. 'It's *mine*, Molteni!'

For some unexplained reason I was conscious, all at once, of a desire to offend Rheingold: his false, ceremonious smile, his real dictatorial hardness, his psychoanalytical obtuseness, all became at that moment intolerable to me. I said furiously: 'No; Homer's *Odyssey* is not yours, Rheingold . . . And I'll say more, since you force me to it: I find Homer's *Odyssey* altogether enchanting and yours altogether repulsive!'

'Molteni!' This time Rheingold appeared really indignant.

'Yes; to me it's repulsive,' I went on, becoming heated now; 'this desire of yours to reduce, to debase the Homeric hero just because we're incapable of making him as Homer created him, this operation of systematic degradation is repulsive to me, and I'm not going to take part in it at any price.'

'Molteni . . . one moment, Molteni!'

205

'Have you read James Joyce's *Ulysses*?' I interrupted him angrily. 'Do you know who Joyce is?'

'I've read everything that concerns the *Odyssey*,' replied Rheingold in a deeply offended tone, 'but you . . .'

'Well,' I continued passionately, 'Joyce also interpreted the *Odyssey* in the modern manner . . . and he went much farther than you do, my dear Rheingold, in the job of modernization – that is, of debasement, of degradation, of profanation . . . He made Ulysses a cuckold, an onanist, an idler, a capricious, incompetent creature . . . and Penelope a retired whore . . . Aeolus became a newspaper editor, the descent into the infernal regions the funeral of a boon companion, Circe a visit to a brothel, and the return to Ithaca the return home at dead of night through the streets of Dublin, with a stop or two on the way to piss in a dark corner . . . But at least Joyce had the discernment not to bring in the Mediterranean, the sea, the sun, the sky, the unexplored lands of antiquity . . . He placed the whole story in the muddy streets of a northern city, in taverns and brothels, in bedrooms and lavatories . . . No sunshine, no sea, no sky . . . everything modern, in other words debased, degraded, reduced to our own miserable stature . . . But you – you lack Joyce's discretion . . . and therefore, I repeat, between you and Battista, I prefer Battista, in spite of all his papiermâché . . . Yes, I prefer Battista . . . You wanted to know why I don't wish to do this script . . . Now you do know!'

I fell back in my armchair, damp with sweat. Rheingold was now looking at me with a hard, serious expression and a deep frown. 'You do, in fact, agree with Battista,' he said.

'No; I do *not* agree with Battista . . . I *dis*agree with him.'

'On the contrary,' said Rheingold suddenly, raising his

voice, 'you're *not* in disagreement with me . . . and you *are* in agreement with Battista.'

All at once I felt the blood leave my cheeks and knew that I had gone deathly pale. 'What d'you mean?' I asked in an uneven voice.

Rheingold leant forward and hissed (that is the only word for it) just like a snake when it sees itself threatened: 'I mean what I said . . . Battista came to lunch with me today, and he did not conceal his ideas from me, nor the fact that you share them . . . You are *not* in disagreement with me, Molteni, and you *are* in agreement with Battista, whatever Battista may desire . . . To you, art does not matter; all you want is to be paid . . . That's the truth of it, Molteni . . . all you want is to be paid, at any cost!'

'Rheingold!' I cried all of a sudden, in a loud voice.

'Oh yes, I understand, my dear sir,' he insisted, 'and I repeat it to your face: at any cost!'

We were face to face now, breathless, I as white as paper and he scarlet. 'Rheingold!' I repeated, still in the same loud, clear voice; but I became aware that it was not so much scorn that was now expressed in my voice as a kind of obscure pain, and that that cry: 'Rheingold!' contained a prayer rather than the anger of an offended person who is on the point of passing from verbal to physical violence. Yet at the same time I was conscious of the fact that I was going to hit him. I had no time. Rheingold – strangely, for I thought him an obtuse kind of man – appeared to discern the pain in my voice and, all of a sudden, seemed to check and control himself. He drew back a little and said, in a low, deliberately humble tone: 'Excuse me, Molteni . . . I said things I didn't mean . . .'

I made an agitated gesture, as much as to say 'I excuse you', and felt at the same time that my eyes were filling with tears. After a moment's embarrassment Rheingold resumed: 'All right, it's understood, then . . . You won't take part in the script . . . Have you told Battista yet?'

'No.'

'Are you intending to tell him?'

'Please tell him yourself . . . I don't think I shall see Battista again.' I was silent a moment, and then I added: 'And tell him also to start looking for another script-writer . . . Let it be quite clear, Rheingold.'

'What?' he asked in astonishment.

'That I shall not do any script of the *Odyssey* either according to your ideas, or according to Battista's ideas . . . either with you, or with any other director . . . D'you understand, Rheingold?'

He understood, at last, and a light of comprehension came into his eyes. Nevertheless, he asked cautiously: 'To put it shortly, is it that you don't want to do *my* script, or that you don't want to do this script in any way at all?'

After a moment's reflection, I said: 'I've already told you: I don't want to do *your* script . . . However, I quite realize, on the other hand, that if I account for my refusal in that way, I should do you harm in the eyes of Battista . . . Let's put it like this, then: for you, it's *your* script I don't want to do . . . but, for Battista, let it be understood that I don't want to do the script *whatever* interpretation may be given to the subject . . . Tell Battista, then, that I don't feel like it, that I'm tired, that my nerves are worn out . . . Is that all right?'

Rheingold appeared at once to be much relieved by my suggestion. He insisted, nevertheless: 'And will Battista believe it?'

'He'll believe it, don't worry . . . you'll see, he'll believe it.'

A long silence ensued. We both felt embarrassed now:

our recent quarrel still hung in the air and neither of us could quite manage to forget it. At last Rheingold said: 'Yet I'm very sorry you're not going to collaborate in this work, Molteni . . . Perhaps we might have come to an agreement.'

'I don't think so.'

'Perhaps the differences were not so great, after all.'

Feeling perfectly calm now, I said firmly: 'No, Rheingold, they were very great indeed . . . It may be that you're right to see the *Odyssey* in that way . . . but I myself am convinced that, even today, the *Odyssey* could be made as Homer wrote it . . .'

'That's an aspiration on your part, Molteni . . . You aspire after a world like that of Homer . . . you would like it to be so . . . but unfortunately it isn't!'

I said conciliatingly: 'Let's leave it at that, then: I aspire after that sort of world . . . You, on the other hand, do not!'

'Oh yes, I do, Molteni . . . who doesn't? But when it's a question of making a film, aspirations are not enough.'

There was a further silence. I looked at Rheingold and realized that, even though he understood my reasons, he was still not altogether convinced. Suddenly I asked him; 'No doubt you know the Ulysses canto in Dante, Rheingold?'

'Yes,' he answered, a little surprised at my question, 'I know it . . . but I don't remember it exactly.'

'Do you mind if I recite it to you? I know it by heart.'

'Please do, if you care to.'

I did not know precisely why I wanted to recite this passage from Dante – perhaps, I thought afterwards, because it seemed to me the best way of repeating certain things to Rheingold without running the risk of offending him afresh. While the director was settling himself in his armchair, his face assuming a submissive expression, I added: 'In this canto Dante makes Ulysses relate his own end and that of his companions . . .'

'Yes, I know, Molteni, I know; recite it then.'

I concentrated my thoughts for a moment, looking down on the floor, and then began: *Lo maggior corno della fiamma antica'* – continuing steadily in a normal voice and, as far as I could, without emphasis. Rheingold, after considering me for a moment, with a frown, from beneath the peak of his cloth cap, turned his eyes in the direction of the sea and sat without moving. I went on with my recitation, speaking slowly and clearly. But at the line: *'O frati, dissi, che per cento milia . . .'* I felt that my voice, in spite of myself, was trembling with sudden emotion. I considered how there was contained, in those few lines, not merely the idea I had formed of the figure of Ulysses, but also of myself and of my life as it ought to have been and, alas, was not; and I realized that my emotion arose from the clarity and beauty of this idea in comparison with my own actual powerlessness. However I more or less succeeded in controlling the tremor in my voice and went on, without stumbling, to the very last line: *'Infin che il mar fu sopra noi richiuso.'* The moment I had finished I jumped to my feet. Rheingold also rose from his armchair.

'Allow me, Molteni,' he said at once, hastily, 'allow me to ask you . . . Why did you recite this fragment of Dante to me? . . . For what purpose? It's very beautiful, of course – but why?'

'This, Rheingold,' I said, 'this is the Ulysses I should have liked to create . . . this is how I see Ulysses . . . Before leaving you I wanted to confirm it unmistakably . . . I felt I could do this better by reciting the passage from Dante than in my own words.'

'Better, of course . . . but Dante is Dante: a man of the Middle Ages . . . You, Molteni, are a modern man.'

I did not answer this time, but put out my hand. He understood, and added: 'All the same, Molteni, I shall be very sorry to do without your collaboration . . . I was already getting accustomed to you.'

'Some other time, perhaps,' I answered. 'I should have liked to work with you, too, Rheingold.'

'But why, then? Why, Molteni . . . ?'

'Fate,' I said with a smile, shaking his hand. And I walked away. He remained standing beside the counter, in the bar, his arms outstretched as if to repeat: 'Why?'

I hurried out of the hotel.

20

I returned home as hurriedly as I had come; and with a feeling of impatience and of pugnacious elation which prevented me from reflecting calmly over what had happened. In fact, as I ran along the narrow ribbon of cement under the burning sun, I did not think of anything. The deadlock in an unbearable situation had already lasted too long, and now I knew I had broken it; I was aware, too, that in a short time I should at last know why it was that Emilia had ceased to love me; but beyond the establishment of these facts I could not go. Reflection belongs either to the moment after, or to the moment before, the taking of action. During the time of action we are guided by reflections already past and forgotten, which have been transformed in our minds into passions. I was acting; therefore I was not thinking. I knew that I should think later, when action was over.

When I reached the villa, I ran up the stairs leading to the terrace and went into the living-room. It was empty, but a magazine lying open in an armchair, some red-stained cigarette-stumps in the ash-tray, and the sound of subdued dance-music coming from the radio indicated to me that Emilia had been there until a few moments before. And all of a sudden, owing perhaps to the softened, pleasing brilliance of the afternoon light, perhaps to the discreet music, I felt my anger subsiding, though the causes which had inspired it, remained firm and clear. I was struck, particularly, by the comfortable, serene, familiar, inhabited look of the room. It looked as if we had been living in the villa for months, and as if Emilia had become accustomed by now to regarding it as her settled abode. The radio, the magazine, the cigarette-stumps, all reminded me, for some reason, of her old love of home, of the pathetic yearning, wholly instinctive and feminine, that she had had for a hearth. a stable resting-place of her own. I saw that, notwithstanding all that had happened, she was preparing for a long stay, and that she was, in reality, pleased to be at Capri, in Battista's house. And now, instead, I was coming to tell her that we had to go away again.

Thoughtfully I went to the door of Emilia's room and opened it. She was not there; but here too I noticed signs of her domestic instinct – the dressing-gown carefully laid out on the armchair at the foot of the bed, the slippers placed neatly beside it; the numerous little bottles and pots and other accessories of beauty tidily arranged on the dressing-table, in front of the mirror; on the bedside table a single book, an English grammar, the study of which she had embarked upon some time before, and with it an exercise-book, a pencil, and a small bottle; and no trace at all of the many suitcases she had brought from Rome. Almost by instinct I opened the wardrobe: Emilia's dresses – not very many of them – were hanging in a row on coat-hangers; on a shelf were arranged handkerchiefs large and small, belts, ribbons, a few pairs of shoes. Yes, I thought, it did not really matter to Emilia whether she loved me or loved Battista: what mattered more than anything was to have a house of her own, to be able to count upon a long, quiet stay, without worries of any kind.

I left the room and went along a short passage towards the kitchen, which was in a little annexe at the back of the house. When I reached the threshold, I heard the voice of Emilia in conversation with the cook. I stopped,

213

automatically, behind the open door and listened for a moment.

Emilia was giving the cook instructions for our dinner that evening, as I immediately realized. 'Signor Molteni,' she was saying, 'likes plain cooking, without a lot of gravies and sauces – just boiled or roast, in fact . . . It'll be better for you; you'll have less to do, Agnesina.'

'Well, signora, there's always plenty to do . . . Even plain cooking isn't as plain as all that . . . What shall we have this evening, then?'

There was a short pause. Evidently Emilia was reflecting. Then she asked: 'Would there still be any fish at this time of day?'

'Yes; if I go to the fishmonger who serves the hotels.'

'Well, then, buy a nice big fish – two or three pounds, or even more . . . But it must be a good-quality fish, without too many bones . . . a *dentice*, or, better still, a *spigola* . . . in fact, the best you can get . . . And I think you'd better bake it . . . or boil it . . . You know how to make *mayonnaise* sauce, Agnesina?'

'Yes; I do.'

'All right . . . then if you boil it, make some *mayonnaise* . . . and then a salad, or some kind of cooked vegetables – carrots or *aubergines* or French beans . . . whatever you can find . . . And fruit, plenty of fruit . . . and put the fruit on the ice as soon as you get back from your shopping, so that it will be very cool when it's served . . .'

'And what shall we do about a first course?'

'Oh yes, there's the first course too! . . . Let's have something quite simple for this evening. Buy some ham – but be sure you get the best quality . . . and let's have some figs with it . . . There *are* figs to be got?'

'Yes; you can get figs.'

I don't know why, but while I was listening to this domestic conversation, so quiet, so easily foreseeable, I suddenly remembered the last words I had exchanged with Rheingold. He had said that I aspired after a world like that of the *Odyssey*; and I had agreed with him; and then he had retorted that this aspiration of mine could never be satisfied, that the modern world was not the world of the *Odyssey*. And now I thought: 'Yet here is a situation that might have occurred just as well thousands of years ago, in the days of Homer . . . the mistress talking to her serving-maid, giving her instructions for the evening meal.' This idea recalled to my mind the lovely afternoon light, radiant but soft, which filled the living-room, and, as though by enchantment, it seemed to me that Battista's villa was the house in Ithaca, and that Emilia was Penelope, in the act of speaking to her servant. Yes, I was right; everything was, or might have been, as it was then; and yet everything was so bitterly different. With an effort, I put my head in at the door and said: 'Emilia.'

She scarcely turned, asking: 'What is it?'

'You know . . . I want to talk to you.'

'Go and wait in the living-room . . . I'm not finished with Agnesina yet . . . I'll be there in a minute.'

I went back into the living-room, sat down in an armchair and waited. I now had a feeling of remorse in anticipation of what I was going to do: Emilia, to all appearances, was expecting to stay a long time at the villa; and I, on the other hand, was about to announce our departure. I remembered at this point, how she, not so many days before, had made up her mind to leave me; and, comparing her almost desperate attitude that day with her present serene bearing, I thought that after all she must have decided to live with me, even if she did despise me. In other words, she was still, at that time, rebelling against an intolerable situation, whereas now she accepted it. And yet this acceptance was far more offensive to me than any kind of rebellion; it indicated, in her, a decline, a collapse, as though now she despised not only me but herself as well. This idea sufficed to banish the slight feeling of remorse from my mind. Yes, indeed, both for my sake and for hers, we had to leave, and I had to announce our departure to her.

I waited a little longer; then Emilia came in, went and turned off the radio and sat down. 'You said you wanted to talk to me.'

'Have you unpacked?' I asked in return.

'Yes. Why?'

'I'm sorry,' I said, 'but you'll have to pack again . . . We're going back to Rome tomorrow morning.'

She remained quite motionless for a moment, hesitating, as though she had not understood. Then, in a harsh voice, she asked: 'What's happened now?'

'What's happened,' I replied, rising from my armchair and going over to shut the door that led into the passage, 'is that I've decided not to do the script . . . I'm throwing up the whole thing . . . And so we're going back to Rome.'

She seemed to be really exasperated by this piece of news. Frowning, she enquired: 'And why have you decided to refuse this job?'

I answered dryly: 'I'm surprised that you should ask . . . It seems to me that, after what I saw through the window yesterday evening, I could hardly do otherwise.'

She at once objected, coldly: 'Yesterday evening you were of a different opinion . . . and you'd already seen.'

'Yesterday evening I allowed myself to be persuaded by your arguments . . . but afterwards I saw that I ought not

216

to take them into account . . . I don't know for what reason you advise me to do the script, nor do I wish to know . . . I only know that it's better for me, and for you too, that I shouldn't do it!'

'Does Battista know?' she asked unexpectedly.

'No, he doesn't,' I replied; 'but Rheingold does . . . I've just been to see him and I told him.'

'You've made a very great mistake.'

'Why?'

'Because,' she said, in an uncertain, discontented tone of voice, 'we need this money to pay the instalments on the flat . . . Besides, you yourself have said, over and over again, that to break a contract means cutting yourself off from other jobs . . . You've made a bad mistake: you shouldn't have done it.'

I, in turn, became irritated. 'But don't you understand,' I cried, 'don't you understand that my situation has become intolerable . . . that I cannot go on taking money from the man . . . from the man who is in the process of seducing my wife?'

She said nothing. I went on: 'I am refusing the job because it would not be decent for me to accept it, in the present circumstances . . . but I am refusing it also for your sake, on account of you, in order that you may change your opinion about me . . . You – I don't know why – at present consider me a man capable of accepting a job under such conditions . . . Well, you're wrong . . . I'm not that sort of man!'

I saw a hostile, malicious light come into her eyes. 'If you're doing it for your own sake, well, I don't know . . . but if you're doing it because of me, you still have time to change your mind . . . You would be doing a useless thing, I assure you . . . it would serve no purpose except to damage yourself – that would be all.'

'What d'you mean?'

'I mean just what I say – that it would serve no purpose.'

I felt cold about the temples, and knew I was turning pale. 'And so – ?'

'You tell me first what effect this sacrifice of yours is supposed to have on me.'

I realized that the moment of final explanation had arrived. It was she herself who was offering it to me. And all of a sudden I had a feeling of fear. I began, nevertheless: 'You said, some time ago, that . . . that you despised me . . . that was what you said . . . I don't know why you despise me. . . . I only know that people get themselves despised when they do despicable things. . . . Accepting this job, at the present moment, would in fact be a despicable thing . . . and so my decision will prove to you, more than anything, that I am not what you believe me to be – that's all.'

She answered promptly in a tone of triumph, pleased, one would have thought, at having at last made me fall into a trap: 'On the contrary, your decision won't prove anything to me . . . that's why I advise you to go back on it.'

'What d'you mean, it won't prove anything?' I had sat down again and, with an almost automatic gesture, in which my distress was visibly expressed, I put out my hand and took hers as it lay on the arm of the chair. 'Emilia, tell me that.'

She pulled her hand away awkwardly. 'Please leave all that alone . . . in fact. . . please don't touch me, don't try and touch me again. . . . I don't love you and it will never be possible for me to love you again.'

I withdrew my hand and said in a resentful voice: 'Don't let's talk about our love; never mind that . . . let's talk

218

instead about your . . . your contempt . . . Even if I refuse the job you'll go on despising me?'

Suddenly she jumped to her feet, as though seized by a violent impatience. 'Yes, certainly I'll go on . . . And now let me alone.'

'But why do you despise me?'

'Because I do,' she cried all at once; 'because you're made like that, and however hard you try, you can't change yourself.'

'But how am I made?'

'I don't know how you're made – *you* ought to know . . . I only know you're not a man, you don't behave like a man.'

I was struck by the contrast between the genuineness, the sincerity of feeling that sounded in her voice and the common-place, sweeping nature of her words. 'But what does it mean to be a *man*?' I demanded, with a rage in which irony was mingled. 'Don't you realize it means nothing at all?'

'Nonsense – you know perfectly well.'

She had gone over to the window now, and her back was turned to me as she spoke. I clasped my head in my hands and gazed at her for a moment in despair. She had turned her back upon me, not only physically, but also, as it were, with the whole of her mind. She had no wish to explain herself, or perhaps, I suddenly thought, she was unable to do so. Clearly some reason for her contempt existed; but it was not so clear that she was able to indicate it precisely; and so she preferred to attribute her feeling of contempt to some original, innately despicable quality in me, a quality that was motiveless and therefore irremediable. All at once I remembered Rheingold's interpretation of the relationship between Ulysses and Penelope, and a sudden enlightenment made me wonder: 'Supposing

Emilia had had the impression that during these last months I knew Battista was paying court to her, that I was trying to take advantage of it, and, in fact, that instead of expostulating, I was sanctioning Battista's purposes for my own interest?' The impact of this idea left me breathless; even more so because I now recalled certain ambiguous episodes which might have confirmed her in such a suspicion; amongst others, my own lateness, the first evening we had gone out with Battista – due, in reality, to a taxi mishap, but which she might have attributed to a clever plan for leaving her alone with him. As if to corroborate my reflections, she suddenly said, without turning round: 'A man who is really a man would not, for example, have behaved as you did yesterday evening, after seeing what you saw . . . But you came to me, as if butter wouldn't melt in your mouth, and asked me my opinion, pretending not to have seen anything . . . in the hope that I would advise you to go on with the script . . . and I gave you the advice you wanted and you accepted it . . . Then, today, goodness knows what happened with that German, and you come and tell me you're giving up the job for my sake, because I despise you and you don't want me to despise you. But I know you, by this time; and of course I can see that it's not you who've given up the job, but he who made you give it up . . . Anyhow, it's too late . . . I've made up my mind about you, and you can give up all the jobs in the world and I shan't change it . . . So don't make such a fuss about it now; accept the job and leave me in peace, once and for all.'

So here we are, back at the beginning again, I could not help thinking: she despised me, but refused to tell me the reason. It was deeply repugnant to me to try and formulate the reason myself, both because the reason itself would inevitably be repugnant to me, and also because, in formulating it, I should feel I was in some way accepting its validity. However I intended to get to the bottom of this question, and there was nothing else to be done. I said, as calmly as I could: 'Emilia, you despise me and you won't tell me why . . . perhaps you don't even know yourself . . . But I have a right to know, so that I can explain to you that it isn't true, and so that I can justify myself . . . Now listen: If *I* tell you the reason for your contempt, will you promise me that you'll tell me whether it's true or not?'

She was still standing in front of the window, with her back to me, and for a moment she said nothing. Then, in a tired, irritable voice, she said: 'I don't promise anything . . . Oh, do leave me alone!'

'The reason is this,' I said very slowly, as though I were spelling it out. 'You have imagined, on a basis of deceptive appearances, that I . . . that I knew about Battista, and that, for my own interest, I preferred to close my eyes – that, in fact, I actually tried to push you into his arms . . . isn't that so?'

I raised my eyes in her direction, as she stood with her back towards me, and awaited her answer. But no answer came: she was gazing at something on the other side of the window-panes, and she did not speak. All at once I felt myself blushing right up to the ears, in sudden shame at what I had said; and I saw that, as I had feared, the actual fact of my having said it could not but be interpreted by her as yet another proof of a valid foundation for her contempt. In desperation, I added hastily: 'But if this is true, Emilia, I can swear to you that you're wrong . . . I never knew anything about Battista until yesterday evening . . . Of course you're at liberty to believe me or not to believe me . . . but if you don't believe me, it means that you want to be able to despise me at all costs, that you want *not* to be convinced, that you want me *not* to be able to justify myself.'

Once again she did not speak; and I saw I had hit the mark. Perhaps she really did not know why she despised me, and in any case preferred not to know but to continue looking upon me as a contemptible figure – just like that, without reasons, without any reference to my behaviour, just as one might happen to have dark hair or blue eyes. I saw also that I had not achieved the effect I desired; but, I thought, innocence does not always succeed in being convincing. Urged on by an impulse beyond control, I felt the necessity of adding a physical argument to my words. I rose and went over to her – she was still standing by the window, looking out – and seized her by the arm, saying: 'Emilia, why do you hate me so? . . . Why can't you let things go, even for a moment?'

I noticed that she turned her face aside, as if to hide it. But she allowed me to hold her arm; and, when I came close to her, so that my side was touching hers she did not draw back. Then I grew bolder and put my arm round her waist. At last she turned, and I saw that her whole face was wet with tears. 'I shall never forgive you,' she cried; 'never shall I forgive you for having ruined our love . . . I loved you so much, and I'd never loved anyone but you . . . and I shall never love anyone else . . . and you've ruined everything because of your character . . . We might have been so happy together . . . and instead of that, it's all quite impossible now . . . How can I possibly let things go? How can I possibly not dislike you?'

A faint hope was born in me: after all, she was saying that she had loved me, that she had never loved anyone but me. 'Now listen,' I suggested, seeking to draw her to me. 'You go and pack now, and we'll leave tomorrow morning . . . and when we get to Rome I'll explain

222

everything to you . . . and you'll be convinced. I'm sure of that.'

This time she freed herself, almost furiously, from my grasp. 'I'm not going,' she cried. 'What's the point of my going back to Rome? I should have to leave the flat, and, since my mother doesn't want me, I should have to go and live in a furnished room and become a typist again . . . No, I'm not going . . . I'm staying here . . . I need quiet and rest, and I'm staying here . . . You go, if you want to . . . I'm staying here . . . Battista told me I could stay as long as I like . . . so I'm staying.'

Now I became furious too. 'You're going with me,' I cried. 'Tomorrow morning.'

'You poor thing, you're quite wrong; I'm staying here.'

'Then I shall stay here too . . . and I shall see to it that Battista turns us out of the house, both of us.'

'No you won't.'

'Yes; I shall.'

She looked at me for a moment; then, without saying a word, she left the room. The door of her bedroom banged violently; and then I heard the sound of the key being turned in the lock.

21

And so I now found myself bound by a declaration made in
a moment of anger: 'I shall stay here.' In truth, as I realized
after Emilia had left the room, it was impossible for me to
stay there any longer: the one person who had to leave was,
in fact, myself. I had broken off relations with Rheingold, I
had broken off relations with Battista, and now, in all
probability, I had broken them off with Emilia too. I had
become – to put it briefly – superfluous, and it was up to
me to go. But I had cried to Emilia that I intended to stay,
and in my heart, whether as a last hope, or out of pique, I
felt I wanted to stay. Such a situation, in other circumstances, would have been positively ridiculous; but, in my
desperate state of mind, it was deeply distressing: it was
like that of a mountaineer who having reached a particularly dangerous point in his ascent, realizes that he can
neither stay where he is, nor go backward nor forward. In a
sudden access of anxiety and agitation, I started walking up
and down the room, wondering what I ought to do. I knew
that I could not sit down to dinner that evening with Emilia
and Battista as though nothing had happened; I thought for
a moment of going to dine in Capri village and not coming
home till late; but I had already been four times that day
over the path leading thither from the house, each time at a
run, each time under a burning sun, and I felt tired and had
no desire to face it again. I looked at the clock: it was six.
There were still at least two hours before dinner. What
should I do? At last I made up my mind. I went to my own
room and turned the key in the lock.

I closed the shutters and, in the dark, threw myself on the bed. I was truly tired, and, as soon as I lay down, I felt that my limbs were instinctively seeking the best positions for sleep. At that moment I was grateful to my body, which was wiser than my mind and gave, without effort, its own mute response to the painful question: What shall I do? After a few moments I fell into a deep sleep.

I slept for some time, dreamlessly; then I awoke and, from the complete darkness that surrounded me, judged that it must be very late. I got up from the bed, went over to the window and threw it open, and saw that night had indeed fallen. I turned on the light and looked at my watch: it was nine o'clock. I had been asleep for three hours. Dinner, I knew, was at eight, or at latest, half past eight. Again I was faced with the question: What should I do? But now I felt rested, and the question at once found its own confident, light-hearted answer: 'I am in the villa; I have no reason to hide myself; I shall present myself at the dinner table and let come what may.' I even felt quite warlike and ready for a quarrel with Battista and, as I had threatened, prepared to act in such a way that he would turn Emilia and me out of the house. Quickly I tidied myself and left the room.

But the living-room was deserted, although the table was laid, in the usual corner. I noticed that it was laid for one person only. Almost immediately, to confirm my growing suspicions, the servant appeared in the doorway to tell me that Battista and Emilia had gone off to dine in the village. If I wished, I could join them at the Restaurant Bellavista. Otherwise I could dine at home; dinner, in fact, had been ready for half an hour.

I saw that Battista and Emilia had also put the question to themselves: What is to be done? And that they had solved the problem with the greatest ease, by going away

225

and leaving me master of the field. This time, however, I felt neither jealousy nor annoyance nor disappointment. It seemed to me, on the contrary – and not without a feeling of considerable sadness – that they had done the only thing they could do, and that I ought to be grateful to them for having avoided an unpleasant encounter. I realized also that this tactic of absence and emptiness was intended to make me go away; and that if they continued to make use of it on the ensuing days, they would undoubtedly succeed in their purpose. But that was a matter for the still uncertain future. I told the servant to serve me, that I would dine at home; and sat down at the table.

I ate little and unwillingly, tasting no more than one slice of ham out of the many that covered the dish, and a small piece of the big fish that Emilia had ordered for the three of us. My dinner was over in a few minutes. I told the servant to go to bed, as I should not need her again. And then I went out on to the terrace.

There were some deck-chairs in a corner. I unfolded one and sat down beside the balustrade, facing the dark, invisible sea.

I had promised myself, on my way back to the villa after my meeting with Rheingold, that I would reflect calmly over everything after I had talked to Emilia. At that moment I had realized that I still knew nothing about the reasons for which she had ceased to love me; but it certainly did not enter my head that, even after I had had my explanation with her, I should continue to be ignorant of them. On the contrary, I was sure – albeit without reason – that the explanation would bring about a clarification which would in some way reduce and mitigate an issue in which, hitherto, I had seen only a frightening obscurity; so that, in the end, I should be forced to exclaim: 'Is that all? . . . And is it for so unimportant a reason that you refuse to love me any more?'

But, instead of this, things had turned out exactly as I had not expected them to turn out; the explanation had taken place – or at least such explanation as was possible between us two – and I knew just as much as I had known before. Worse still: I had discovered that the reason for Emilia's contempt could quite possibly be established through an examination of our past relations; yet she herself was not disposed to recognize this and wished, in her heart, to go on despising me without a reason, thus depriving me of all possibility of exculpating and justifying myself, and shutting herself off, on her side, from any possible return to esteem and love of me.

I realized, in short, that in Emilia the feeling of contempt had preceded, by a long way, any justifications for it, either real or imaginary, that I might have provided by my behaviour. The contempt had been born out of the daily proximity of our two characters, regardless of any important, recognizable test, in the same way as the purity of a precious metal is established by contact with the touchstone. And indeed, when I had hazarded the theory that her ceasing to love me might have had its origin in a mistaken estimate, on her part, of my demeanour towards Battista, she had neither accepted nor rejected it, but had taken refuge in silence. In reality, I thought suddenly, with a stab of pain, she had considered me, from the start, to be capable of this and of even more; and all she asked was that I, by my theories, should confirm her in her feeling. In other words, in Emilia's attitude towards me there was an appraisement of my worth, an estimate of my character, quite independent of my actions. The latter, it so happened, had appeared to confirm her appraisement and her estimate; but, even without such a confirmation, she would not, in all probability, have judged me differently.

And indeed the proof, if there was any need of one, lay in the mysterious strangeness of her conduct. She could, from the very beginning, have dissipated the cruel misunderstanding upon which our love had been wrecked, by talking to me, by telling me of it, by opening her heart to me. But she had not done this, because – as I had cried out to her a short time before – she did not really want to be undeceived, she wanted to go on despising me.

Up till now I had been lying in the deck-chair. But, in the uncontrollable agitation which these thoughts caused in me, I rose almost automatically and went and stood by the parapet with my hands resting on it. I wanted, perhaps, to calm myself by contemplating the calmness of the night. But, as I held up my burning face to catch a faint puff of air that seemed to breathe from the surface of the sea, I thought suddenly that I did not deserve such relief. And I realized that a man who is despised neither can nor ought to find peace as long as the contempt endures. He may say, like the sinners at the Last Judgement: 'Mountains, fall on us, and hills, cover us'; but contempt follows him even into the remotest hiding-places, for it has entered into his spirit and he bears it about with him wherever he may go.

I went back, then, and lay down again in the deck-chair, and with a trembling hand lit a cigarette. It seemed to me, however, that, whether I was despicable or not – and I was convinced that I was not – I still retained my intelligence, a quality which even Emilia recognized in me and which was my whole pride and justification. I was bound to think, whatever the object of my thought might be; it was my duty to exercise my intelligence fearlessly in the presence of any kind of mystery. If I abandoned the exercise of my intelligence, there was indeed nothing left to me but the disheartening sense of my own supposed, but unproved, despicableness.

And so I started to think again, in a manner both determined and lucid. In what could it consist, this despicableness of mine? There returned to my mind now, inescapably, the words with which Rheingold, without realizing it, had described my position in relation to Emilia, thinking, instead, to describe that of Ulysses in relation to Penelope: 'Ulysses is the civilized man, Penelope the primitive woman.' Rheingold, in short, after having, by his strained interpretation of the *Odyssey*, unintentionally precipitated the supreme crisis in my relations with Emilia, had then consoled me – rather in the manner of Achilles' spear which first wounded and then healed – by informing me, by means of the same interpretation, that I was not despicable, but civilized. I was aware that this consolation was valid enough, if only I was willing to accept it. I was, in effect, the civilized man who, in a primitive situation – a crime in which honour is concerned – refuses to resort to the knife; the civilized man who prefers to use reason even in face of things that are sacred and considered as such. But no sooner had I shaped it in my own mind than I realized that such an explanation – a 'historical' explanation, let us call it – could never satisfy me. Apart from the fact that I was not at all sure that the relationship between Emilia and me really resembled the one the film director had imagined in the case of Ulysses and Penelope, this explanation, valid, no doubt, in the historical field, was not so in the highly intimate and individual realm of conscience, which is outside time and space. Here it is only our own interior spirit that can dictate laws. History could not justify or absolve me except in the sphere proper to itself, which, in the situation in which I found myself, whatever the 'historical' reasons for it may have been, was not really the sphere in which I desired to operate and to live.

Why, then, had Emilia ceased to love me? Why did she despise me? And, above all, why did she feel the need to despise me? Suddenly there came back to me the phrase she had used, 'Because you're not a man', which had struck me because of its sweeping, commonplace character in contrast with the genuine, frank tone in which it had been pronounced; and it seemed to me that the phrase perhaps contained the key to Emilia's attitude towards me. There was, in fact, in that phrase, a negative indication of Emilia's own ideal image of a man who – to use her own words – was a man: that is to say, of what, according to her, I was not and never could be. Yet on the other hand the phrase, so sweeping, so slovenly in character, itself suggested that this ideal image had not arisen in Emilia's mind from any conscious experience of human values, but rather from the conventions of the world in which she had found herself living. In that world, a man 'who was a man' was, for instance, assuredly Battista, with his animal-like force and his gross successes. That this was true had been proved to me by the looks almost of admiration that she had directed towards him at table, the day before; and by her having finally surrendered to his desires, even if only out of desperation. In fact, Emilia despised me and wished to despise me because, in spite of her genuineness and simplicity, or rather just because of them, she was completely ensnared in the commonplaces of Battista's world; and amongst these commonplaces was the supposed inability of the poor man to be independent of the rich man, or in other words, to 'be a man'. I did not know for certain whether Emilia really suspected me of having, out of self-interest, favoured Battista's aims; but, if this was true, she must clearly have thought on these lines: 'Riccardo depends on Battista, he is paid by Battista, he hopes to get more work from Battista; Battista is paying court to me, therefore Riccardo suggests that I should become Battista's mistress.'

I was astonished at not having thought of this before. It was indeed strange that I myself, who had so clearly recognized, in Rheingold's and Battista's interpretations of the *Odyssey*, their two different ways of looking at life, should not have realized that Emilia, in constructing an image of me so different from the truth, had done, fundamentally, the same thing as the producer and the director. The only difference was that Rheingold and Battista had set out to interpret the two imaginary figures of Ulysses and Penelope; whereas Emilia had applied the despicable conventions by which she was dominated to two living creatures, herself and me. Thus, from a mixture of moral straightforwardness and unconscious vulgarity there had sprung, perhaps, the idea – not accepted by Emilia, it is true, but not contradicted by her either – that I had wished to push her into the arms of Battista.

In proof of all this, I said to myself, let us imagine for a moment that Emilia has to choose between the three different interpretations of the *Odyssey* – Rheingold's, Battista's, and mine. She is certainly capable of understanding the commercial motives for which Battista insists upon a spectacular *Odyssey*; she can even approve Rheingold's debasing psychological conception; but, with all her naturalness and straightforwardness, she is certainly quite incapable of achieving the level of my own interpretation, or rather, that of Homer and Dante. She cannot do this, not only because she is ignorant, but also because she does not live in an ideal world, but rather in the perfectly real world of people like Battista and

Rheingold. Thus the circle closed in. Emilia was at the same time the woman of my dreams and the woman who judged and despised me on the basis of a miserable commonplace; Penelope, faithful to her absent husband for ten long years, and the typist, suspecting self-interest where there was none. And, in order to have the Emilia I loved and to bring it about that she judged me for what I was, I should have to carry her away from the world in which she lived and introduce her to a world as simple as herself, as genuine as herself, a world in which money did not count and in which language had retained its integrity, a world – as Rheingold had pointed out to me – after which I could aspire, certainly, but which did not in fact exist.

In the meantime, however, I had to go on living – that is, moving and operating in that same world of Battista's and Rheingold's. What should I do? I felt that in the first place I ought to free myself from the painful sense of inferiority inspired in me by the absurd suspicion of my own innate and, so to speak, natural, despicableness. For, when all was said and done, this – as I have already mentioned – seemed to be the underlying idea in Emilia's attitude towards me, the idea of a baseness which was, so to speak, constitutional, and due not to behaviour but to nature. Now I was convinced that no one could be said to be despicable in himself, irrespective of all outward appearance and all relationship with others. But in order to free myself from my sense of inferiority I had also to convince Emilia of this.

I recalled the threefold image of Ulysses which the *Odyssey* script had held out to me and in which I had discerned three possible modes of existence – Battista's image, Rheingold's, and finally my own, which I felt to be the only true one and which, in substance, was that of

Homer. Why did Battista, Rheingold and I myself have three so very different conceptions of the figure of Ulysses? Precisely because our lives and our human ideals were different. Battista's image, superficial, vulgar, rhetorical and senseless, resembled the life and the ideals – or rather, the interests – of Battista; Rheingold's, more real, but diminished and degraded, was in accordance with the moral and artistic possibilities of Rheingold; and finally mine, without doubt the loftiest yet the most natural, the most poetical yet the most true, was derived from my aspiration, impotent perhaps but sincere, after a life that was not tainted and crippled by money or reduced to a purely physiological and material level. In a sense it was comforting to me that the image I preferred should be the best. I had to try and live up to this image, even if I had not been able to turn it to good account in the script, even if it was most improbable that I should be able to turn it to good account in life. Only in this way should I be able to convince Emilia of my reasons and so regain her esteem and her love. And how was I to accomplish this? I saw no other way than that of loving her still more, of proving to her once again, and every time it might be necessary, that my love was pure and disinterested.

I came to the conclusion, however, that for the moment it would not be a good plan to try to force Emilia. I would stay on until the next day and leave by the afternoon boat, without seeking to talk to her or to see her. Later, from Rome, I would write her a long letter, explaining all the many things I had not been able to clear up by word of mouth.

At this point in my thoughts I heard quiet voices coming, apparently, from the path below the terrace, and soon I recognized them as those of Emilia and Battista. Hurriedly I ran back into the house and went and shut myself in my room. But I was not sleepy; moreover, it seemed to me it would be too painful for me to stay shut up in that stuffy room while those other two were talking and moving about the villa, all around me. Since I had been suffering from sleeplessness, especially during these last weeks, I had brought with me from Rome a very strong sleeping-draught, very speedy in its effect. I took a double dose of it and threw myself down again – in real anger this time – on the bed, fully dressed as I was. I must have fallen asleep almost at once, for I don't think I heard the voices of Battista and Emilia for more than a few minutes.

22

It was late when I awoke – judging, at least, by the rays of sunshine which penetrated into the room between the slats of the shutters – and for a moment I lay listening to the profound silence of the place, so different from silence in a town which, even when it is complete, seems always somehow to retain wounds and aches from sounds already past. Then, as I lay motionless on my back, I listened more carefully to this virgin silence, and suddenly it seemed to me that there was something lacking – not just one of those quiet sounds such as that of an electric pump drawing up water into the cistern in the morning or the servant sweeping the floor, which seem to stress the silence and make it more profound, but rather a presence. It was not, in fact, a silence that was complete yet full of life, but a silence from which something vital had been withdrawn. A silence, I said to myself, finding the right word at last, a silence of abandonment. This word had barely crossed my mind before I had jumped from the bed and gone to the communicating door that led to Emilia's room. I opened it, and the first thing my eyes lit upon was a letter lying on the pillow at the head of the wide, disordered, deserted bed.

It was brief.

Dear Riccardo, Seeing you do not want to go away, I am going myself. Perhaps I might not have had the courage to go all alone: but I am taking advantage of Battista's departure. Also because I am afraid of being left alone; and Battista's company, after all, seems preferable to solitude. But in Rome I shall leave him and go and live on my own. However, if you hear that I have become Battista's mistress, don't be surprised: I'm not made of iron, and it will mean that I haven't been able to manage it and couldn't stand it. Good-bye, Emilia.

After reading these lines, I sat down at the head of the bed with the letter in my hand and stared straight in front of me. I saw the wide-open window, and, beyond the window-sill, a few pine trees, and, behind the trunks of the pine trees, the wall of rock. Then I removed my eyes from the window and looked all round the room: all was in disorder, but it was an empty, blank disorder; no clothes, no shoes, no toilet articles, nothing but open, or half-open, empty drawers, gaping wardrobes with bare, dangling coat-hangers, vacant chairs. I had often thought recently that Emilia might leave me and I had thought of it as one thinks of some dreaded calamity; and now, here I was in the midst of such a calamity. I had a dull feeling of pain which seemed to start from the very depths of my being; just as an uprooted tree, if it felt pain, would feel it in the roots that had held it upright in the ground. I had, in truth, been suddenly uprooted, and my roots, like those of the tree, were up in the air, and the sweet earth, Emilia, who had nourished them with her love, was far away from my roots, and those roots would never again be able to sink themselves in that love and feed upon it but would gradually dry up, and I felt that they were already drying up and it made me suffer unspeakably.

Finally, I rose and went back into my room. I felt stunned and distracted, like one who has had a bad fall from a height and who feels a dull pain and knows that this pain will soon burst forth into an acute spasm, and fears this moment, but does not know when it will come about. Carefully watching this hidden pain as one watches a wild

236

beast which one fears may leap upon one at any moment and tear one to pieces, I automatically took my bathing costume, went out of the house, walked along the path that runs round the island and reached the village *piazza*. There I bought a newspaper, sat down in one of the cafés, and, almost to my own surprise, since it seemed to me that in my situation I would not have been able to think of anything except the situation itself, I read the whole newspaper through, from the first to the last line. In the same sort of way, I reflected, a fly whose head has been torn off by some cruel child seems, for a time, to feel no effect from the mutilation but walks about or cleans its feet, until suddenly it collapses and dies. At last midday struck, and the clock in the campanile filled the square with the din of its chimes. A bus was on the point of leaving for the Piccola Marina, and I got into it.

Shortly afterwards I was in the open, sun-filled space where, amid a sharp smell of urine, stood the little carriages with their horses, while their drivers sat together in a group, quietly chattering. I went off with a light step down the stairs leading to the bathing-huts, and looked down from above upon the short stretch of white, shingly beach and the sea lying blue beneath the tranquil sky. Utterly calm was the sea, smooth and glossy as satin right to the horizon, with great, diaphanous current-tracks winding idly over its surface in the dazzling sunlight. I thought it would be good to go out in a boat that morning; rowing would be a distraction, and then I should be completely alone, which, on the already frequented beach, would be impossible. When I reached the bathing-huts, I called the attendant and asked him to get a boat ready for me. Then I went into one of the huts to undress.

When I came out, I walked barefoot along the little

terrace in front of the huts, looking down and taking care not to hurt myself on the roughness of the warped, salt-worn planks. The June sun blazed overhead, enveloping me in its strong light, burning my back. It gave me a sensation of well-being which was in bitter contrast with my mental state of stunned suspense. My eyes still lowered, I went down the steep steps and walked towards the edge of the beach over the scorching stones. It was only when I was at a short distance from the edge that I raised my eyes; and then I saw Emilia.

The attendant, a thin, vigorous old man, brown as leather, with a big straw hat pulled down over his eyes, was standing beside the boat which he had already pushed half into the water; Emilia was sitting in the stern wearing a two-piece costume that I knew well, of a rather faded green. She was sitting with her legs pressed closely together, her arms stretched backwards to support herself, her bare, slender waist slightly twisted in relation to her hips, in an attitude that was insecure yet full of feminine grace. Aware of my surprise, she was smiling and looking straight into my eyes, as much as to say: 'I'm here . . . but don't say anything . . . Pretend you knew I was here.'

I obeyed this unspoken advice and, in silence, more dead than alive, deeply troubled, my heart in a tumult, mechanically took the hand which the attendant held out to me and jumped into the boat. The attendant came into the water up to his knees, slipped the oars into the rowlocks and pushed the boat off. I sat down, took hold of the oars and started rowing with my head down, in the burning sun, towards the promontory that enclosed the little bay. I rowed with energy and in about ten minutes reached the promontory, still in silence and still without looking at Emilia. I felt a kind of restraint at the thought of talking to her as long as the beach, with its huts and its bathers, was still in sight. I wanted solitude round myself and her, as I had wanted it in the villa, as I always wanted it when I wished to say certain things to her.

But, as I rowed, I became aware that, in a sudden overflowing of bitterness mingled with a new, strange joy, tears had started flowing from my eyes. I rowed on and felt my eyes burning with tears and my face burning each time one of these tears detached itself from my eyes and slid down my cheek. When I was opposite the end of the promontory, I rowed more strongly so as to make head-way against the current, which at that point made the water rough and boisterous. On my right was a small black rock with a jagged crest sticking up out of the water, on my left the high, rocky wall of the promontory; I thrust the bow of the boat into this passage, rowed vigorously through the swirling water and thus passed the end of the point. The rock, where it plunged into the sea, was white with salt, and each time the water ebbed one could see green beards of seaweed, brilliant in the sun, and here and there a red fruit like a sea tomato. Beyond the promontory appeared a huge amphitheatre of fallen rock, backed by the perpendicular mountain wall, and here and there between one mass of rock and the next, little beaches of white shingle, completely deserted. The sea, too, was deserted, with neither boats nor bathers; and the water, in this inlet, was of a thick, oily blue that appeared to indicate great depth. Farther off, other promontories were outlined one behind the other upon the flat, sunfilled sea, like the wings of some fantastic natural theatre.

I slowed down at last and lifted my face towards Emilia. And as though she too had been waiting to speak until we had rounded the promontory, she smiled at me and asked in a gentle voice: 'Why are you crying?'

239

'I'm crying for joy at seeing you,' I replied.

'You're glad to see me?'

'Very, very glad . . . I was sure you had gone away . . . but after all you haven't!'

She lowered her eyes and said: 'I had made up my mind to go away . . . and I went down to the harbour this morning with Battista . . . Then at the last moment I thought better of it and stayed.'

'And what have you been doing all this time?'

'I wandered about down by the harbour . . . I sat in a café . . . Then I went up to the village in the funicular and telephoned to the villa . . . I was told you had gone out . . . Then I thought perhaps you'd gone to the Piccola Marina, so I came here . . . I undressed and waited for you . . . I saw you asking the attendant to get you a boat . . . I was lying in the sun and you passed quite close to me without seeing me . . . Then, while you were undressing, I got into the boat.'

For some moments I said nothing. We were now half-way between the promontory we had passed and another point which enclosed the inlet. Beyond that point, I knew, was the Green Grotto, in which, in the first place, it had been my intention to bathe. Finally, I asked in a low voice: 'Why didn't you go away with Battista, as you had decided? Why did you stay?'

'Because this morning, on thinking it over, I saw I had been mistaken about you . . . and that the whole thing had been a misunderstanding.'

'What was it made you see that?'

'I don't quite know . . . lots of things . . . chiefly, perhaps, the tone of your voice yesterday evening.'

'And are you really convinced now that I've never done all those dreadful things you accused me of?'

'Yes; I *am* convinced.'

There still, however, remained one thing I had to know, perhaps the most important of all. 'But you,' I said, 'you don't think I'm a despicable person do you? . . . Even though I haven't done those things . . . despicable because made of despicable stuff . . . Tell me, you don't believe that, Emilia?'

'I've never believed it . . . I thought you'd behaved in a certain way, and that's why you lost my esteem . . . But now I know that it's all been a misunderstanding . . . Let's not talk about it any more, if you don't mind.'

This time I said nothing, and she was silent too, and I started rowing with greater energy, with an energy that was now redoubled, it seemed to me, by a feeling of joy which gradually, like a rising sun, grew and mounted within me, warming my spirit which till then had been aching and numb. Meanwhile we had reached a point opposite the Green Grotto, and I steered the boat towards the cave, already visible and appearing to hang, dark and crooked, above an expanse of cold green water. 'And you do love me?' I went on.

She hesitated and then answered: 'I've always loved you . . . I always shall love you'; but she said it with a kind of sadness that surprised me.

'Why,' I insisted in alarm, 'why do you say that in such a sad way?'

'I don't know . . . perhaps because it would have been better if no misunderstanding had ever come between us and we had always loved one another as we did in the past.'

'Yes,' I said; 'but all that's over now . . . We mustn't think about it any more . . . Now we're going to love each other for ever.' She appeared to nod her head, but without raising her eyes, and still rather sadly. I stopped rowing for a moment, and, leaning forward, added: 'We'll go to the Red Grotto now . . . It's a smaller cave and very deep, beyond the Green Grotto . . . There's a little beach at the end of it, in the dark . . . We'll make love there, shall we, Emilia?'

I saw her lift her head and nod her assent, in silence, gazing fixedly at me, with a look of discreet, and even rather bashful, complicity. I started rowing again energetically. We entered the grotto, beneath the great vault of rugged rock upon whose surface water and sunlight threw gay reflections, casting upon it a close net of quivering emerald. Farther on, at the place where the sea penetrated only at intervals, making the vault resound with hollow reverberations, the water was dark, with a few smooth, black rocks emerging from it like the backs of amphibious beasts. Here was the tortuous opening, a narrow passage between two rocks, that led through to the Red Grotto. Emilia was sitting quite still now, looking at me and following each one of my movements with her eyes, in an attitude of sensual but patient docility, like a woman who is ready to give herself and is only awaiting the signal. By thrusting, first with one oar then with the other, against the walls of the channel, beneath the stalactite-hung vault, I brought the boat through into the open and then steered it towards the dark mouth of the Red Grotto. 'Look out for your head,' I said to Emilia; and then, with one stroke of the oars, I propelled the boat over the smooth water into the cave.

The Red Grotto is divided into two parts. The first, like an entrance hall, is separated from the second by a lowering of the vault overhead; beyond this point the cave bends sharply and runs a considerable distance back to the beach at its farthest end. This second part is plunged in almost complete darkness, and one's eyes have to become accustomed to the gloom before one can discern the little

242

subterranean beach, which is strangely coloured by the reddish light that gives its name to the Grotto. 'It's very dark inside the cave,' I went on to say, 'but we'll be able to see as soon as our eyes get used to it.' In the meantime, carried along by the force of my initial stroke, the boat slid along in the darkness, under the low vault of rock; and I saw nothing more. At last I heard the bow strike the beach, thrusting into the gravel with a moist, resonant sound. Then I let go of the oars and, half-rising, put out my hand towards the point in the darkness where the stern of the boat should be, saying: 'Give me your hand and I'll help you to get out.'

No answer came to me. I repeated, in surprise: 'Give me your hand, Emilia!' and for the second time leant forward, holding out my hand. Then, since there was again no reply, I leant still farther forward and, cautiously, so as not to strike the face of Emilia, whom I knew to be sitting there in the stern, I felt about for her in the darkness. But my hand met nothing but empty air, and when I lowered it I felt beneath my fingers, at the spot where they should have encountered Emilia's seated figure, nothing but the smooth wood of the empty seat. My astonishment was mingled, all at once, with a feeling of terror. 'Emilia!' I cried, 'Emilia!' The only answer was a thin, icy echo; so, at least, it appeared to me. In the meantime my eyes had become accustomed to the darkness and could at last distinguish, in the thick gloom, the boat with its bow lying on the beach, the beach itself, of fine, black gravel, and the glimmering, dripping vault curving over my head. And then I saw that the boat was completely empty, with no one sitting in the stern, and that the beach was empty too, and that all round me there was no one, and that I was alone.

Looking towards the stern, I said, in astonishment:

243

'Emilia!' but this time it was in a low voice. And I repeated again: 'Emilia, where are you?' – and at that same moment I understood. Then I got out of the boat and threw myself down on the beach and buried my face in the moist pebbles and I think I fainted, for I remained motionless, almost without feeling, for a time that seemed endless.

Later I rose to my feet, automatically got into the boat again and pushed it out of the cave. At the mouth of the grotto the strong sunlight, reflected off the sea, smote me. I looked at the watch on my wrist and saw that it was two o'clock in the afternoon. I had been in the cave for more than an hour. And I remembered that noon was the hour for ghosts; and I realized that I had been talking and weeping in the presence of a ghost!

23

My return to the bathing-huts was slow; every now and then I stopped rowing and sat still, resting on my oars, my eyes fixed dreamily upon the blue, shining surface of the sea. It was clear that I had had a hallucination, of the same kind as I had had two days before, when Emilia was lying naked in the sun and I had imagined that I had bent over her and kissed her, whereas in reality I had not moved nor gone near her. This time the hallucination had been far more precise and articulate; but that it was in truth a hallucination and nothing more no further proof was needed than the conversation I had imagined myself to have had with Emilia's ghost – a conversation during which I had made Emilia say all the things I wanted her to say, and assume exactly the attitudes I wished her to assume. Everything had begun and ended with myself; the only difference from what usually happens in such circumstances being that I had not confined myself to a wishful imagining of what I wanted to happen, but, from the sheer force of feeling that filled my heart, had deluded myself into thinking it really had happened. Strange to say, however, I was not in the least surprised at having had a hallucination of a kind that was not merely uncommon but perhaps unique. As though the hallucination were still continuing, I turned my attention, not so much to the question of its actual possibility, as to its details, reconstructing them one by one, dwelling with an almost sensual pleasure upon those which gave me most pleasure and comfort. How beautiful Emilia had been, sitting in the stern of my boat no longer hostile, but full of love; how sweet her words; how disturbing, how violent the feeling I had experienced when I told her I wanted to make love to her and she had answered me with that faint nod of agreement! Like one who has had a voluptuous and very vivid dream and who, on awakening, lingers with relish over all its aspects and sensations, I was, in reality, still caught up in my hallucination, believing in it and joyfully reliving it in my memory; and little did it matter to me that it was a hallucination, seeing that I was experiencing all the feelings with which one usually remembers a thing that has really happened.

As I dwelt with inexhaustible pleasure upon the details of my vision, it suddenly occurred to me to compare once again the time at which I had left the Piccola Marina in the boat with the time at which I had come out of the Red Grotto, and I was again struck with the great length of time that I must have spent at the far end of the cave, on the little subterranean beach: allowing three-quarters of an hour for the journey from the Piccola Marina to the Grotto, it must have been more than an hour. As I have already said, I had attributed this length of time to a fainting fit, or at any rate to some kind of collapse or unconsciousness very like a fainting fit. But now, on re-examining my hallucination, which had been so complete and at the same time had corresponded so obligingly with my most profound desires, I wondered whether, perchance, I had not, quite simply, dreamed the whole thing. Whether, that is to say, I had not embarked from the bathing-beach alone and without any ghost on board, and whether I had not penetrated, still alone, into the Grotto, and finally lain down on the little beach and gone to sleep. During my sleep – if this were so – I had dreamed that I had started off in the boat with Emilia sitting in the stern,

246

that I had talked to her and she had answered me, that I had suggested making love, that we had gone together into the cave. And then I had also dreamed that I had put out my hand to help her out of the boat, that I had failed to find her, that I had been frightened, that I had thought I must have had a ghost with me on my boat excursion, and that I had finally thrown myself down on the beach and fainted.

This supposition now seemed to me to be probably true; but no more than probably. Now that it had been obscured, side-tracked and confused by my subsequent fancies, it seemed to me almost impossible to search out the dividing line between dream and actual reality, a dividing line that must be located in that moment when I lay down on the beach. What had really happened at the precise moment when I lay down on the little beach at the far end of the cave? Had I fallen asleep and dreamed that I had been with Emilia, the real Emilia of flesh and blood? Or had I fallen asleep and dreamed that I had been visited by Emilia's ghost? Or, again had I fallen asleep and dreamed that I was asleep and dreaming one or the other of the aforesaid dreams? Like those Chinese boxes each one of which contains a smaller one, reality seemed to contain a dream which in its turn contained a reality which in its turn contained yet another dream, and so *ad infinitum*. Thus, again and again, pausing and resting on my oars out at sea, I wondered if I had dreamed or had had a hallucination, or – more singularly – if a ghost had indeed appeared to me; and in the end I came to the conclusion that it was not possible for me to find out, and that, in all probability, I should never find out.

I rowed on and came at last to the bathing-huts. I dressed in great haste, went up again to the road, and was in time to board a bus which was on the point of leaving for the *piazza*. I was in a great hurry now to be home again: somehow, for a reason I could not explain, I felt convinced that when I reached the villa I should perhaps find the key to all these mysteries. I was in a hurry to get there also because I had still to have lunch and pack my bag and then catch the six o'clock boat; and I had wasted time. I left the *piazza* at once, almost at a run, by the usual path; in twenty minutes' time I was at the villa.

I had no time, as I entered the deserted living-room, to succumb to the sadness of desolation and loneliness. On the already laid table, beside the plate, was a telegram. Unsuspecting but vaguely troubled, I took the yellow envelope and opened it. Battista's name surprised me and, for some reason, seemed to give me a hope of favourable news. But then I read the text: it announced to me, in a few words, that, as the result of a serious accident, Emilia was 'dangerously ill'.

I realized, at this point, that I have almost nothing more to say. It is useless to describe how I left that same afternoon, how, when I reached Naples, I learnt that in reality Emilia had been killed in a motor accident a short distance south of Terracina. Her death had been a strange one. Owing to fatigue and the great heat, she had, apparently, fallen asleep, with her head down and her chin resting on her chest. Battista as usual, was driving extremely fast. Suddenly an ox-drawn cart had come out of a side road. Battista had jammed on the brakes; and, after an exchange of abuse with the driver of the cart, had driven on. But Emilia's head was swaying from one side to another, and she had not spoken. Battista had spoken to her, but she had not answered; and at a bend in the road, she had fallen on top of him. He had stopped the car, and had then discovered that she was dead. The sudden jamming on of the brakes to avoid the cart had caught her body in a moment of complete abandonment, with all the muscles relaxed, as indeed happens during sleep; and the jolt of the suddenly-stopped car had caused an abrupt jerk of the neck, fracturing the spinal column outright. She had died without knowing it.

It was extremely hot – a wearisome thing for sorrow, which demands, like joy, that there should be no rivalry in any other feeling. The funeral took place on a day of unrelieved sultriness, beneath a cloudy sky, the air damp and windless. After the funeral, in the evening, I closed the door behind me as I entered our apartment – for ever useless and empty now – and I understood at last that Emilia, truly, was dead, and I should never see her again. All the windows in the flat had been opened wide in the hope of increasing even the faintest breath of air, but I felt I was suffocating nevertheless as I wandered from one room to another, over the polished floors, in the twilight gloom. Meanwhile, the brightly lit windows of the adjoining houses, their inhabitants visible inside the rooms, drove me almost to frenzy, their quiet lights reminding me of a world in which people loved without misunderstandings and were loved in return and lived peaceful lives – a world from which it seemed to me that I was for ever shut out. The re-entry into such a world would have meant, for me, an explanation with Emilia, her conviction of my innocence, the creation once again of the miracle of love which, in order to exist, must be kindled not only in our own hearts but in those of others as well. But this was no longer possible, and I felt I should go mad when I thought that perhaps I ought to recognize, in Emilia's death, a last, supreme act of hostility on her part against myself.

But I had to go on living. Next day I took up the suitcase which I had not yet opened, locked the door of the flat with the sensation of closing a grave, and handed the keys to the porter, explaining that I intended to get rid of the apartment as soon as I returned from my holiday. Then I started off again for Capri. Strange to say, I was driven to return there by the hope that, somehow or other, in the same place where she had appeared to me, or elsewhere, Emilia would again show herself to me. And then I would again explain to her why everything had happened, and I would again declare my love, and would again receive her assurance that she understood me and loved me. This hope had a quality of madness about it, and I was aware of this. Never, indeed, was I so near to a kind of reasoned insanity as I was at that time, balanced precariously between a loathing for reality and a longing for hallucination.

Emilia, fortunately for me, did not reappear to me, either when sleeping or waking. And, when I compared the time at which she had appeared with the time at which she had died, I discovered that they did not correspond. Emilia had been still alive at the moment when I thought I had seen her sitting in the stern of the boat; but she was, in all probability, already dead during the time of my unconsciousness on the little beach at the far end of the Red Grotto. So, in death as in life, there was no true conformity. And I should never know whether she had been a ghost, or a hallucination, or a dream, or perhaps some other illusion. The ambiguity which had poisoned our relationship in life continued even after her death.

Driven on by longing for her and for places where I had last seen her, I made my way one day to the beach below the villa, where I had come upon her lying naked and had had the illusion that I had kissed her. The beach was deserted; and as I came out through the masses of fallen rock with my eyes raised towards the smiling, blue expanse of the sea, the thought of the *Odyssey* came back into my mind, and of Ulysses and Penelope, and I said to myself that Emilia was now, like Ulysses and Penelope, in those great sea spaces, and was fixed for eternity in the shape in which she had been clothed in life. It depended upon myself, not upon any dream or hallucination, to find her again and to continue our earthly conversation with renewed serenity. Only in that way would she be delivered from me, would she be set free from my feelings, would she bend down over me like an image of consolation and beauty. And I decided to write down these memories, in the hope of succeeding in my intention.

THE WORLD'S GREATEST NOVELISTS NOW AVAILABLE IN GRANADA PAPERBACKS

Angus Wilson

Such Darling Dodos	£1.50	☐
Latecall	£1.95	☐
The Wrong Set	£1.95	☐
For Whom the Cloche Tolls	£1.25	☐
A Bit Off the Map	£1.50	☐
As If By Magic	£2.50	☐
The Strange Ride of Rudyard Kipling (non-fiction)	£1.95	☐
Hemlock and After	£1.50	☐
No Laughing Matter	£1.95	☐
The Old Men at the Zoo	£1.95	☐
The Middle Age of Mrs Eliot	£1.95	☐
Setting the World on Fire	£1.95	☐

J B Priestley

Angel Pavement	£2.50	☐
Saturn Over The Water	£1.95	☐
Lost Empires	£1.95	☐
It's an Old Country	£1.95	☐
The Shapes of Sleep	£1.75	☐
The Good Companions	£2.50	☐

GF581

THE WORLD'S GREATEST NOVELISTS NOW AVAILABLE IN GRANADA PAPERBACKS

Alberto Moravia

Time of Desecration	£1.95	☐
Bitter Honeymoon	£1.25	☐
Mother Love	60p	☐
The Wayward Wife	£1.25	☐
Conjugal Love	50p	☐
Roman Tales	£1.25	☐
Time of Indifference	£1.25	☐
The Empty Canvas	£1.50	☐
Two Adolescents	£1.00	☐
The Fancy Dress Party	95p	☐
The Voice of the Sea	£1.95	☐

Henry Miller

Black Sprint	£1.95	☐
Tropic of Cancer	£1.95	☐
Tropic of Capricorn	£1.95	☐
Nexus	£1.95	☐
Sexus	£1.95	☐
Plexus	£1.95	☐
The Air-Conditioned Nightmare	£1.95	☐

GF981